£1.50

PARTING SHOT

Also by Richard Greensted

Coming to Terms
Lost Cause

PARTING SHOT

Richard Greensted

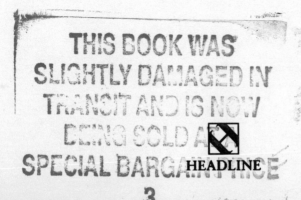

First published in 1997
by HEADLINE BOOK PUBLISHING

10 9 8 7 6 5 4 3 2 1

British Library Cataloguing in Publication Data

Greensted, Richard
Parting shot
1. Detective and mystery stories
I. Title
823.9'14 [F]

ISBN 0-7472-1810-2

Typeset by
CBS, Felixstowe, Suffolk

Printed and bound in Great Britain by
Mackays of Chatham PLC, Chatham, Kent

HEADLINE BOOK PUBLISHING
A division of Hodder Headline PLC
338 Euston Road
London NW1 3BH

For Julie
Not Fade Away

ONE

Barry knew immediately that something was wrong.

Mr Mercer always stood at his bedroom window, but he wasn't standing there this morning. In fact, there was no sign of life at the house, and it worried Barry so much that he called in to his controller to check that he had the right time and date. Having confirmed the job, he pulled the Mercedes into the drive and parked in front of the garage.

Barry drummed his fingers on the steering wheel and considered his options. He checked his watch: five-thirty a.m. on the dot, and Mr Mercer should, by rights, be ready and waiting for him. He was not like other punters, some of those jumped-up little bank executives that kept you waiting for ever and didn't even apologise. Some jobs, you just knew they were relying on you for a wake-up call and probably hadn't even bothered to pack. But Mr Mercer was different: in all the years Barry had driven him to and from the airport he had never been late and was unfailingly courteous – and he knew how to tip.

Now Barry was at a loss: he could get out, go up to the big white front door and ring the bell, but this seemed to him like an unwarranted intrusion into Mr Mercer's privacy. He could call him on his mobile phone, but he didn't fancy that much either. What if Mr Mercer were otherwise engaged? He'd be well pissed off then, and Barry certainly didn't want any of that at this time of the morning. Reluctantly, carefully, he pushed his door open and crunched on to the gravel drive, stepping lightly to try and avoid making too much noise. As he approached the front door a brilliant halogen lamp flashed on, temporarily blinding him. He stopped and pulled the knot of his tie tighter towards his neck; now used to the flooding light, he stared at the door and the big brass knocker on it.

What to do, what to do? Lacking the confidence to advance, he went back to the car and reached in for his phone. He knew Mr Mercer's number off by heart, even though he had never used it. He punched the numbers slowly and his finger hovered over the 'send' button briefly before he pushed it. After a short moment he could hear the phone ringing inside, a hollow noise that unnerved him. He listened for what seemed an eternity before cancelling the call. Then he got back into the car and left his door open, looking up hopefully at the bedroom window to where Mr Mercer's face would normally be.

He called in to the controller again on the radio, and was told that no cancellation had been received. Mr Mercer's firm was one of their top clients and they weren't about to jeopardise that income by recalling Barry, so they told him to sit tight and wait. He flicked through the newspaper, then folded it neatly and replaced it on the passenger seat: he always had a fresh copy for Mr Mercer. He liked to read it, and always commented on the proportions of the girls inside. Barry wondered what Mrs Mercer would have to say about that – she seemed like a really nice lady, refined and polite. Caroline, wasn't that her name?

More in hope than expectation, Barry got out to have a recce around the house. He reckoned it must have cost a small – no, a big – fortune. Set back from the road, it was double-fronted and had a garage attached to one side; the drive had two entrances, both gated but always open, which swept around a large flower bed and lawn behind the front wall. In this area, the house must have cost close to a million, he speculated, and he'd seen all the extra work they'd had done and all the builders' rubble, over the five years he'd been driving for Mr Mercer.

He walked over to the garage. The up-and-over door was freshly painted white to match the front door and window frames; inside, he knew, was stored a vintage MG. Mr Mercer had shown it to him once, proud as anything he was, like it was his baby. Looking down casually, Barry noticed the door was not fully closed and his heart leapt. With all the security systems around the house, this seemed like an odd lapse and he was intrigued by it. He glanced to either side and behind him before crouching down and putting his hand under the lip of the door. He waited a long time before finding the courage to pull very slowly and raise the door, anxious not to make any noise. It glided silently upwards until it was over Barry's head.

In the pre-dawn darkness it was hard to make out anything. He could just see the silhouette of the car, wrapped tightly in its protective tarpaulin, but nothing else was clear. As he stepped in his face brushed against a light cord and he grasped it: the neon strip took a couple of seconds to burst into life. The garage was typical: there were rows of shelves with old paint tins and tools, and several different-sized bicycles were leaning against one wall. But Barry's eye was drawn towards the far corner of the room, where he could see the back of an old green armchair.

He walked towards it, the crown of a head just protruding from the top. He paused, his heart racing, and wondered what the hell was going on. From the colour of the hair it looked like Mr Mercer, although he couldn't be sure.

'Mr Mercer?' he said quietly. 'Is that you?'

Receiving no reply, he ventured closer until his foot hit something sticky on the floor; looking down, he could only make out that it was some kind of dark brown liquid, possibly paint. He wiped his foot on a clean patch of floor and stepped around the mess until he was beside the armchair.

His stomach jumped and his eyes watered when he finally took in what he was looking at. Dressed in a blue double-breasted suit, Mr Mercer lay in the chair, his right arm hanging limply over the side. His eyes bulged in their sockets, and his neck was mottled and deeply bruised. His body was set at an odd angle to his legs, which were splayed out in front of him, as if he had been snapped at the waist. He looked terrified, his mouth agape in horror even as he lay inert.

Barry put his hand forward to touch him but then pulled it back when he saw Mr Mercer's left arm, which was folded over his lap. Where there should have been a hand there was none; instead, there was a clean cut at the wrist and Barry could see bone and muscle and blood, so much blood that it had flooded down his trousers and on to the floor. Barry vomited then and reeled backwards as he did so, crashing into the car behind him. He stayed there, unable to take his gaze away from the body and too terrified to move.

By the time Caroline Mercer steered the big Volvo on to Hammersmith Bridge she was ready to scream. The two children,

4

Hugh and George, had been good for the first half of the journey but their patience had worn thin, and they had amused themselves by fighting over everything they could imagine. She had shouted, she had played I-Spy, she had threatened, but they took no notice. All she wanted was to get back home, tip them out of the car and pour herself a very large gin and tonic. Guy could look after them for the rest of the evening; he deserved them, and she silently cursed him for crying off from this trip at the last moment, weakly claiming pressure of work. She'd taken them alone to the house in Minster Lovell, on the edge of the Cotswolds, on Friday night, avoiding the rush-hour traffic so that they only reached the place at ten o'clock at night. By then, of course, they had both slept in the car and were bright as buttons and ready for action. From there it had been all downhill, and now she was fit for nothing.

Sunday evenings were always difficult: Mira, the au pair, had the weekend off and Guy was frequently absent, travelling to God knows where or holding important meetings in the City. She desperately hoped that he'd be there, and in a good mood, so that he could relieve some of the pressure. Love him as she might, she still felt that his contribution to family life lacked a certain vigour.

'We're home, boys,' she shouted as they edged along Castelnau towards the house. She was so tired that she hardly noticed the two policemen standing at the gates until she was turning into the drive. One put his hand up to stop her and she rolled down her window.

'What's going on?' she asked, her concern breaking through the weariness.

'Can I ask who you are?' the policeman replied.

'Yes, I'm Caroline Mercer and this is my house. What's happened?'

'Right. Sorry. Please go ahead.' He whispered into the radio on his lapel as she pulled into the drive. Still frowning, she saw a dark blue car parked outside the front door and a lot of tape fluttering across the open garage. She stopped the car quickly and jumped out as a man walked across to meet her.

'Mrs Mercer?' he said.

'Yes. What's going on here?' She was aware of the children piling out behind her but couldn't worry about them.

'I'm Detective Chief Inspector Grass. I think you'd better come inside,' he said, leading off before she had a chance to ask him anything more. He pushed the front door open and led her into the front sitting room. 'Please sit down.'

'I don't want to sit down,' she shouted. 'Just tell me what's going on.'

He nodded and adjusted his face to what he thought was a proper expression in the circumstances. 'Mrs Mercer, I've some very bad news for you. I'm afraid your husband's been murdered.'

After Hugh and George had been steered away into the kitchen to sit with a policewoman, Caroline sat alone with Grass in the sitting room. Her first reaction had been flat denial. Over and over again she had told the inspector that there must be some mistake, that it couldn't possibly be Guy. She sought defence from the miasma of his information through contradiction. Grass took this well, inured to the reaction through practice and training, and he did not try to argue with her. He simply waited.

'Why?' she asked simply, when she had finally realised that

his news could no longer be ignored.

'At the moment, we have an open mind about motive,' he replied.

'Which is a nice way of saying you don't have a clue.'

'Pretty much. But perhaps you can help us on that, when you're feeling up to it.'

'I wonder when that will be,' she said wistfully. 'Now's as good a time as any, if you want to interrogate me.' He pulled out a little black notepad, and she felt a small surprise; he was behaving exactly as she might have expected in the circumstances, as if real life were mirroring the fiction she'd seen on television or read in books. A woman came into the room and nodded briefly at both of them; she closed the door and stood with her back to it.

'This is Detective Sergeant Jane Fox,' Grass said. 'She'll be helping me with the investigation.' Jane flashed a small, formal smile at Caroline. 'Can you think of any reason why your husband might have been murdered?' Grass asked.

'Nothing specific springs to mind, but I'm not sure I'm the best person to ask. If he had enemies, he never told me about them.'

'Did he have any problems that you are aware of – I mean, serious problems that might have led to this?'

She paused then, and he studied her reaction closely. His interest was partly professional, but he was also fascinated by her reactions. She had gone through the denial phase very quickly, and was now rational and calm; he wondered if this show of strength was superficial, or if she were really as tough as her demeanour suggested. Here she was, discussing her husband's death less than an hour after she'd heard about it; he read nothing sinister into this, but it engaged his attention nonetheless.

She smiled weakly. 'Does the bank send round the heavies if you haven't paid your mortgage?' she said.

'You had money problems?' This was more promising.

'We had a continuing crisis. Every month was the same – who gets paid? I know, you're looking around and thinking to yourself that we can't be short of a bob or two, but that's all on tick. Actual folding stuff is the problem. We never have any.' To him it seemed that this was volunteered by her almost in relief, as if she were glad to be telling someone that, under the patina of wealth, there lurked a real despair.

'Would he have used . . . unconventional means of finance?' Grass asked. She frowned before getting the drift.

'You mean loan sharks? I doubt it. He was a City financier, after all, so I think he'd have known the trouble that could bring.'

'But if it were really as desperate as you say? In that case, might he not have taken whatever option he could?'

She shook her head vaguely. 'I doubt it. He always used to work on the principle that something would turn up. I was the one who lost sleep over it.'

Grass scribbled something in his notebook and then flipped it shut. He stood up and looked down at her. 'Someone was angry enough, or upset enough, to want him dead, Mrs Mercer. We have to find out who and why. I'd like you to think very carefully about his friends, his business colleagues, anything that could give us a lead. Go through his papers when you have a chance, and see if you can find anything unusual. Will you do that for us?'

She recognised the kindness in his voice and was touched by

it. In spite of his job, he still cared a little for the victims and she appreciated that. 'I'll do my best.'

'Good. I'll let you get on now. My lads are finished here, but we'll leave someone on the gates tonight. Is there anything else we can do for you?'

'Not for now,' she said. But she did need something more, a final affirmation of what he had told her; she struggled to find a way to ask for it. 'My husband,' she began.

Grass understood. 'We will need you to identify the body, when you're feeling up to it.'

'Can I see him now?' She was torn between the horror of what lay ahead and the need to set things straight.

'As soon as you're ready. It's . . . he's in the ambulance.' At this, Jane opened the door and left the room to prepare for the identification.

'Give me a minute alone, will you?' Caroline asked.

Grass could tell from the way she said this that a small fissure was appearing in her façade and that he would do well to leave before it grew. He walked to the door and left her to her private thoughts.

Caroline stayed seated and the emptiness suddenly hit her. 'Oh Guy,' she said under her breath, and she closed her moistening eyes to the pain.

TWO

His blunt indifference was understandable – after all, his could hardly be described as one of the better jobs – but Caroline still felt that he might have made more effort with his appearance. He looked as if he had slept in his clothes, and his hair stood up at odd angles; the smell of him was overpowering, a pungent concoction of stale and fresh sweat, alcohol and tobacco. Breathing carefully to avoid the full blast of this, Caroline waited for him to react.

'Yeah, unit 327A. I'll get the keys and take you down,' he said at last as he ran his finger down a register.

Unit 327A: she had seen that symbology for the first time earlier that morning when she'd opened the mail. Unable to sleep in the early aftermath of Guy's death, Caroline had wandered restlessly from room to room, opening drawers and finding more evidence of his life. She had felt the urge to clear out the house, but had lacked the energy to begin or the means to bring any order to the process. She stared at photos of him and cried; she held his pillow against her face and wept into it; and she ran her fingers across the line of suits that she had hung so neatly in his wardrobe. It was as if she needed to confirm that he was more than a trick of her imagination, and her final, longest act was to look in on the boys and see their father in their faces.

Wearily she had flicked through the mail when the au pair, Mira, delivered it to the kitchen table. It was left to Mira to deal with the children and keep them from coming too close to their mother's grief. Twenty-two years old and enjoying the freedom and wealth she'd never had in Belgrade, Mira had become a trusted companion, too young and fresh to be a friend but supporting Caroline with kindness and devotion. Mira bubbled with vigour and exuberance, energetic to the point that she could exhaust Caroline simply by association. But Guy's murder had affected her, much as she tried to hide it for Caroline's sake. Her eyes were sore from crying, a sadness that stemmed both from her respect for Guy and her understanding of how it would harm this kind and gentle family. But, without complaint or question, she engulfed George within her ample and comforting bosom. Hugh remained aloof, acutely proud of his maturity and intimidated by his nascent hormonal response to Mira's physique.

Caroline sifted through the letters, mainly addressed to Guy, before she arrived at one envelope for her. It was a small padded package, and the writing was unmistakable – it was from Guy. She squeezed it tentatively, wondering what he could possibly have sent her through the mail, and checked the postmark; it was dated Saturday, the day before he'd been murdered. She could see him walking down the street to the post office, buying the stamps and licking them, and she held the envelope to her cheek. She blinked at her own stupidity and weakness, and ripped off one end of the package. She pulled out a letter and a small key with an orange rubber handle. His writing was untidy and irregular across the page.

Caro–

It's difficult to know how to say this, so forgive me if I'm less than eloquent and coherent.

Bad things have happened with the business and they now require my urgent attention. This means that I need to go away for quite a long time – how long is anyone's guess. I have to lie low until I've got things sorted out and I really have no way of knowing how long that's going to take.

It's better if you know nothing about my whereabouts. I don't for one second believe that you'll be in any danger, but we can't be too careful. I realise how much pain this is going to cause you and the boys, and I wish to God there was a better way of doing things. But I can't think of a better solution, so you'll have to trust me on this one.

As always, my thoughts are with you and those little bun-scoffers. I shall miss you all desperately but you have my word that I'll return just as soon as I can. You know I love you all madly, and can't bear to be without you.

Don't worry about me – I'll be fine, just as I always am! But I've taken certain measures to make sure that you and the boys are looked after in the interim. The key in this package is for a self-storage centre in Battersea – unit 327A at Castle Containers, on the river by the bridge – and I want you to go there on Monday morning. They'll know you're coming – just take your passport and show it to them. When you get inside you'll see a large fireproof filing cabinet (4-drawer) in the far left corner. The key is taped under the desk next to it. In the bottom drawer you'll find something that'll help.

Sorry to be so clandestine, but it's the way it's got to be for now. This won't last for ever, I promise. You are still my little chocolate peppermint cream!

All my love and a thousand kisses and cuddles to those little horrors –
Guy

She had always trusted Guy; he had never done her any harm and had devoted himself to the family, however haphazardly. But the letter had shocked her almost as much as his murder. It was so out of character for him to have considered taking this action without ever discussing it with her. They talked about everything and he relied greatly on her advice. Now it seemed as if he had chosen to ignore her, a slight that she felt as keenly as the news of his death. Was he so alone, so desperate, that he couldn't bear to share his anguish with her? How could he even have imagined that she would not understand? Under the bravado of his words she could almost touch the fear and hopelessness.

But, obedient to him even in death, she had driven to the Castle Containers Self-Storage Centre straight after breakfast, telling Mira to comfort the boys and give them whatever they wanted. Caroline had only briefly spoken to the boys about what had happened, leaving out many of the details although Hugh had already worked it out. George was easily puzzled, frightened by what he could not understand: he was just ten and often seemed younger, retaining the innocence of a very small boy. He always needed cuddles, even at the best of times, and hated disruptions to his routine. Hugh, at thirteen, was trying to shake off the last vestiges of childhood, caught in that awkward zone where his body and mind were always fighting each other for control. To her credit, Mira could read the boys' moods and needs: she had a brilliant empathy with both, a casual and unforced friendship which was now more critical than ever. She gave Hugh the space he needed, and held George close to her.

Caroline was now walking down a long corridor which ran between huge metal containers, all with padlocks and security-key access. She was in the wake of the attendant, catching his tang as she followed him until they reached unit 327A.

'All yours,' he said as she put the key in the lock. 'Press the button by the door when you're done and I'll come and fetch you.' He reached inside the unit and switched the light on for her, then shuffled away without looking inside.

Caroline took one step in and stopped. The unit had been set out like an office: down both side walls there were metal storage cupboards, and at the far end was the desk and the four-drawer cabinet. The desk was tidy, with a laptop computer in the centre and an anglepoise lamp to one side. She shook her head, unable to take in the information this was sending her; Caroline was standing in the middle of something so alien and unknown that she had no way of accepting its existence.

She forced herself to approach the desk and walked behind it, resting her hands on the top of a high-backed chair. She received another jolt when she saw a framed photo of herself on the desk, a snap taken in the garden some years ago. She looked thinner and happier then, and that impression depressed her still further. Her limbs felt heavy and she wanted to sit in the big chair and cry or sleep – and she knew then how much she needed Guy's huge arms to surround her and take the pain away.

After several minutes of silent inactivity, Caroline pushed herself up and went to the edge of the desk, feeling underneath until she found a sliver of masking tape. She pulled the key away from the desk and turned to the filing cabinet. It unlocked noisily and she crouched down to pull open the bottom drawer. Inside was a black leather briefcase with brass fittings, another of Guy's things she had never seen. She snapped the catches open and lifted the top. Then her legs started to give way as she saw what was inside, and she collapsed into the chair. She had never seen so much money.

She sat in the car, oblivious to the rumble of traffic as it raced past her. She could not recall how she had managed to drive to this spot, parked in a street that ran between Clapham and Wandsworth Commons; they had lived here once, many years ago, and she often came back to see how their house looked now. But she had no interest today: instead, she merely stared through the windscreen as a light summer shower passed over and dotted the glass. She could not bring herself to reach over to the passenger seat and open the briefcase again. In the corner of her eye it looked like some malevolent package – a ticking bomb, a smoking gun – and she wanted to block it from her mind.

Caroline had cried for ten minutes, clutching the steering wheel as the tears soaked her face and dripped down on to her blouse. She was wounded, but she couldn't tell what had hurt her more: Guy's death or the discovery of his dark secrets. She needed the space and peace of an empty car to try and confront the horror of it all. Had Guy died from a heart attack she felt she would have been better able to cope; but murder was so removed from her experience, so dislocated from her existence, that she was ill-equipped to accept the fact and grieve for him as she should. There were too many questions that needed resolution before she could yield to the absolute misery of her loss. The money merely added to her confusion, so that she floundered in an emotional vortex that defied a reasoned response.

She had not tried to count it; there were too many notes and the amount seemed almost irrelevant. In truth, she was reluctant to touch it in case she assumed some guilt from that simple act, but she still felt dirty from carrying the briefcase out of the unit. She had not stayed long once she'd opened the case: her mind swimming with a thousand possibilities, she had wanted to get away as soon as she could and suck in fresh air to clear her head.

Her thoughts returned to the previous day. Much as she fought against it, the image of Guy would not go away: she saw him at home, working at his desk or making coffee; she thought of him on the phone, his huge laugh filling the house as he shared a joke with a colleague; and she remembered him standing on the pavement and waving his white handkerchief as she drove away with the boys, both of them waving back furiously. Her last sight of him had been in the rear-view mirror, too small to capture him fully.

And what had happened when he had gone back into the house? Had he known what lay ahead? Had he sat down straight away and written her that letter? Had he made some urgent calls? Did he know he might never see them again? As long as Caroline was ignorant of the answers, she felt she could never properly deal with his death.

17

After an hour she started the engine. Grass would need her and she, in turn, needed him. He might have critical knowledge, information that could dissolve her quandary and rescue her from this turmoil. She wanted to know the truth, even though the prospect frightened her; she had to put everything in order before she could start to mourn for Guy and deal with everything his death would deliver. She wiped her eyes with her fingertips and blinked away the remaining tears. She looked across at the briefcase and clenched her teeth; she had no idea of how to deal with it and that, more than its simple presence, was what terrified her.

Gerry Grass had his feet up on the desk and was sucking a pencil. He would not normally have taken much interest in the death of a banker – other than to say that it was a good start – but he had been disconcerted by his brief conversation with Mrs Mercer, and he was already more involved than he wanted to be.

'The hand's got to be a clue, hasn't it? I mean, it must be some kind of signal.' Grass had hardly noticed that Jane Fox was in the room and was surprised when she spoke; as his assistant, she would do all the laborious and repetitive work needed to solve a case like this, and he didn't expect her to exercise her brain too much.

'It definitely sent a signal to him,' Grass said as he pulled the pencil out of his mouth. 'He was alive when they chopped it off.'

'Right. But why did they strangle him? They could just as easily have left him to bleed to death.'

'Perhaps he didn't get the message. Or maybe they wanted a

bit of fun before they finished him off. Either way, I'm not too concerned about the modus operandi. And I'm not convinced that the hand has any real significance, other than showing that we're dealing with some sick bastard who carries round an electric saw.'

Jane Fox suffered much intolerance and discrimination in the force, but she resented only one particular aspect: most men assumed that she had little brain and rarely asked for her opinion, let alone paid attention to it when it was offered. Grass was not a bad boss, but he still evidenced a lingering reluctance to listen to her.

'It could be significant for another reason,' she suggested, ignoring his put-down.

'Which is?' he replied, without showing the least interest in her idea.

'Perhaps he had something attached to his arm – like a case that was chained on.'

Grass considered this and put the pencil back in his mouth to demonstrate his attention. 'That's not such a bad idea,' he said. 'Yeah, I like that. Why don't you get on to it, see if you can come up with something? Maybe the wife could give you some help.'

She glowed a little at this, grateful for any scrap of acknowledgement or praise. 'I'll go round and see her later,' she said.

'Good. I was due to go, but you can handle it. And after you're finished with her, you should go to his office and talk to some of his mates, see if there's anything there.'

Jane realised he was being lazy, but she didn't mind. This was a case she felt well able to deal with on her own.

THREE

Caroline Mercer was thirty-nine, three years younger than Guy. She had always battled to keep her figure but, having delivered two boys, she had been fighting against the odds. She would laugh and tell friends that she was planning to have her stomach surgically removed, but secretly she despised herself for her lack of discipline. She wanted to be thin, even though Guy had told her a thousand times that he loved her as she was; she wanted to be a size 10 and look like she did when she'd met him. She remembered those courting days with great affection, when their raw emotion overruled even basic needs like food and drink.

Guy was a catch, a prize that she valued in those early times. He was big and loud in public, eighteen stone, six foot four and with an appetite for everything to match, but privately he could be tender and gentle and she loved these counterpoints to his character. He was liked by all, though she never resented the easy way in which he acquired new friends; in their moments alone, he made her feel like the only one who mattered to him. People would marvel at his lust for life, calling him the consummate *bon viveur*; he was every man, every colleague, every friend they wanted him to be. Guy was a legend come true.

Part of the legend was his climb to the top of the mountain of money. By the time he was twenty-nine, Guy was a partner in an American investment bank, the head of a global business which Caroline barely understood but which involved a lot of entertaining and even more money. Every March Guy would come home and tell her how much he had made the previous year as his bonus; he would show her the bland computer-generated statement of his partner's account, indicating a balance that ran into millions. But that balance was locked away, carefully protected by the firm so that he couldn't simply cash it in and retire in comfort or take his expertise across the street. A Byzantine plan had been established so that only a small percentage of any bonus could be taken in cash; the rest was deferred, and the wealth that they had was nothing more than an IOU on a slip of A4 paper. They could borrow against it – and did – but the cash remained entombed, not in some huge vault but on a large IBM mainframe in New Jersey.

She would say to herself that all things were relative, that they were relatively rich and secure, but she never completely convinced herself. Whilst he earned an enormous salary, they took on equally huge obligations: having started out in a small flat in Putney when they married, they had soon moved up to the house in Castelnau via the terrace in Clapham. They'd bought the cottage in the Cotswolds, and filled both homes with expensive furniture and fittings. Neither had the strength or patience to wait for the good life, feeling the pressure to live their lives as they saw others live theirs. They took the luxury holidays, committed themselves to private education for the children: nobody told them to stop, and no one suggested that the tap of money might eventually run dry before their dream was complete.

Then, one March some five years ago, Guy had come home in a different mood. They had established a ritual: they would go to a smart West End restaurant, drink the finest wine and eat caviar and lobster. He would produce the statement with a flourish over brandy, simultaneously delivering an expensive gift for her. In the mist of that moment they would both believe that they had made it, that they would never have to worry again. Both knew it was just an illusion, but it was warm and beguiling nonetheless.

But he did not follow the ritual that evening. They went out as usual, but he was clearly anxious to discuss something else.

'I've been thinking,' he said as the main course arrived.

'That can be very dangerous for your health,' she replied.

'Seriously, Caro, I want to get out. I'm treading water where I am.'

'I thought you walked on it. That's what everyone says, isn't it?' She didn't like his tone: it was serious, and Guy rarely wasted time on reflective contemplation. She wanted to swipe it away like an irritating fly.

'You're right, in a way,' he said. 'I've built up a bloody good reputation in the City, and I'm not properly rewarded for it. I need to cash in on that, and I've been trying to work out a way to do it.' He paused for effect. 'And now I think I might have found one.'

'What do you mean?'

'Do you remember when I went on that trip to Chicago last year, to talk to a bunch of investors over there?'

'Vaguely.'

'I met one guy who represented a private investment group. He gave me his card and said he'd be in touch. I never heard another word from him – until last month. Then he gives me a call and says he's in town and wants to see me for dinner. We meet, and he comes up with this proposal. His investors will back me to start my own firm. They'll put up all the necessary finance and give me sole authority in running the business – they'll remain as silent partners. And they won't ask for any dividends from their shareholding until the firm is really well established and profitable.'

'Sounds too good to be true,' Caroline said. 'Is it?'

'I don't think it is. I've checked them out and they seem kosher. They have some closed-end funds registered in Netherlands Antilles and total assets of about five billion dollars, so they're not short of a bob or two. The word is that they're very conservative and prudent and believe in long-term partnerships. I can't see a problem.'

'And you want to do this?' Caroline was surprised that he had even given this much thought to the idea without mentioning it to her first. He had never demonstrated any desire to work for himself; he had always seemed so happy to work for someone else and have them worry about all the trivia of business management.

'That's the problem, if there is one,' he said. 'I just don't know. The money could be stratospheric, and it would be ours. The downside is that I'd have to work my tail off and I'd still be beholden to other people. But it might be the opportunity of a lifetime.'

'Have you talked to anyone else about it?'

'I've had very informal discussions with some clients – you

24

know, the ones I can really trust – and they seem broadly supportive. On the other side, the brokers would be keen because they know I can give them an excellent service. So I don't think there would be any problem with the success of the business. It's really down to me – to us.'

Caroline waited. She knew he valued her opinion, and she knew he needed her support to make him take things any further, but she wasn't armed with enough facts or imagination to give him a satisfactory answer.

'What happens if you say no?' she said, stalling.

'Life goes on as normal. Nothing will change.'

'But you'd like to say yes?'

'I'd like to say maybe. I'd like to see whether it could really work, and I won't know that unless I talk to them some more. At the bottom of it all, I'd like us to be secure, and I don't know the best way of ensuring that. But the way things are at the moment, I just can't see where we're going to end up. The bonuses are locked up for so long that, by the time we can cash them in, we'll only be interested in gold-plated Zimmer frames and GTI wheelchairs. I don't want that to happen.'

'How bad is the money situation?' Caroline asked tentatively. He was never more than opaque about their finances, and she had no reason to believe he'd change now.

'To be honest, it's a disaster. We're up to our necks in debt and the repayments just about eat up all our income. We've made no provision for school fees either. And God knows what we'll do when the final bill comes in from Lloyd's.'

The mention of their insurance losses sent a shiver through Caroline. At the time it had seemed such a good idea to be a Lloyd's Name, and the money had flowed in so regularly that they had come to rely on it. They had never truly considered the meaning of unlimited liability – now they were having to confront it.

Ridiculous as it sounded, they were broke. However much Guy earned, it wasn't enough. They had always thought the next pay rise, the next promotion, would be the one that dug them out of the hole and yet, when it arrived, they'd already spent it. For him to admit this was new, however: in other circumstances he'd laugh and pretend that everything was fine. Now, quite possibly because it suited his argument, he was laying his cards on the table.

'Would things be different – better – if you went in with these people?'

He sighed. Guy was showing her a side of himself that she rarely saw, a thoughtful and tentative aspect he normally kept well hidden. It didn't fit with the image he had constructed for himself, and she suspected she was the only one who had ever seen it.

'Who knows?' he shrugged. 'My best guess is that it would be up to me, and that's the way I'd like it. I know I'm good, and I know what I'm worth. I could move to another bank, but in five years' time we'd be facing the same crisis, maybe even worse.'

'Let's say you did do it. Several things need to be considered. For a start, what would happen to all the equity you've got in the partnership now?'

'You mean this?' he said, pointing at the bonus statement that still lay on the table. 'Most of it would vanish. They've designed the bonus scheme to stop me from leaving. I don't know the exact number, but I'd probably only get about five per cent back.'

'Well, five per cent of a lot is still better than a slap in the belly with a wet fish,' she said encouragingly. 'But let's discount that. What about us? What's the downside? If it all fails, where does that leave your career?'

'I think I'm young enough to take that risk. I'd still be good at my job, and I wouldn't have lost contact with the market. And these guys would pay me a salary whilst it was getting going, so we wouldn't be any worse off in the early days.'

'So you have discussed this in some detail, haven't you?' Caroline said, and she couldn't help smiling. He returned her look.

'Sorry. Yes, it is quite advanced. But there's still time to back out gracefully.' He poured her some more wine and then held her hand across the table. 'I won't do anything unless you're completely in agreement. You know that.'

'Guy, what are you waiting for? If you truly believe this is our great chance, you've got to take it. You know I'll support you. God knows why, but I love you too much to do anything else.'

And that was it. Within six months the deal had been signed and Guy had his own business – Asset Management Strategies – and an office in Finsbury Circus. They threw a huge party to celebrate the inauguration and Caroline met some of his new partners, buttoned-up Americans with stilted manners and identical blue suits. She didn't like them much, but what did she know?

Caroline was in the kitchen, thinking of that evening, when the doorbell rang. Mira was preparing macaroni cheese and bacon for the boys whilst they sat and watched a video in the family room in the basement; she cursed in her own language – Caroline picked up the sentiment if not the exact meaning – turned down the heat under the pasta and went to answer the door. She returned with Detective Sergeant Jane Fox.

'You want I should go?' Mira asked Caroline.

'No, that's fine. The boys have to eat.'

Jane waited for the exchange to finish. 'I'm sorry, I've come at a bad time,' she said.

'No worse than any other,' Caroline replied. 'Please, sit down. Would you like coffee, or a drink?' Jane shook her head and sat down at the table while Caroline poured herself a coffee from the cafetière. 'Do you have any news for me?'

'Early days, Mrs Mercer. I'm here because I think you might be able to help us with our investigations.'

'I doubt it. I'm so totally confused at the moment I don't even know what day it is. But I'll try.'

'Thank you. I'm sorry to have to do this, but we need to talk about your husband's death. Are you up to that?' Caroline nodded. 'You know about his hand?'

'His hand?'

'Yes. I thought you knew. His left hand was severed from his arm.'

'Oh God,' Caroline gasped, and she had to swallow back the bile. She breathed heavily and irregularly as she tried to compose herself. 'Why?'

'That's what we're trying to work out. We think your husband might have had a briefcase attached to his wrist with a chain. If we're right, we need to know what was in that case, because it was obviously very important to someone. We were wondering if you knew anything about that.'

Every internal organ appeared to be malfunctioning within Caroline's body; she shook and began to sweat as the image of this mutilation took hold. The horror was intensified by the knowledge that she had stared at Guy, looked into his face as the covering sheet was pulled back, and she had been unaware of what had happened to him. She could barely take in what she had been told; she stammered and faltered as she tried to respond. 'I . . . it's . . . Christ, I had no idea.'

'Take your time, Mrs Mercer.' Jane glanced at Mira, who had stopped her work and was following the conversation closely. Mira's eyes met Jane's and, for a brief moment, Jane could see the fear and the sorrow. Then Mira moved and went to the sink, retrieving a glass from the draining board and filling it with cold tap water. She passed it to Caroline, who took the glass and sipped very slowly from it.

'Was he . . . would he have known?' Caroline asked, part of her not wanting the answer.

'He was alive when they did it, but we think he may have been unconscious.'

Caroline winced from the related pain of this information and drank the rest of the water. Then she stood up and hurried out of the room. Jane waited and scanned the notes on her pad. Mira clattered pots and pans noisily at the sink; Jane wondered how much she understood of the conversation. She was obviously distressed, and Jane wanted to ask her some questions. She was trying to find the right approach when George ran into the kitchen. He stopped in his tracks when he saw Jane, looking uncertainly at her and then at Mira. 'When's supper going to be ready?' he asked.

'Five minutes,' Mira replied. 'Go, little Georgie. Go and

watch your video. I'm bringing it soon.' George waited for one beat, giving Jane a worried look, then scuttled away.

'Sorry about that,' Caroline said when she returned, her eyes red and swollen. 'I think I need a more substantial drink.' She pulled a bottle of wine from the fridge door and filled the empty water glass before sitting down.

'I realise this is all very distressing for you, and I apologise for it,' Jane said quietly. 'But you'll appreciate that we have to find out what happened. If you'd like me to come back later . . .'

'No. No, I understand. You've got your job to do. Go on.'

'Perhaps it would help if I tell you what we already know. Your husband was booked on the Sunday morning flight to Nice. As far as we know, he was not due to travel with anyone else. We're getting the phone records to verify all the calls that were made and received during the weekend, and we'll be speaking to his colleagues. But we don't know what was in the case – or if there even was a case. That could be central to the entire investigation.'

'Well, I can't help you there at all.' The news about Guy's flight to Nice was surprising, but he had always been one to make last-minute plans and he might, she supposed, have been going on an urgent business trip. She didn't want to discuss it: with her emotions under better control, Caroline's thoughts turned to the briefcase she had discovered that morning and which was now locked in her car. That, too, could be central to the whole investigation, and yet something restrained her from mentioning it. Her earlier fears returned and she became more cautious.

'Well, it was a long shot anyway,' Jane said. 'But if you do think of anything, you will let us know, won't you?'

'Of course,' Caroline replied.

Jane got up and smiled at her. 'Before I go, there is one other thing,' she said. 'We found this in your husband's pocket.' She pulled out a clear plastic bag from her jacket pocket and pushed it across the table. Inside was a scrap of paper with 'L – 0181 347 9904 (H)' scribbled on it in Guy's handwriting. 'Does this mean anything to you?'

'Should it?'

'Just thought you might recognise this number, or know why he was carrying it. The number's in the name of Linda Betts, but we've rung it and there's no reply. Do you know her?'

'Linda Betts?' Caroline said. 'That's not a mystery at all. She works for Guy. She'll be at the office – you can get hold of her there.'

'Well, that's the funny thing,' Jane said. 'She rang in sick and nobody knows where she is. You'd think if she were ill she'd be at home. But she isn't.'

'I can't help you there either,' Caroline said, sensing this was significant but unable to shed any more light on the matter.

'No problem. Thanks for your time. We'll be in touch soon.' Jane let herself out, and Caroline was left to deal with her own turmoil.

FOUR

It was not what Jane had expected. She had imagined that the office of Asset Management Strategies would be an oasis of calm, with an abundance of pinstripe suits, Hermès ties and Gucci loafers attached to smart young whizz-kids who toiled before silent screens. Instead, she walked into a large open-plan room where ten or so men and women sat in various poses of relaxed inertia or frantic phone activity. There were screens – dozens of them piled on top of one another – but they bleeped and flashed colourfully and insistently against a backdrop of detached voices that squawked from powerful loudspeakers built into the desks. The men were uniformly scruffy, ties loosened and hanging like sad oriflammes around their necks, whilst the women were dressed in regulation wool skirts and blouses, some having kicked off their shoes the better to flex their toes during their stressed working day.

'Yeah, it's quite a sight, isn't it?' Alan said, catching her look of surprise. Alan Apostle was the office manager, with a job description that covered everything from making sure the coffee machine was fully charged to seeing that the castors were securely fixed to the chairs. He had greeted Jane at the communal reception area and was clearly the nominee for dealing with her questions. His soft pink face was in stark contrast to the blackened teeth within his mouth, stained from years of nicotine and neglect. He had a bulging gut that was out of proportion to his skinny legs and narrow shoulders, and his receding hairline was accentuated by the way he slicked back his hair with gel.

'Come on, let's go to my sumptuous office.' He led her to a small airless room with no natural light: on every available surface there were piles of papers, folders and files, and his desk looked as if a hurricane had recently swept across it. In the middle was an ashtray that contained probably fifty stubs, and Alan lit a cigarette as he sat down. 'Take a pew,' he said, motioning Jane to a grubby brown chair.

'Thanks.' She sat down uncertainly, wondering if she would stick to the fabric.

'We're all in a state of shock here, as you'd imagine. Guy was just about the most popular man in the City. If he had any enemies, we certainly didn't know about them. I just can't figure it out.' He took a long drag on his cigarette. 'But then, I suppose that's your job, isn't it?'

'Precisely,' Jane replied as she pulled her notebook out of her pocket. Alan couldn't help noticing her legs, and made no effort to disguise his interest. He liked the visitor's chair, because it forced women to display their goods whether they wanted to or not – and, in his considered opinion, most did. Her legs were particularly fine specimens, and he wondered whether she might be wearing stockings rather than those passion-killing tights they found so popular. In any event, he was impressed: a copper with good undercarriage was an unexpected bonus.

'So, what can I do for you?' he asked, addressing her knees.

Jane was aware of the look, but she'd dealt with enough closet perverts to ignore it.

'We're at a very early stage of our investigation, and we're still trying to piece together various aspects of Mr Mercer's life. I'm hoping you'll be able to fill in some of the gaps.'

'Where do you want to start?'

'Mr Mercer was here on Friday, I believe?' Jane asked. 'Did you notice anything unusual about his manner or behaviour?'

'Depends what you mean by unusual,' Alan replied. 'Everything Guy did was unusual. He wasn't your regular kind of boss. If we'd had a good week, as likely as not he'd send one of the girls out to get a case of champagne, or we might go down the pub to celebrate. He was a bloody good manager. He was the sort of guy who could give you a right good bollocking and there'd be no hard feelings on either side, and he was just as quick to praise you if you'd done a good job. People here had a lot of respect for him. Most of us are refugees from places where it wasn't so easy to get along with your employers. I haven't been here that long, but I tell you, it's a bloody sight better than any other shop I've worked in. So to answer your question, I wouldn't be able to say if there was anything different about him on Friday.'

'Did you know he was planning a trip?'

'Guy wasn't much of a planner. He did things on the spur of the moment. Like, he'd come in one morning and announce he was going to Eastern Europe for a week, and nobody knew a bloody thing about it. His secretary used to climb up the wall, but she'd organise it all anyway. Where was he off to?'

'The South of France. Did he have clients down there?'

'Not my speciality, clients. You'd have to ask one of the

traders – or Linda, if she ever gets her miserable arse in here.'
He stubbed out the cigarette and snorted disdainfully.

'That's Linda Betts, right? What's her role here?'

'She's head of administration. She's been with Guy since he
set up.' His body language made it clear that he had a low opinion
of her.

'What exactly does that involve?' Jane was anxious that her
total lack of knowledge of the financial markets should not be
too obvious.

'Perhaps I should give you a quick rundown on what we do
here,' Alan said. The legs encouraged him to appear helpful
and compliant, and Jane nodded gratefully. 'Basically, we're a
securities lending operation – an agent, if you like. Our
customers are all big investors on the world's stock markets –
pension funds, insurance companies, fund managers and banks.
When they decide to hold on to those investments, they can
earn some extra cash by lending them to people who need them,
like brokers. The brokers may have sold securities they don't
have, and they need to borrow them to make up the shortfall.
What we do is match up the lenders and borrowers so that they
all get what they want. We also manage the collateral that
borrowers put up as security against the loans. That's normally
treasury bills, bonds, blue-chip stocks or, occasionally, cash. It
all flows through us, and a little sticks to the sides. That's how
we make our money. Linda's job is to make sure that everything
turns up in the right place at the right time after the deals have
been struck.'

'And that's what the people out there are doing?'

'In short. They're on the phone to their clients, finding out
what they've got to lend today, and they're also fielding calls

from brokers who want to borrow.'

'Why do they use you? Why don't they just deal with each other directly?' Jane hoped the questions didn't sound too stupid.

'Two reasons. First, the borrowers may need a large amount of stock. They won't necessarily find all that by going to one lender. So we save them the bother of phoning round everyone they can think of by aggregating all the holdings that we know are for loan, then offering them one deal to satisfy their whole requirement. That saves them time and money, even after they've paid our commission. The same principle applies to the lenders. They know that they're putting their securities into a big pool, and there's more chance that they'll get lent.'

'And the other reason?'

'Anonymity. Some lenders don't want their name in the market, for whatever reason. So they use us as an intermediary, and they deal in our name. The borrower never knows where the stock came from and, quite frankly, doesn't give a toss as long as the deal works.'

'OK. I've got it. And this is presumably a very big business?'

'Mega. We run a twenty-four hour service here: as well as Europe, we deal with the Far East and America from this one location, so we can be lending securities even when our clients are tucked up in bed. We're talking about billions of dollars of loans every day.'

'So it's a profitable activity for you?'

'We rub along,' Alan said as he bared his teeth in an ugly grin.

'And Mr Mercer owned all this?'

'Ah, no, well, now we're on to some shaky ground,' he replied, suddenly turning more serious. 'I'm not privy to that kind of information. I think there are some other shareholders, but we never see them. I don't really know who to ask about that. Jim, the finance director, would be the man to help you on that score.'

'OK. I'll talk to him later.'

'Not unless you've got a very powerful mobile phone. Last I heard, he was somewhere in the Mediterranean on a big yacht. He's recovering from heart bypass surgery. Won't be back for another six months or so, lucky sod.'

'Surely the news of Mr Mercer's death will bring him back, if he's a director?'

'Well, he's not a director of the holding company, the one that has all the power and voting rights. He's only finance director of some of the operating companies.'

'So who is in charge right now?'

'That's what we're trying to work out. Truth to tell, it's a bloody mess around here today. We're running round like headless chickens. That's why you ended up with me, I'm afraid.'

Jane scribbled some notes and looked up. 'Tell me, Alan, can you think of any reason why Mr Mercer should have been murdered – anything at all?'

He shook his head slowly and thoughtfully. 'It really beats me. He was such a nice guy. He had a good honest business here, and his clients liked him. So did the staff. He had a lovely family, too. It's a crying shame, it really is.'

Jane flipped her notebook shut. 'You've been very helpful, and I appreciate it. I won't take up any more of your time. Can I just ask you one more favour, and then I'll get out of your hair? If Linda Betts appears, we'd really like to talk to her. Could you let us know?'

'Sure thing. I'd really like to talk to her too,' he said.

Jane stumbled out of the building, her mind reeling from her rapid lesson in high finance. She needed a strong coffee and a quiet corner to try and work it all out.

The sickness wouldn't go away. Caroline felt a bolus trapped in her lower throat but it didn't want to come up or go down. She rocked herself on her hands in front of the kitchen sink, her eyes and mouth watering in anticipation of an explosion that wouldn't arrive.

The boys had gone out with Mira to the cinema. She had stood at the gate and watched them disappear before feeling confident enough to unlock the car and pull out the briefcase, looking all around her as she scuttled back into the house. She felt an inexplicable sense of guilt and shame, and this grew as she snapped open the case on the kitchen table, having first locked all the doors and windows. It took her forty-five minutes to count it all: one million pounds exactly. She had washed her hands carefully, the distinctive smell of fresh money nauseating and overpowering, and now she was anchored to the sink as she tried to purge herself.

She blinked away the tears and attempted to bring some reason and order to her thoughts. The money, quite clearly, was not hers: if it had been free and unencumbered, Guy would not have made such clandestine arrangements for it. But possession was nine-tenths of the law, she recalled, and no one else had stamped their name on it. That was the beauty of cash, as Guy had told her on so many occasions. Whoever owned it hadn't come forward to claim it, and she was convinced she could find a good home for it without their help.

But, just as clearly, the money held the key – or, at the very least, a key – to Guy's murder. Another cliché attacked her: follow the money and you'll find the villain. Were she to tell the police, they would doubtless be greatly assisted in their hunt for his killer. Almost as an afterthought, she accepted that she might feel substantially less ill and frightened if she did tell them. But then what? She had no means of supporting herself. The overdraft was up to its limit, and she couldn't get any money out of the business. In the house there was about a hundred pounds in cash, including the boys' piggy-bank savings: that was enough for a brief whizz around Sainsbury's and nothing more.

Caroline's sickness did not originate solely from grief. She was smart enough, even in the midst of her confusion and anguish, to realise that Guy's murderer had been looking for something, something that might still remain unclaimed. Was it the money? Was she now in danger herself, blameless as she was? This insecurity, and her inability to do anything to lessen it, merely heightened the nausea.

These questions continued to churn her guts when the phone rang. 'Mrs Mercer?' a man said vaguely.

'Speaking. Who's this?'

'My name's Anthony Tilt. I'm your husband's solicitor.'

'Yes?' She had never heard of him, but she was getting used to surprises. He had a beautiful voice, she noticed, well educated without being too plummy.

'I was very sorry to hear about your husband. Please accept my condolences.'

'Thanks. Is that why you called?'

'No. Mrs Mercer, we need to talk urgently. I have a number

40

of instructions from your late husband – and I also have his latest will.'

'Latest?'

'Exactly. That's one of the reasons I need to see you. Would it be possible for me to come round this evening?'

'Well, I suppose so. Do you know where I am?'

'Yes. Shall we say eight o'clock?'

'Fine. I'll see you then.'

She dropped the receiver back on to its cradle and turned to face the neat piles of cash in the case. On impulse, she decided to wait for Mr Tilt's visit before calling the police to tell them about the money.

FIVE

When she saw him, she realised why he was half an hour late. Everything about him suggested chaos – the wild curls of black hair unbrushed, the tie knot askew, the shirt heavily creased and the suit crumpled – and she knew that he would be as casual with his timekeeping as he was with his appearance. He stood on the doorstep, smiling, and Caroline wondered how this dishevelled man could possibly help her.

'Mrs Mercer? I'm Anthony Tilt.'

'Come in,' Caroline said. She led him towards the sitting room and directed him to the least-stained armchair. The boys had spilt a selection of fruit juice, yogurt, chocolate mousse, cola, pizza and ketchup over everything in the house, and Caroline had long since abandoned the battle to remove the evidence. Guy and she had always promised themselves new furniture when the boys had attained a reasonable level of coordination, but they had never reached that stage. Early on they had maintained that the boys should not even be allowed in the room but, like many other good intentions, this had not stood the test of time or the children's perseverance.

Tilt slumped into the chair and dropped his bag, a battered canvas holdall, on to the floor next to him. 'Am I very late?' he asked. 'I'm afraid my watch is at the mender's.'

'Not a problem,' she said. 'Would you like a drink?'

'A Scotch would be nice.'

She fixed their drinks and sat opposite him on the big Chesterfield, which had once been a crisp ivory colour but was now mottled with grey patches. 'So – where do we start?' she asked.

Tilt sipped his drink and the action seemed to relax him. 'I've brought all the documents, and we can go through those later if you like. But I do need to ask you some questions first. Is that all right?'

'Fire away. I'm getting used to interrogation.' She shrugged and smiled at him to show how amenable she could be, even in the face of adversity.

'Before we start, I wanted to say how sorry I am about all this. I know it must be very painful for you, and I'll try my best to keep my questions to the bare minimum. Have the police got anywhere with their investigation?'

'Not as far as I'm aware. Early days, they say.'

'Well, let's hope something turns up. It's hard to grieve when nothing's finalised, isn't it?' He took another gulp of his drink – longer and deeper this time – and Caroline felt that he was speaking from personal experience. She was intrigued, but too polite to push it.

'You're right. I would like some answers, if only so that I can sort it all out in my mind.'

'Perhaps I can help you a bit. Did you know that Guy was using me as his solicitor?'

'I'm afraid not.'

'No, I suspected as much. That's probably not important,

though. He came to me about eighteen months ago. His accountant is a mutual friend and he introduced us. He was very concerned about getting his affairs in order. I assumed that he was worried about his health – you know, men of his age often start to get feelings of mortality and the will is one of the things they finally get around to. He didn't have a will, so that's where I came in.'

'He never mentioned any of this to me,' Caroline said.

'I suppose he didn't think it necessary. Whatever – I did the work for him and that, I guessed, would be that.'

'And it wasn't?'

'This is what I wanted to ask you about. It's none of my business, but I was wondering if your circumstances have changed dramatically in the last three months.'

'How do you mean?'

'Have you inherited a lot of money, or found some long-lost relatives? You know – something exceptional that would force a drastic rearrangement of your finances?'

She shook her head slowly, trying to take in what he was saying. 'Nothing springs to mind.' She watched Tilt finish his drink and stare into the bottom of the glass. 'Can I get you another one?'

'Oh, that'd be lovely,' he replied, sounding rather relieved. When she came over to retrieve his glass she caught the smell of him for the first time – a combination of cigarettes, wine, whisky, eau de Cologne and that distinctive and slightly stale odour of a City worker – and the redolence was almost too much for her to bear. It was too like Guy's, too close for comfort, and she pulled herself away before she was overcome by it.

'This is the part I don't pretend to understand,' he said when

45

she gave him the drink. 'Guy came back to me about three months ago. He said there had been some developments and he needed to update the will. He wanted to establish a number of trusts. That, in itself, is not unusual. But . . . well, the beneficiaries of these trusts aren't entirely straightforward.'

'Go on.'

'There are trust funds for Hugh and George – no problem there. And all the life assurance policies have you as the named beneficiary, which is quite normal. But he also established two other trusts, leaving no instructions as to how they should be managed. It's not clear to me exactly what he intended to do with them, or how he intended to fund them. He simply told me that the beneficiaries would know all about them and that they'd contact me directly if and when he died.'

'So you're saying you don't know who the beneficiaries are? I don't get it.'

'That's a shame. I was rather hoping you would. Guy may have decided to set up these trusts as another way of passing his estate to you, but I can't see the logic in that. They wouldn't serve any purpose just because they're oddly named or the beneficiaries are unspecified. But I thought he might have told you – or at least left instructions for you – so that you'd know what he was trying to do.'

'You've lost me,' Caroline said. 'In what names are these two mysterious trusts?'

'One is simply called Hartmann Number One. The other is called the Shadowlawn Foundation Trust.' Tilt leant over and pulled his case on to his knees. He searched through different folders before apparently finding what he was looking for, and handed a blue plastic file to Caroline. 'It's all in here.'

Caroline opened the file but she couldn't focus on it. Further news of Guy's secrets had confused her to the point where she wanted to block it all from her mind, and this man's partial knowledge merely exacerbated her frustration. She dropped the file wearily on to her lap and looked at him. 'You have no way of finding out any more?' she asked.

'Well, once the news of Guy's death gets out, I'm hoping that we'll see the beneficiaries crawl out of the woodwork – that is, if they know anything about it. Other than that, I can't see what else I can do.'

Caroline thought of the cash that was still lurking in the kitchen, hidden in the cupboard under the sink behind bottles of disinfectant and buckets. She wondered whether she should tell him about it: having reached the stage where she trusted nothing and no one, she wanted to believe that there was someone who could help, and he was at least available. She decided to test him.

'How much do you know about Guy's business affairs?'

'I was his personal lawyer. I had no involvement in the business side, and I didn't ask him about it. But I got the feeling that things were not going too well.'

'What makes you say that?'

'Nothing more than a hunch. Everything just seemed so urgent, as if these matters had to be sorted out very quickly. He was on the phone to me the day after we'd met to find out if the changes had been made, and he kept on stressing how important it was to get things done promptly. He offered to pay me more to speed up the process.'

Caroline immediately understood. 'Forgive me for asking, but how much did he pay you?'

'He didn't. I sent him a bill for three hundred pounds. It's still outstanding. But don't worry about that now. We can settle all that later.' To cover his embarrassment he drank some more, and Caroline gave him the benefit of the doubt: he had not come here simply to get the money from her. He seemed genuinely perplexed by the task he'd been given by Guy and was looking for guidance. She reappraised him: the clothes, though poorly cared for, were good quality and well cut. His face betrayed too many years of bad living, yet he might still be considered as handsome, in a craggy sort of way. To Caroline, it looked as if there was much more beneath his weathered exterior, and she felt herself warming to him.

'Is there anything else I should know?' she asked, dreading the answer.

'The will is pretty straightforward otherwise. The house is already in your name and, as I said, you'll get all the proceeds from his life assurance policies. You also get his shares in the business, and you'll need to sign some papers for that. He drew up a list of other assets and there are no big surprises there. We can go through it, if you like.' He shrugged as if to suggest that this would not be productive and he had no inclination to do so. 'I suggest you keep that file and have a look through it. Something may jog your memory. And you should also go through all his personal papers to see if there's anything that makes sense of all this.'

She nodded and thought about what to do and say next. An idea came to her. 'Look,' she said, rather apologetically, 'I need a lot of help. How would you feel about working for me? There are some issues that need resolving, and I could use some professional advice. Would you do it?'

He finished his drink and looked at his shoes. 'I'm not sure,' he replied. 'I'd like to help, but . . . to be frank, this is not a good time for me. I don't know if I can take on any more work at the moment.'

'Oh,' Caroline said, trying to sound reasonable and understanding.

'Perhaps it would help if you told me a little bit more about what you had in mind?'

Caroline decided to lay her cards on the table. 'Every time I talk to someone about Guy I find out something I didn't know before. There are so many things I don't understand. To tell you the truth, I'm half scared out of my wits by all this. You see, he wrote to me just before . . . just before it happened, but what he said wasn't very clear. He seemed to be in serious trouble, danger even. I need someone who's completely independent to come in and have a look, to try and work it all out.'

'Shouldn't the police be doing that?'

'Yes and no. It's stupid, but I don't want them delving into our personal affairs. I want them to find the person who did this to Guy, and that's it. Anything else is between me and him. Can you understand that?'

'I suppose I can.' He looked uncertain, glancing at her and then at his glass. 'Look, I want to be helpful. Professionally, I owe that to you and your late husband. If you could tell me a little bit more, anything that might be relevant, I could see if there's anything that comes out of it that may be useful. But . . . I will have to charge you, I'm afraid.'

'I'd expect nothing less,' Caroline said. 'I'm not ready for charity just yet.'

He grinned reassuringly and Caroline felt that she had finally found someone to put her faith in. He was all she had, but it was a start. She had, initially, judged him too harshly, and now she was beginning to warm to him. She wanted to tell him more, and was ready to disclose her secret: he would have to know about the money.

'I'd better get you another drink,' she said. 'This could be a long night.'

Jane had decided that Mrs Mercer was not all that she seemed. Although she was sad and shocked, there was something deeper going on, some bigger emotion that warranted investigation. Was it fear? Jane felt she had something to be afraid of, a backdrop to her obvious pain that suggested she knew more than she was saying. It wasn't necessarily the keystone of the case, but it needed to be pursued, and Jane would follow the line cautiously and persistently.

Mira offered a different set of problems. A young girl, out of her natural environment, enjoying a standard of living she probably wasn't used to: could she have had some closer relationship with Mercer that went beyond professional boundaries? Jane didn't know enough about her, didn't even know if she had an alibi, and she wanted to tie up this particular loose end. She made a mental note to resolve it.

As for the business, Jane struggled to make a connection between Mercer's death and his commercial activities. On the face of it there was little to be gained from spending too much time at his office, but her training told her that it was another avenue that demanded further work. Her problem, as always, would be to gain enough access to information that could tell her whether Asset Management Strategies formed part of the equation. What they did there was so remote from her own experience that she just couldn't say if it needed the full blast of a major inquiry.

Grass came over to her desk as she was writing neat notes on her pad. 'Get anywhere?' he asked innocently.

She dropped her pen on the pad and looked up at him. 'The wife's up to something, and I don't know what,' she said.

'Should she be a suspect?'

'I honestly don't see how,' Jane answered. 'She was miles away when it happened and I can't see a motive. But I think she knows more than she's letting on. I think she has some information that would help us sort out why he was topped, if not who did it.'

'Are you going to bring her in for questioning?'

'That would probably be counter-productive right now. She'd clam up if she thought we were on to her. No, much better that we just play it softly and show her we're deeply warm and caring individuals. We're more likely to catch her off guard that way.'

'OK.' Grass changed his tone to show he was still in charge. 'Forty-eight hours, then we take the gloves off. Our sympathies can only stretch so far. So if I were you I'd get back over there and find out what she's got.'

'Exactly what I had planned,' she said. 'Oh, and by the way, we've got the phone records for Linda Betts. No calls out since two days before Mercer's death. And one other interesting item. She bought French francs from her bank two weeks before the murder – five thousand pounds' worth – and she put her flat up for rent at about the same time, with a local estate agent.'

'Meaning?'

'Meaning wherever she's gone she didn't intend coming back

51

in a hurry. What I don't know is whether it means anything more than that, or whether it's just coincidence.'

Grass smiled, but it was a smile of condescension rather than complicity. 'One of the things you'll learn is that there's no such thing as a coincidence in a murder inquiry,' he said. 'I'd say that Miss Betts is pretty critical to this investigation. *Cherchez la femme*, as they say.'

Jane did everything she could to ignore his attitude. 'I'm dealing with it, sir. We're checking with the credit-card companies to see if she charged any flights to them.'

'Keep me posted, Jane,' he said. 'We can't afford to screw this up.'

As he sauntered off Jane curled her toes tightly and counted to ten, her determination supplemented by Grass's tacit hostility. 'I'll show you,' she said under her breath as she picked up her bag and stuffed her papers into it.

SIX

Being married to Guy had not been easy. With his huge circle of friends and acquaintances he was always affable, the laughing cavalier they expected and loved, but, behind closed doors with Caroline, he could be moody and irritable. To herself she often described her life as a giant roller coaster, riding incredible highs and lows with Guy as the motor. Sometimes he was the perfect lover, the attentive father and the consummate family man; at others, he was withdrawn and sullen, barking at all of them and wearing a thick veil of depression. She often wondered if he would ever attain a state of true contentment: within his large frame he seemed to harbour frustrations that threatened to explode, and she believed that the eczema from which he suffered was a manifestation of this. His skin would erupt into weeping crusts and he would scratch them in his sleep and smother them with cortisone creams. Strangely the condition was always at its worst after a particularly stressful time, as if his sheer willpower could control it while he battled with a crisis and it would appear only after he had dealt with the problem and his defences were weakened.

She loved him no less for all this; in fact, she felt that she loved him more because she knew his deeper, darker side and how hard he struggled to control it. When he was irascible she consoled herself with the thought that this was the price she paid – was willing to pay – for everything he had delivered to her. He could bring her joy, make her laugh, give her the feelings of warmth and comfort that she craved; he knew how to push her buttons and she was glad of it. Guy was the only man she had ever known with the instinctive sense of how to treat her, of how to make her feel special, beautiful and wanted. From this she drew strength, knowing that she was as valuable to him as he was to her.

Guy's mother, a little woman whose obvious wisdom was often obscured by too much gin, had once discussed his weaknesses with Caroline. 'You have to accept that all men are flawed,' she had said. 'There are so many things to lead them off the straight and narrow and you have to decide which ones you can live with. I think you should count your blessings with him. After all, there are worse things in life than drinking too much and spending money you don't have. He could sit naked in the cupboard sniffing your underwear.' As men's foibles went, it was an odd example to give, but Caroline understood the sentiment and agreed with it: his failings were manageable and he made ample compensation for them.

Guy was dynamic, forceful, energetic, invigorating – whilst it had not been easy for Caroline to cope with her whirling dervish, as she often referred to him, she knew that the alternatives could have been so much worse. She might have been stuck with a little man with little habits and little aspirations, and her own life would have been smaller and duller as a consequence.

Guy and she had once discussed, after too many drinks, their biggest regrets, and she amazed herself by admitting that she honestly had none. He reminded her of something she said when she was consumed with baby blues after George was born, that he was her greatest mistake; at the time she had truly believed it, not because he was a bad baby, but because his effect on her was so deleterious. She put on weight she couldn't lose; she slept only fitfully and lightly; her breasts seemed to hover somewhere near her navel; and her moods swung so violently that even she couldn't predict how she might feel about anything. It took her two full years to recover from George, something Guy never understood.

When he confronted her with this, she tried to explain. 'At the time that's how I felt. I know now it was a silly thing to say, but you have no idea of what George did to me.'

He seemed to take this to heart, and never raised it again. Even if he didn't appreciate what she had gone through, he was at last aware of the pain it had caused and did not want to recall it for her. Instead, he changed the subject to talk about his own regrets – of how he wished he had taken a job in Hong Kong that was offered to him when they only had Hugh because he thought it would have secured them financially for good, and other such professional disappointments – but he didn't stray into his personal feelings. If there were things he rued about their life together, he kept them very private, and Caroline chose not to probe. She knew of some, but they had always remained unspoken. He was desperately sad about his relationship with his father, for instance: he died when Guy had just gone up to university, well before she met him, and she always sensed that he carried a special guilt about the fact that they were so remote from each other, so far removed by the four decades between them that nothing could pull them together. He never directly referred to it but, through his own actions with the boys, Caroline could see how keen he was to prevent history repeating itself.

In the early days of their marriage he was wary of letting her meet his family. He had an older brother, Charlie, who had left home as soon as he finished his A levels and worked in Edinburgh for an insurance company; his mother turned to drink when his father died, sold the family home and moved to a flat in the town nearby where she spent her days in a placid, slightly sozzled state. He was close to neither and only duty made him stay in touch. To Caroline this was a paradox that she couldn't reconcile with the character she knew and loved, but she let it rest. If that was how he wanted it to be, there was little to be gained from trying to change it.

She had spoken to both Charlie and his mother on several occasions after Guy was murdered. Both were concerned, but neither offered her much practical support. For this she was quietly grateful, as she didn't need the additional trouble of dealing with them on top of all the other crises. In any case, the support they might have given was not what she required: only Guy could have fulfilled those demands.

Her own family was slightly less complicated. Her mother, Joan, was still both sensible and reasonable, in spite of the fact her husband had run off with his secretary less than a year after Caroline was born. Caroline lost all contact with her father after she finished school: he had paid for her education and, once it was over, felt he had discharged all his responsibilities. She didn't ask her mother what had happened to him, although she had the occasional twinge of interest when she would wonder how things had turned out for him. They had become a self-sufficient unit, mother and daughter, and Caroline had grown up very quickly, almost missing awkward adolescence altogether. Inevitably, however, her life with Guy and the children steadily eroded the closeness between them, to the extent that she rarely found time to see Joan on her own.

Joan's own appraisal of her worth seemed to validate this remoteness. Caroline had sought comfort from her mother and had called her frequently after Guy's death, but Joan could offer nothing more than sympathy: there was no advice, no wisdom, in what she had to say. 'I'm afraid I can't be of much use to you,' she had said in one of their rambling phone conversations. 'My own experience with men should have made you realise that.' It was a blunt and unkind judgement, but it had a strong and positive effect on Caroline. If her mother felt unable to make things better, then who could?

If anything, Guy had been keener on starting a family than Caroline. He was determined to have children and didn't want to wait too long to begin. Though he never admitted it to her, she suspected that this sprang from his own experience: his father had been forty-three when Guy was born, and he died eighteen years later. Guy remembered him only as an old man, not as a father who played football with him instead of mowing the lawn, and he wasn't prepared to offer his children the same fate. He wanted to be their friend, their special mate to whom they could turn for their every need; he didn't wish to be seen as distant and forbidding, administering only redundant advice and parental justice. By default, that task fell to Caroline.

They were not, in truth, natural parents. They suffered from the frustrations of broken nights and broken dreams and were surprised by the different ways in which the boys developed.

Hugh was bright and small: he had started talking very early and was an avid reader, loving nothing more than to curl up on the sofa in his father's big arms and go through a pile of books. Guy would often come home from work with a bag full of new books to keep Hugh amused, only slightly sad that his son and heir was not more interested in train sets and Meccano.

George was such a contrast that they wondered how they could have produced him: he was quiet and shy, a very fat baby who turned into a beautiful fair-headed toddler with confused brown eyes. With Hugh, they only needed to tell him something once and he would understand and remember it; but George seemed dislocated from reality, unable to grasp even the most basic concepts of life and living. They hugged him more to protect him from the horrors he would one day have to face. They knew it was wrong, but they did it anyway.

Guy loved them both and accepted their differences without demur, and they loved him back with a passion that bordered on fixation. They craved his approval for everything they did and competed fiercely for his attention, a commodity in short supply. He struggled to find the quality time he and Caroline had read so much about and could often do no more than take them to the cinema or play soccer with them on a Sunday afternoon. Their disappointment was well concealed, their naive optimism never dimmed; Dad could do no wrong in their eyes.

Hugh understood about Guy's death. It hurt him, but he was too proud to show it; instinctively he tried to assume his new role as the man of the house, tough and reliable. With a wisdom beyond his years, Hugh decided to shield his brother from the truth, to let George hold on to the hope that Dad might return until he realised the futility for himself. With Caroline Hugh was sombre and, in rare unguarded moments, tearful, more bent on vengeance than even she was; with George, he played a game he thought was right and tried to hide his grief.

Caroline was at a loss as to how best to deal with them, offering cuddles that she knew she needed more than they and striving to keep their squabbles to a minimum. By default she devolved much more responsibility to Mira, entrusting the boys' care to her as she battled with her own fears. Vivacious and tireless, Mira relished the challenge, cooking more than ever and keeping George occupied as much as she could. She gave Hugh only what he asked for; she sensed his confusion and his struggle to find a place for himself in the disjointed family where he was neither man nor boy. Caroline was grateful for her intuition, and wondered how she had lost her own.

In spite of driving rain, Mira had taken both boys to the playing fields on Rocks Lane, once more leaving Caroline to brood in an echoing and lifeless house. She craved the peace but once it arrived she missed the noise – can't live with them, can't live without them, she'd say – and she resorted to sitting at the kitchen table with a list of things to do, without doing any of them. The endless flow of correspondence had produced a mountain of papers that she knew she should deal with, but she lacked the will to attack it. Who really cared if she failed to renew the guarantee on the dishwasher, or apply for another store credit card?

Only three documents nagged her sufficiently to initiate some activity. She had found Guy's life assurance policies stuffed in a drawer and, distasteful as she found it, she knew she must call and set the wheels of a claim in motion. She dragged herself to the wall phone and started to make the calls. The conversations were brief, similar and equally depressing.

'I'm sorry, Mrs Mercer, but the premiums have not been paid for three months and the policy is no longer in force. We sent several reminders but received no payment.'

She found herself shouting: 'Bastard!' She knew, in spite of her protestations to the faceless paper-pushers, that there was no error. She had seen the bank statements: direct debits and standing orders were always going unpaid and she had no doubt that the bank would happily bounce them and charge her for the privilege, further increasing the debt. Her one lifeline – an ironic description in the circumstances – had been brutally and casually severed. Guy had been reckless to the end.

The cash: inevitably, its presence burned through to reach the front of her thoughts. It sat malevolently, like a rotting carcass, more pungent by the second. One million pounds – how many bad pennies was that? It could solve every problem, but what new ones could it create? It was someone else's money, and they would still be wanting it. She needed it too: she could pay off the mortgages, loans and overdrafts, put aside enough to cover the boys' school fees and still have some left over. But what price would she have to pay? It was a question to which she could find no answer, an equation with no solution, and her fear increased with every minute that she failed to come up with the formula.

The balcony café was bustling with travellers, meeters and greeters. Like any gateway airport, Amsterdam's Schipol processed a continuing tide of people on the move, on the make and on the run. The two men who sat opposite each other attracted no particular attention, business executives discussing a major deal or finalising their itinerary. They spoke in German.

'You know what to do?'

Christian Lemmerich nodded briefly. 'It's all in hand.'

'You'll go straight to her house?'

'No. That's not the plan. I need to make contact with our friends first.' Lemmerich seemed annoyed that he had to rehearse this strategy once again.

'But you will see her?'

'All in good time. Don't forget, we still cannot be sure that she has our property. We need to move carefully. I don't want her alarmed or put on guard. That will just make everything more problematic.'

'Chris, I don't need to remind you of the exposure we're facing. Twenty-five million dollars is at stake. It has to be recovered.'

Lemmerich removed his wire-framed glasses and rubbed the bridge of his nose. 'I'm fully aware of the problem.' The finality with which he said this precluded any further discussion, and they sat in silence until the flight was called. 'KLM announces the departure of flight 763 to London City Airport from gate six. All passengers should now proceed to the gate.'

Lemmerich stood up and gathered his coat and briefcase. 'If she has the money, I will get it back for us. That's all you need to know. Don't trouble yourself to come to the gate. I'll call you.'

'Do that. Good luck.'

SEVEN

Linda Betts sat in the gloom of her hotel room, her satin dressing gown untied to reveal bare flesh that she had no reason to cover up. On the bed she had carefully laid out all the papers – passport, money, travellers' cheques, plane ticket, directions to the flat – which she had thought she would be needing. She went through the plans one more time – Guy's plan, and her undisclosed alternative – just to make sure she was not being stupid.

In Guy's plan, she would fly down to Nice on the Saturday, catch the connecting plane to Corsica and go to the apartment on a hill outside Ajaccio. He would follow on the Sunday, and she'd meet him at the airport. That was the simple plan; hers was more complicated. She had never intended to fly to Corsica without knowing that he was already there. In her complex moral code, Linda had no time for naked trust; she loved him, and she thought he loved her, but she'd felt the burn of disappointment too often in her life to let that belief be sufficient. He was a married man with much to lose, perhaps too much when it came down to it, and she was not prepared to be let down at the last minute. Even in the final flush of excitement, Linda had kept her head.

She had gone to Heathrow early on Sunday and waited patiently for the check-in desk for Nice to open. She watched every passenger as they heaved their luggage on to the scales, handing over their passports and tickets to the pretty girl at the counter. She never took her eyes off it until the flight had taken off. Guy was not on the plane. All the doubts she'd suppressed during their planning now flooded back: after all, she told herself, he had so many commitments, so many reasons not to come, that she began to convince herself that it had all been too good to be true.

Analysing everything back in the hotel by the airport, she could see the pattern of deceit which confirmed her doubts. If he could lie to everyone else, then why not to her? He had withheld so many vital details from her that she was no longer sure of where she stood. Was she part of the problem or part of the solution? Much as she tried to convince herself of his sincerity when he had told her that this was it – their place in the sun, as he'd described it – she couldn't stop herself from thinking that he was merely playing an elaborate game to keep her quiet and protect his own interests. He was smart enough to fool much bigger fish than her, and her insecurity peaked as the thought of betrayal dawned on her.

Twice she'd been on the verge of calling, dialling his number before hanging up as her courage evaporated. Perversely it was better not to know, not to be given the final confirmation of all her fears: this way, at least, she could hang on to the slender hope that everything would work out as planned. She couldn't be sure that he had let her down yet, and maybe he wouldn't. There were a thousand perfectly sensible explanations for his delay, any of which she would calmly accept as part of their deal, and the thought of him, and what he could do for her and to her, should have been enough to sustain her. How many times had he told her how much she meant to him? Was this the pillow talk of a man who was only interested in getting her knickers off? She'd had enough experience of those to believe that he was different, a man who would not make such statements lightly if his only motive was lust. No, he had played it straight so far. He would come through – wouldn't he?

With Guy she was a different person, the way she had always wanted to be but had never had the courage. He made her soft and feminine, blind to her thin outer hide and delving beneath to reveal a version of herself that he could love and she could be proud of. Simply in the way he would say, 'Good morning', he could cut through her so that she was exposed and vulnerable, a silly girl with none of the pretensions she'd worked so hard to cultivate. To her he never tried to exploit this skill, but seemed only to use it naturally. There were other women in the office equally affected by his presence, but he was oblivious to their simperings. She was the only one with whom he had gone further, the only woman who had caught him in her delicate, charmed web. Of that she was quite sure; she didn't need him to tell her – although he had on numerous occasions – since her intuition was strong enough to know it.

And Guy was the only man who could make her cry by his absence. Linda's tears were at a premium; she was not a waterworks fan, believing that crying was wasted effort which rarely achieved more than a runny nose and smudged mascara. Her mother had never cried, so why should she? But she made an exception for Guy. He alone, of all the men she had known, could hurt her just by not being there, and that injury would bring her sufficient pain that she had no alternative but to weep. Contrary to all her best intentions, she could never bring herself to blame him for her misery for more than a few moments and now, faced with the prospect of living without him for ever, she cried without rancour or recrimination. It was not his fault, she reminded herself as she sniffed and dabbed. He had ties that were too strong to break; he was a victim.

She got up and tightened the robe around her. She looked out of the window to the airport, watching planes with their lights winking as they took off and landed. She had been so close, and she so wanted to keep the dream alive. All she needed was his strong embrace and soft words in her ear. She could not forget those final words of his when they had last been together, and her skin tingled at the memory: 'I'm going to take care of you, Linda.'

Caroline was learning about grief. She knew it was irrational and inconsistent, and she knew it took many forms. Applied to her, it was working on many levels, sometimes striking when she least expected it. She would be in the bath and she would cry without warning. She would be on the phone to her mother and the tears would flow as they talked of nothing to do with Guy. Her knowledge of grief did not mean she could control it, but she tried to avoid it. She didn't want friends or relatives to be near her: they would smother her with overdone emotion and then leave her when she most needed them, as was always the case. It was only when everything was back to normal, and the mourning process had run its course, that the true emptiness and sorrow would engulf her. As yet, she had no indication of when that might occur. There was no body to bury, and the funeral would be a critical stage. The police weren't sure when they would be finished with Guy, so her life stayed in limbo while she waited.

Even had she wanted to, she barely had time to concentrate all her thoughts on her loss. The boys were a constant drain on her attention: there had been a fight, a stupid argument between Hugh and George over who was going to go first on the PlayStation. In the heat of it, Hugh had told George the truth – 'You're so stupid, you don't even realise Dad is dead' – and George, stunned as if clipped on the temple by a tracer bullet, had come to Caroline. Mira had tried to intercept him but Caroline waved her away; it was time to deal with it directly. Perversely, she felt useful at last.

'Is Hugh right? Is he winding me up?' George asked, not wanting to cry until he heard it from her lips.

No perfect explanation would come, no simple form of words that could soften the blow. 'Oh George,' she whispered as she cradled his head against her breast. 'Daddy has died, yes. I'm sorry. I'm so sorry.' He wriggled free from her embrace, whether in anger at being excluded from this secret or simply from shock she couldn't say. He ran away, up the stairs to his room, and stayed there sobbing. After half an hour Mira followed and managed to persuade him to come down. His smudged eyes were filled with hatred for Caroline, for the whole world, as he tried to digest this information that had been concealed from him.

'It was wrong and I'm sorry,' Caroline said. 'But I've been so upset and I didn't know how to tell you.'

'You told Hugh,' George said accusingly. 'You just treat me like a baby.' It was a remark that stung her, for she knew it to be true but could do nothing to change it. George was, in her eyes, still a baby, incapable of independent thought and action.

'I won't in future, I promise. Come here and give me a cuddle. I need one, and I expect you do too.' George put up a brief show of resistance but yielded. He was sniffing and Caroline had nothing to say to stem the flood of tears; it almost hurt her more to see him like this, in full knowledge, than it had when she had learnt of Guy's death. At least, she thought, she had the emotional maturity to deal with it.

But deep down she doubted that. Her own defences were weakened by so much collateral information – the money, the fact that Guy was murdered, the will – that she couldn't cope with any of it. She was frightened for herself and the boys, and had no way to mitigate that fear. The police were slow and clinical, seemingly ignorant of her own predicament; Anthony Tilt was a nice man, but why should he care or put himself out? Everything rested on her. The loneliness of her role gripped her like a fever.

Baths had been taken and George was painting a model of an alien warrior on the kitchen table. He was sulking and quiet, and Caroline hated it. She needed to see him release his misery, but he would not accommodate her. Hugh had retired to his room after a cursory apology for his disclosure to George. Caroline did not expect to see him again until the morning.

People without children never made allowances: Jane Fox had called to say she'd be round at eight o'clock – 'just to follow up on a few things' – the worst possible time for a meeting at the Mercer household. The prospect of a further interview was precisely what Caroline didn't need: she needed a hot bath and someone to scrub her back as she sipped a large gin and tried to bring some order to it all.

As a compromise, she stood under the shower and let the jets of hot water do their best to revive her. Although her thoughts were still dislocated and unfocused, she had at least decided to come clean with the police. Jane's involvement in the case was rather comforting: she seemed bright and interested, as if nothing else mattered and she had all the patience and energy necessary to effect a just resolution of Guy's murder. Caroline could talk to her.

Mira let Jane in when she arrived. 'Mrs Mercer, she's having a shower,' she said. 'She won't be long.'

Jane saw the opportunity and took it. 'That's OK,' she replied as Mira showed her into the sitting room. 'I wanted to have a word with you anyway. Do you mind?'

'Me?' Mira said, putting her hand on to her bosom. 'Why?'

'Let's sit down. Don't worry, there's nothing to be afraid of.' Mira sat on the edge of a sofa opposite Jane. 'I just wanted to know a little bit more about you, and how you got on with Mr Mercer, that's all. Maybe you know something that will be helpful to us.' Mira looked blankly at her: did she understand, Jane wondered? 'Do you like working here?'

'Yes, oh yes,' Mira replied. 'Very nice. The Mercers are so kind. Mr Mercer, he was very special. I'm very sad.'

'Mr Mercer – you were very close to him?' Jane didn't know quite how to ask such a sensitive question, especially when she wasn't sure how much Mira could take in.

69

'No, not very close. He was good to me, very kind, yes, very kind. But not close, I don't think.'

'OK. That's good. And can you remember what you were doing on the weekend when Mr Mercer was murdered? You had some time off, didn't you?'

Mira thought about this. 'Yes. That's right. I went to Oxford with my friend. I had a lovely time, then I come back and all this is happening.'

'And your friend can confirm this?'

'Sorry?'

'Can I speak to your friend?'

'Sure, why not? You want her number? I get it for you.'

'Not now, that's all right. Maybe later.' Jane saw this particular trail going very cold and was prepared to leave it. Then Mira started to sob.

'It's no good, this,' she said through her tears. 'You're going to catch him, right, the man who done this terrible thing?'

'Yes, we're going to catch him,' Jane replied, realising that Mira had nothing more to offer her.

Caroline walked into the sitting room with a tray of coffee and saw Mira crying. 'What is it?' she asked, shooting a quick glance at Jane.

'Sorry, sorry,' Mira said as she got up and ran out of the room. Caroline stayed by the door and gave Jane a puzzled look.

'My fault, Mrs Mercer. I had to ask her a few questions, and I don't think I handled it very well.'

'Mira?' Caroline said. 'Surely not.'

'We have to explore all the possibilities, however remote. It has to be done.'

70

Caroline sighed, put the tray on the table and sat down. 'Help yourself,' she said. 'Now, I hope you've got some good news for me. I could use some.'

'In all honesty, Mrs Mercer, I can't tell you that this is an easy case,' Jane began. 'There's no obvious motive, and very little hard evidence. I'm telling you this because I need to ask you some fairly unpleasant questions, and you deserve to know why.'

'OK,' Caroline replied. 'I'm getting used to it.'

'There are several lines of inquiry. One of them concerns Linda Betts. She's gone missing, and we think she could be useful to our investigations. Maybe we're putting two and two together and making five, but it's too much of a coincidence for us to ignore. Do you know anything about Linda that might help us?'

'Only what I've already told you. She worked for Guy.'

'Did you and he ever talk about her – other than as it related to business?'

It took a little time to sink in, but Caroline finally got the message. 'You're suggesting . . . God, are you saying what I think you're saying?'

'I'm not saying anything – I'm asking. We have to know, however painful it may be for you.'

Caroline shook her head and grimaced. 'That's absurd,' she said angrily. 'It's such a stupid idea that it would be funny if it weren't so offensive. No – my husband was not having an affair with Linda Betts.'

'How can you be so sure? Do you have something that would prove that?'

'I have a woman's intuition,' Caroline snapped. 'I'd have

71

known if something were going on, and it wasn't. Guy may have had his faults, but adultery wasn't one of them.'

'What were they then – his faults?'

'Is that relevant?'

'I don't know. That's why I'm asking. You told us that you had money problems. Perhaps that has something to do with the murder. We really need to know everything.'

Caroline calmed herself, breathing through her nose in a deep, steady rhythm until she regained her composure. 'You can speak to a dozen families in this road and you'll find they're all in the same boat as us. No one's got any money. We're all broke and living the big lie. But that's hardly a motive, is it? I mean, what are you looking for, for Christ's sake?'

'One possibility is that your husband was planning to run off with Linda Betts. We know the extent of your debts, Mrs Mercer. I'm sorry, but we have to look into that kind of thing. He may have decided to cut and run. It does happen.'

'I'm sure it does, but not to us. Guy was devoted to us. He'd never have left us.' Even as she said this, Caroline knew that she was sinking. The force of evidence to the contrary made it impossible to accept her own denials, and she was becoming overwhelmed with the weakness of her position. She sobbed heavily and dug her nails into the palms of her hands. 'I'm sorry,' she said. 'I know you have a job to do.'

'Take your time. I apologise if I sound a little insensitive, but we really need to clear this up. Can you think of any reason why your husband might have been going to the South of France?'

Caroline gave a small shake of the head. 'Business?' she said weakly.

'We don't think so, although that's one possibility. Have you found anything of his in the house, anything at all, that might help us?'

Caroline recovered slightly. She thought about Guy's note and the money: now was the time to tell everything and seek protection. But Guy had not done this; he had sought to find a way out of his problems without involving the law, and she didn't know why. There were too many puzzles like this for her to give up just yet. In spite of her terror, she felt unwilling to let strangers come too close, even if they wore uniforms and carried badges and guns. This was private, a secret that Guy had not even wanted to tell her. She calculated the risks and rewards of non-disclosure. Guy had been murdered for something – the money? information? revenge? – and now she was next in line. How could she escape? But when she looked at Jane, so young and fresh-faced and eager, she decided that nothing, nobody, could offer her what she really needed – safety. In that moment she started to come to terms with her new situation, recognising how isolated she was.

Caroline made a decision. 'There is one thing,' she said. 'It's a facility, a self-storage unit in Battersea. Guy used it to keep things in.'

'What sort of things?'

'Mainly office papers, I think. I went there on Monday, you know, to look for something like you asked.'

'And what did you find?'

'To be perfectly honest, I didn't look very hard. I wasn't thinking straight, as you can imagine.'

'Isn't it rather strange, having a facility like that? Why didn't he keep everything here, or at the office?'

'You tell me,' Caroline said. 'It was something we never discussed.'

'We'll need to search it. Can you give me the details?'

'Of course. But look, I don't understand what you're trying to do. Do you think that Guy's death is somehow linked to his business?'

'We just don't know. We're looking at everything right now. It's a process of elimination. It takes time, but we'll get there.'

'And in the meantime? What if the killer decides to come looking for me?'

Jane raised her eyebrows at this and cocked her head. 'What makes you say that?' she asked. 'Why do you think that might happen?'

'Guy was my husband. For all the killer knows, I could have valuable information, or whatever it is he wants. I know I don't, but does he?'

'You're sure about that – I mean, that you don't have anything? If you're hiding something, Caroline, you've got to tell me now. I'm telling you this as a friend, not as a police officer. You may put yourself in considerable danger if you withhold information.'

Again Caroline saw her chance, and again she denied it. She could not explain her reaction, any more than she could work out the difference between fact and fantasy. But, just in this conversation, Caroline had already felt the whiplash of Guy's secret life, and she was not prepared to open it up any wider. 'There's nothing else to tell you. I wish there was.'

'Fine.' Jane shrugged as if unconvinced. 'Give me the details of the self-storage unit, and we'll see what we can dig up.'

Caroline did as she was asked and then saw Jane to the door.

She shivered as she watched Jane get into her car; she almost ran to it in a final act of submission, but some base impulse restrained her. She was set on a course and no rational thought could impede it.

EIGHT

Anthony Tilt stood in front of the bathroom mirror and waited. In a morning ritual that was as predictable as it was uncomfortable, the wave of nausea would move up from his stomach until he retched; then, eyes bulging and blood vessels popping, he would take the second drag of his cigarette and sip a little of the vodka he'd poured. The violent pumping would abate and his head would stop swimming, so that by the time he'd finished his drink he would be feeling halfway decent.

He shaved casually and ran his fingers through his hair, a routine that meant nothing more to him than mere convention. He picked up his suit from the chair by his bed and sniffed the crutch of the trousers, deciding that a quick spray of deodorant would neutralise the smell. He found a shirt that was less creased than most and shook it half-heartedly before putting it on: it was a Jermyn Street shirt and soon, when he had the time and money, he'd take it to the laundry for renovation. He had a little trouble with the buttons as his hands shook so badly, and knotting his tie was equally problematic. The result was predictable; he knew he couldn't have looked worse if he'd slept all night in these clothes, something that in fact he occasionally did.

He checked all the jacket pockets for money and discovered

that he still had a crumpled ten-pound note and some loose change. This encouraged him: it meant that he had not spent as much as he'd feared in the wine bar and he would be able to get to work without going through the fearsome process of putting his card into the cash machine, never certain when it would finally be confiscated. Even as a partner of Tickler Swabey Eckstein, a law firm with a swanky West End address but few swanky clients to match, his income rarely matched his outgoings, eaten up by maintenance and an insatiable appetite for fine – and not so fine – wine.

Anthony had been a high-flyer once, destined to make it to the very top of his profession. He was intelligent, good with clients, and could handle the most complicated of cases with casual ease. His relative downfall – relative to his peers, many of whom had gone on to be highly paid barristers or corporate finance advisers – was self-inflicted. His private life was messy and too often spilled over on to his work. He drank too much and spent money excessively; his marriage had never been strong and, when it ended, he drank even more. He let chances drip through his shaking fingers until he was left with a stalled career. He still had the mental acuity to be brilliant, but was no longer asked or expected to exercise it.

There was always something to nag at him and this morning, as he sucked a mint on the tube and tried to control his flatulence, he couldn't stop thinking about Caroline Mercer. He had not told his partners about her and had no intention of doing so; he reasoned that this was personal and he had a vague notion that there might be considerable gains from the relationship. The will intrigued him: people rarely made such a fuss over their legacy unless there was a lot at stake.

He convinced himself that she needed help and guidance and he was, after all, qualified to offer them. He had rather admired Guy in a grudging way, and he classified the work he would do for Caroline as a private matter, as would be the case if he helped a neighbour. There was no need to look at it as something to be shared with the other sharks at his firm, all of whom were perfectly capable of making their own money.

But Caroline's story represented more than an opportunity: it was also deeply disturbing. It was obvious to Tilt that there was ample scope for danger and, quite possibly, serious injury, neither of which were particularly appealing. If he wanted those he could walk out of his front door in Stoke Newington after dark. So he kept returning to the central question: why had he agreed to help? He couldn't find a satisfactory answer and he tried to prepare himself to call her when he got to the office and cancel the whole deal – 'Sorry, Mrs M., but your case doesn't meet my firm's criteria and we must decline it' – thus alleviating the bad feelings he had about it. What could be easier? And yet . . .

By the time he collapsed into his office chair he was no longer convinced. In fact, he was so ambivalent that he decided he would call her, but that the purpose would be to find out if anything else had happened since they met. Perhaps the police had already solved it; perhaps Caroline had found some vital papers and no longer needed him. He was still imagining the conversation when the phone rang.

'Tony?' He knew at once that it was his ex-wife, Angela; she was the only person who called him Tony, something he hated and she knew it.

'Hallo Angela. Let me guess why you're calling.'

'You never change, do you? You can always be relied upon to screw up. Where is it?' She sounded resigned rather than angry, the consequence of too many discussions like this one.

He did have the money he owed her, for a change, but he had simply not got round to sending it. It gave him a little temporary pleasure to make her ask for it, about the only power he still had over her. 'I'll send it round by bike today, OK? Sorry – I've been very busy.'

'Busy – what, pissing it up against a wall? Maybe I should come round to the office to collect it. I'll bring Sophie with me. That'd look good, wouldn't it, in front of all your colleagues?' The mention of Sophie was her revenge and it was sweetly timed, hitting him square in the guts. She was the only positive product to have come out of their marriage, and he'd rather die than see her caught up in the crossfire.

He tried to calm things down. 'The money's on its way, I promise. I'll get my secretary to do it right now.'

Angela couldn't resist the opening. 'Is that the secretary you've already screwed, or is it the one who's still anxiously waiting for the experience?'

'Mature. That's what I love about you, Angie, you can be so grown-up when you make the effort. I've always admired that in you.'

'Just send the money, or the bailiffs will be round to collect it.'

'Well, great talking to you too, and have a nice day.' He slammed down the phone and looked up to see his secretary Deirdre – a middle-aged spinster with two cats and a full set of Barbara Cartland novels – staring at him in concern. He smiled at her. 'Order a bike, will you?' She nodded and retired, wisely closing the door behind her.

Sophie was all he had to cling on to, and his grip was very tenuous. Having negotiated a divorce settlement with Angela that left him permanently broke, he consoled himself with the idea that he would still have Sophie as a chattel which could not be divided or valued independently. At first Angela was accommodating, giving him unlimited access, but as the temper of their arguments increased she used every means of denial to stop him seeing her. If the monthly payment was late Angela would introduce Sophie as the bargaining chip, coldly calculating that this would be the spur to greater efficiency on his part. He felt castrated by Angela, and would have wished her harm if that would not have presaged a deterioration in Sophie's well-being. So he played the game and continued to cherish the few hours every week that he spent with her; he would even tidy the flat and get an early night before one of her visits.

And possibly it was this that made him so sensitive to Caroline Mercer's plight. His own attachment to his child gave him a better understanding of how she must feel as she struggled to keep her family intact. In his eyes she was a decent woman – and he knew enough indecent women to recognise the difference – brought low by events beyond her control or comprehension. Tilt didn't often deal in noble thoughts or causes, and would never claim to have the constitution for them, but he needed this case for his own reasons, a private agenda which he couldn't explain but didn't resist. He picked up the phone and punched Caroline's number.

There was business to be done and commission to be earned

regardless of all the crap that was flying around; the trading room of Asset Management Strategies harboured little sympathy for past tragedies, especially ones that were almost a week old. After the initial round of comfort calls to clients, in which the message was always 'BAU – business as usual', and the prurient speculation of ghoulish traders over the precise details of Guy's death, the room had quickly returned to its normal pace.

Behind this façade, in the soundproofed offices of senior managers, such equanimity had not been reached. Almost by default, the management had decided to appoint Peter Verity to run the business, pending intervention by the institution which controlled most of the shares. Verity was not an inspirational leader: he had moved with Guy to help set up the operational side of the business and was seen as a safe pair of hands, dealing efficiently with regulators and steering the firm away from some of Guy's more outrageous plans. In his late forties, he was quiet and methodical, the perfect foil for Guy: he made no enemies and cultivated no allies, just doing his job and collecting his pay cheque every month. He had taken on the additional role of finance director when Jim Breach had suffered his heart attack, and was therefore the obvious choice to command the ship during its passage through choppy waters.

Verity was studying a printout in his office when Nancy Armstrong, the firm's head of trading, came in. Her staff had two words to describe her: dried up. Humourless and singularly driven by money, Nancy had no time for anything but business. Her whole appearance gave her away: the long straight hair with a brutal side parting, minimal make-up, harshly cut suits always worn with a bland scarf, sensible low-heeled shoes. Even the most intrepid anthropologist could not have discovered a laughter line on the grainy skin of her face. If she'd been born with emotions, they'd been surgically removed in the maternity ward. The traders would joke – well out of her hearing range – that the combination of being an American woman with a humour bypass could only be worse if she were from an ethnic minority.

'What is it, Peter? I'm up to my neck in shit out there, so let's keep it short, OK?' She had always treated him as a resource and nothing more, a necessary evil whose sole purpose appeared to be to stop her doing profitable deals.

'Sit down, Nancy,' he said, oblivious to her antagonism. She sighed theatrically and sat bolt upright with her arms folded over her chest. 'There's an account on this printout that I don't recognise – AMS666. Do you know anything about it?'

'Should I?'

'With the volume of trades that've gone across it, I'd say you should. Have a look for yourself.' He pushed the printout across his desk and she leant forward to read where he pointed. She frowned and shook her head.

'Are you sure this is right?' she asked. 'I've never passed any entries over that account. What report is this?'

'It's the monthly activity statement. Linda normally reconciles it and she'd only show anything to me if it looked odd or didn't balance. But she's never shown me this. I have no idea what AMS666 is, or where it belongs.'

'Me neither. Who's the client?' In spite of herself, Nancy was interested.

'That's another mystery. I've looked it up on the mainframe directory and it just comes up as "Restricted". That's a code we haven't ever used to my knowledge.'

'What type of deals are they?'

'They're all dollar reverse repos.' Reverse repos were transactions where the AMS client lent cash to a broker in return for securities as collateral, effectively buying and later selling back those securities at a pre-agreed price. 'There's a pattern to them, too. They start off small and get larger – this last one, for instance, was for twenty-five million.'

Nancy was sufficiently puzzled to start an immediate analysis. 'We don't do that many reverses, and I know about all of them. But these haven't come across my desk, I swear. That sort of activity would definitely be highlighted in my trading reports.'

'What we do know is that Linda entered them on to the system and Guy authorised them. We can tell that from the audit trail. Other than that, there's no file, no client agreements, and no documentation.'

'What about the counterparties?'

'Yes, I thought about that too. I checked, and they're all regular borrowers – you know, Lehman, Solly, Merrill. Normally I'd call them to ask, but this isn't a good time to be admitting that we've got some accounting problems. I'd rather try to sort it out internally.'

Nancy thought a little more. 'Is there any way of checking the trader who struck the deals?' she asked.

'As you know, every trader has a unique identifier on the system. When we built it we set up a temporary code – Z1000 – to accommodate any new trader who comes in so that they can start work straight away. When they get their own system ID they just transfer the balance of trades from Z1000 to the new code. All these trades have been booked into Z1000.'

'We haven't had a new trader for, what, six months? The

systems guys aren't that backed up, are they?' Nancy liked to accuse anyone and everyone of chronic sloth and inefficiency, but even she couldn't believe that it would take half a year to establish a new trader on the system.

'No. They maintain that everything is bang up to date. Which leaves us none the wiser.' Peter grimaced and looked at Nancy hopefully. But she offered him nothing.

'It'll give us a major problem with the regulators. They'll fry us if they find these on a compliance visit. We're talking about a major fine.'

'That's the least of our problems for now. We have a delegation arriving from Chicago in two days. Our shareholders have finally decided to take some action, and they've requested full access to all our records. This is going to jump out and bite them on the ankle. I dread to think what they'll have to say about it.'

'Can you . . . disguise it?'

Peter should have been horrified by the suggestion, but panic was beginning to set in and he had already had the same idea. 'It's got to be an option, if only in the short term. Obviously I'd prefer not to do it but, unless we can come up with an alternative, we may have to.'

'I guess we should keep this discussion to ourselves, right?' Nancy knew how to cover her rear better than anyone.

'I think that's best. When – if – Linda comes back, we can go through it all and get it straight.'

'Where is that lazy little bitch, anyway?' Linda and Nancy were frequently at each other's throats, with Guy's intervention sometimes necessary to separate them.

'That's something both the police and I would very much

like to know. In fact, I have a meeting this afternoon with the policewoman running the investigation, and I wouldn't be at all surprised if Miss Betts comes up in our conversation.'

Nancy latched on to the opportunity. 'You going to tell the police about this?' she asked, pointing at the printout.

'Only if she asks. There's no point in getting the police involved in something they couldn't possibly understand. We have our work cut out as it is, and this is purely an internal administrative matter.'

'Your call. I've got to run. Keep me up to speed on this, Peter.'

'I will.' Nancy left his office and Peter returned to his scrutiny of the numbers, but they didn't tell him anything more than he already knew.

NINE

Jane didn't like it. As she sat over a coffee in the canteen she tried to arrange the few pieces of hard information she'd garnered. A man had been killed; whilst superficially wealthy he was actually in hock up to his eyeballs. He had a nice wife, a good job and, possibly, a mistress. The mistress, Linda Betts, had gone absent without leave from the firm he ran and might have something to do with his death. The wife was grieving but, more importantly, was very scared. Was she scared of what she knew, or what she didn't know?

All of this left Jane with so many gaps in her knowledge that she didn't know where to start plugging them. As she waited for Grass to arrive, she became increasingly frustrated by her inability to focus on any particular aspect of the case; no one had told her anything of substance, and she briefly considered the prospect of a major conspiracy of silence. They were all in it together, perhaps – Caroline Mercer, Linda Betts, even that grubby office manager, Alan Apostle – all implicated in some way and determined not to let her discover their secrets.

Grass slumped on to the chair opposite her, shocking her out of her idle musings. 'Cracked it, then?' he asked.

'It's a bugger, this one. It's just going nowhere. No one knows anything.'

'What did Mrs Mercer have to say for herself?'

'Well, there's one bit of good news. She gave me the key to a self-storage unit in Battersea. Apparently he used it as a place to put office papers. She says she's been there and didn't find anything, but then she said she wasn't really looking. I'll have to take a team over there and give it the once-over.'

Grass nodded slowly. 'Come to think of it, I'm down that way later on today. If you like, I'll do it.' The offer was made as if it meant nothing to him one way or the other.

'If you don't mind, that would be great,' she replied, surprised at this gesture of support. Grass hadn't been too involved in the grunt work, and she was caught off guard by his offer. 'Do you want me to come with you?'

'No need. You stay here and get stuck into finding that Linda Betts. *Cherchez la femme*, as they say.' He laughed at his own wit, oblivious to the fact that he had already used this expression with Jane, and she gave him a pale smile in return. Grass was in an unusually good mood; more normally he was short and bad-tempered.

'What do I do if I find her?'

'Bring her in. I reckon she's the key to all this. She must figure somewhere in the scheme of things. He gets topped, she disappears – looks bloody awful, doesn't it? Our Linda may well have exactly what we need to find out who did it.'

'Could it have been her? Is that a line I should be following?' Jane wasn't convinced, but he was in charge.

'Doubt it. But she'll know who did it, I bet you. We just need to get her in an interview room for a couple of hours and she'll tell us.' Grass's interviews were legendary for their remorseless brutality: whilst he rarely resorted to violence, he emanated a threat which few could withstand. Jane knew what he meant and winced at the thought.

'OK. I'll follow that up.' Jane decided to take advantage of his even temper. 'I did have one other idea which might be worth thinking about.'

'Try me,' he said, without too much interest.

'Well, we always say that when someone gets unexpectedly murdered, there's got to be something in it for the murderer – I mean, apart from revenge or passion or whatever. So I just wondered whether there's anything in Mercer's will that we ought to be taking a look at. Was he going to leave all his money to someone other than his family, for instance?'

Grass scratched one ear. 'That's not a bad thought. Do we know if he had a solicitor?'

'I can find out,' she said.

'Then go for it. Yeah, I like that.'

'Thanks, guv.'

Grass got up and looked down at her. 'One day we might even make a good copper out of you.' He wandered off and she was left to ponder the idiosyncrasies of her boss, who could infuriate her with a single word or look. Managing Grass was like catching smoke, but she could handle that: life would be far too simple if she only had to deal with the villains on the outside.

If he had surprised himself with the courage he'd displayed in asking her out, he was even more shocked when she agreed. He didn't even know exactly what had made him do it, and he had plenty of time to ask himself as he sat in the wine bar and waited for her. Tilt was unusually nervous, an agitation that he would normally have quelled with large quantities of alcohol, but he restrained himself: he was her adviser and he must act professionally. He limited his intake to two glasses from the bottle of Chilean red as he watched the other drinkers.

When Caroline arrived she looked very different. She had obviously made an effort: she wore a flattering black dress with a single strand of pearls and had applied a subtle layer of make-up. His immediate reaction was a slight feeling of intimidation, as if she might be sharper than he'd calculated and would know how to manipulate him. Tilt loved women but was in awe of them, especially those he most fancied. Looking at her now, as she smiled at him and walked over to the table, he realised that he had an extra motive for wanting to help her.

He stood up, bumping the table as he did so and spilling his drink. 'Good evening,' he said, shaking her hand softly. 'What would you like to drink?'

'Some of that looks fine,' she replied, nodding at the bottle. They sat down and he filled the spare glass for her.

'So – what news?' He was keen to keep the conversation on a professional level, at least until he could feel the buzz of the wine and gained more confidence.

'Quite a lot has happened, but none of it is really encouraging. The police have been round again. It's all so . . . sordid. It's almost as if they want to find something unpleasant, and won't be satisfied until they do. They don't seem to realise just how painful it is for me. I know they've got a job to do, but even so . . .' She sipped her wine and raised her eyebrows in resignation.

He knew that this was his cue, that he was meant to intercede and show her how strong and compassionate he was, but he had some difficulty in finding the right words. He decided that he would play the silent listener role and lit a cigarette in what he hoped was a thoughtful way, mirroring her perplexed expression.

'So much of what I've heard since Guy's death has been a complete mystery,' she continued, 'as if I've only been involved in a small part of his life. I'm so bloody tired that I'm not thinking straight, and I can't get over this enormous feeling of fear, as if I'm the next victim.'

'What do you mean by that?'

'Well, when your husband gets murdered, I think it's quite natural to be anxious for your own safety. But the police jumped on that when I said it to them, as if I had no reason to be frightened.'

'And do you?'

'Yes. It's completely irrational and unfounded, but of course I am. Wouldn't you be in my position?'

'I suppose I would. Which is all the more reason to help the police as much as you can. Do you think they have any idea who might have done it?' he asked as he refilled their glasses.

'If they have they're not saying. All they've done so far is ask a lot of questions and make it pretty clear that they're not prepared to stop until they've got some satisfactory answers. It's almost as if they think everyone is guilty until proved innocent. For all I know, I'm a suspect.'

'Surely you don't believe that?'

'I don't know, Anthony, I really don't. As I've said, nothing would surprise me. The mere fact that I loved him and was two hundred miles away at the time might not be good enough in their eyes. They make you think like that, they really do. They make you feel as if you're hiding something.'

'Would it help if I was there next time you saw them?' he asked reluctantly.

'That's very sweet of you, and I appreciate the thought, but I don't think it would. If I wheel in my solicitor they're going to be even more suspicious, aren't they?'

'Good point. But I was thinking – they are going to ask about the will. They're bound to. You'll need me around for that.'

'They haven't asked yet. Anyway, what good will that do them?'

'Probably none, but they'll ask anyway. While we're on the subject, have you had any further thoughts about the will?'

'Nothing very profound, I'm afraid. There is something in the back of my mind about Shadowlawn, but I don't know what. It rings a bell, that's all. I've been through all his papers at home and I can't find anything. Sorry.'

'Don't apologise to me. I only wish I could be more helpful. I feel a bit of a fraud, actually. I don't appear to have done anything except muddy the waters.'

'Oh, I wouldn't worry about that. It's very therapeutic just having someone else to talk to about it. That's what I miss most about Guy – the companionship. A dozen times a day I'll think to myself that Guy would have known what to do, or he'd laugh at something I've read in the newspaper, and how much I'd like to talk to him about things. And I do – talk to him, I mean. We knew each other so well that I can still have a conversation with him and I know exactly what he'd say. Does that sound stupid?'

'Not at all,' Tilt said and, for the second time, Caroline felt there was a strange and implicit empathy, a hidden cognisance that hinted at some loss of his own. 'It's perfectly natural.'

'The worst part is that I have no one to blame for what's gone on. This is going to sound very callous, and it isn't meant like that, but if he'd died of natural causes then I could say that he should have been more careful with his diet and lost some weight and I could be angry with him for being so irresponsible. But this isn't his fault – I'm sure he didn't mean to get killed. And until I know who did it I don't think I can fully recover from it. I need that knowledge before I can move on. Like this, I'm just in the twilight zone.'

This was dangerous ground; she was getting far too personal for comfort and Tilt wasn't yet ready for that. He wanted to steer her away from too much emotion. 'What have you done about the money?'

'Nothing. It's where I left it, and I haven't told the police about it. As things stand, that's the only security I've got, and I don't want to give it up lightly.'

'From a professional standpoint I can't condone that. But I think I can understand it. How are you off for money otherwise?' He knew it was impertinent to ask but felt he had a right to know.

'I went to see the bank manager yesterday. He's being very kind, and he's agreed to keep me going until everything's settled. If only he knew.'

'So what would you like me to do next?'

'Hard to say. I did have one idea, but I'll quite understand if you say no. It looks as if the only way of sorting out my finances is to get involved with Guy's business. After all, I'm a shareholder now. I'm not suggesting I go to work there, but I would like to find out more about what they do and who the other shareholders are. Then I can decide whether I want to sell my shares back to them or if I should hang on to them. Could you help me with that?'

Tilt liked her; he felt sorry for her and he wanted to do something, anything, to make her feel better. He also remembered that there was the prospect of a good pay-off at the end of it all, and that helped him to make his decision. He didn't like to admit that he might do more harm than good, and yet he knew he should. But she asked so gently, with those melting eyes to reinforce her plea, that he had no option. He took a good swig of his wine. 'I'd be delighted,' he said.

'Well then,' she said as she smiled at him, 'I'd better buy you dinner.' He liked that idea, too.

There was a school of thought which said that luck played no part in police work, that results came purely from burning shoe leather and gathering the facts until they arranged themselves into a solution. Jane herself adhered to this belief, though she was pragmatic enough to accept the breaks gracefully when they came. She liked to think she was capable of solving a case without relying on chance and coincidence: she thought of herself as a good detective, despite the fact that nobody had ever told her she was. Praise was a scarce commodity and it often needed to be self-administered.

She was sitting in her car with a polystyrene cup of coffee jammed between the dashboard and the windscreen. She was reading a management consultant's report on women in the police force, a study commissioned several years ago that would ultimately gather dust in some chief constable's office without any of its recommendations being implemented. Some of it made a lot of sense and she wondered if the consultants would mind that their intelligent analysis would be largely ignored. There were no names on the cover, so she couldn't tell if it had been written by men or women, and she decided it didn't matter anyway. She looked out of her window towards the house in which Linda Betts had lived. Jane knew she had to go in and poke around in knicker drawers and under the carpet, much as she felt that it was pointless. Grass had told her to do it, and that's what she was paid for.

Just as she opened the car door she saw a black taxi pull up outside the house. She closed the door and watched as a young woman got out and then waited for the driver to deliver two large suitcases on to the pavement. The woman paid him and stood still as the cab drove away. She looked around as if it were the first time she'd ever been in the street; from the other side of the road Jane studied her closely. After some time the woman opened her handbag and pulled out a set of keys, fiddling with them until she found the one she was looking for. Jane restrained herself: she wanted to jump out and arrest her but she resisted the urge until she was sure.

The key went into the front door lock and was turned. Deciding that she'd now seen enough, Jane eased out of the car and looked both ways before crossing the road swiftly and reaching the pavement outside the house. She pulled out her ID and held it ready in her hand. 'Linda Betts?' she said as the woman pushed the door open. Linda looked round to see Jane holding up her badge.

'Oh shit,' she murmured.

'Shall we go in?' Jane advanced until she was next to her.

'Do I have a choice?' Linda replied.

They walked upstairs in silence to the top-floor flat and Linda unlocked the door. The air was stale and Linda opened some windows before throwing off her raincoat. 'I'm sorry but I can't offer you anything to drink,' she said. 'I've been away.'

'We know.'

'So – what can I do for you?' Linda had now recovered her composure and was, if anything, rather dismissive.

'We've been looking everywhere for you. I've come about Guy Mercer.'

Linda sounded interested. 'What about him? He's my boss.'

'Guy Mercer was murdered at his house early last Sunday morning.' Jane waited for a reaction.

Linda looked astonished and fell into an armchair behind her. 'Murdered?' she exclaimed. She had gone very pale.

'Yes. Can I get you a glass of water?'

Linda ignored this and squeezed her eyes shut. Then, after several moments of sitting completely still, she seemed to snap back into the real world. 'Are you sure?'

'Yes, we are. You didn't know, did you?'

'No. Jesus, I had no idea.' She thought a little. 'Do you know who did it?'

'Not yet.'

Linda was beginning to get the picture. 'So . . . what are you doing here?'

'Look, let's cut the crap, OK? We know you and he were having an affair. We know you'd gone to Nice and he was planning to meet you there, or somewhere close by. We're not interested in your private life. That's your business. We just need some information. We need to know what your plans were with him, and what he'd told you.'

'Before I talk to you, I think I should call a lawyer, shouldn't I?' Linda said.

'What for? This is just an informal chat. I'm not arresting you.'

Linda retrieved a pack of cigarettes from her handbag and lit one, inhaling deeply.

'So I don't need to answer your questions then, do I?' she asked.

'Come on, Linda. This is stupid. We need to find whoever did this. You know things that could help us. Be reasonable.'

'Reasonable?' Linda said in a raised voice. 'This whole thing doesn't seem too reasonable to me. My whole bloody life's just disintegrated. I . . .' Linda began to sob, genuine sadness welling up from inside her. Jane felt awkward, not knowing whether to hug her or simply let her get on with it. She hated tears. 'I loved him, you know – I really loved him,' Linda said through her sobs.

'Well, that's a start. Was he going to leave his wife?'

'Look. You've just told me he's been murdered. That's quite hard for me to deal with, and I can't . . . I can't do this, not now.'

'Linda, I'm deadly serious. You can cooperate and everything will be fine. Or you can play silly buggers and I'll have to bring you in for questioning, take a statement, make life generally unpleasant for you. I should add that we haven't entirely ruled out the possibility that you're a suspect.' Jane hoped this might get her attention.

Linda wiped her eyes with her middle fingers, pulled on her

cigarette and thought. 'If I talk to you – and it's a big if – what can you offer me?'

'How do you mean?'

'From where I sit things can't get any worse. How is talking to you going to make it better for me?'

'We don't do deals. I can't offer you anything. Cooperate and we might clear up the case a lot quicker, which will mean we'll be out of your hair sooner. Otherwise . . .' Jane shrugged to demonstrate that the options were too ghastly to describe.

'Give me time, then,' Linda said, almost begging. 'I promise I'll come back to you if you'll just give me a little time. Right now I don't know if I'm coming or going.'

'We don't have that luxury, I'm afraid. Time's the one thing I can't offer.'

Linda closed her eyes and the tears began again. Then, as if something had clicked in her head, she looked at Jane steadily through her watery eyes and nodded. 'OK. Where do we start? What do you want to know?'

TEN

Nothing had prepared Caroline for this. As she stood naked in front of the mirror, examining the evidence of two children, a hundred abortive diets and an amazingly strong gravitational pull downwards, Caroline could hardly believe what had taken place. Anthony Tilt had made a pass at her. True, she said to herself, he was quite drunk when he'd done it, and it was possible that she had misinterpreted his intentions – after all, it had been a long time since anyone had expressed an interest in her, other than Guy – but she was nonetheless convinced that he had been serious. He'd suggested coffee and a nightcap at his flat after dinner; she'd accepted, never for one moment thinking that he had an ulterior motive.

They had sat together on his sofa, the only place they could sit, and he'd rather clumsily put his hand on her knee. At first she took this as a genuine mistake, but he made no effort to remove it until she crossed her legs to move away. Unabashed, he'd simply continued talking and nothing more was said or done. She hadn't really even thought about it until she was lying in her bed; then she laughed out loud at the absurdity of it all, but she fell asleep with a warm glow inside her. Now, as she carried out her routine breast inspection, the brief episode came back to her and she tried to make sense of it. He was, she concluded, rather a dangerous man: you could see that in his wild eyes which seemed to have independent lives, never quite moving in harmony. He gave the impression of a man whose existence hovered between order and chaos, of someone who was struggling to control himself and who secretly wished that he could abandon the façade of normality and react solely on primal urges.

But it was, more than anything, the smell of him that alerted her to his menace. She recalled that first time when she'd been beguiled and repelled by this odour, and how much she'd had to struggle to escape its influence. That heady mix of masculine musk was potent and threatening, and she'd had to sit engulfed by it as they sipped their brandy in his flat. She had found herself assessing him with more interest than was strictly necessary: the bitten nails, the nicotine stains, the facial blotches, and those bloodshot, random eyes. The whole was definitely greater than the sum of the parts, she concluded, but it worried her that she should even be thinking like this.

For Caroline, sex had become a distant memory. After the children, Guy and she had made strenuous pledges to maintain a healthy sex life – it was a perennial New Year's resolution – but they had drifted into that state where, without really noticing, sex was no longer on their agenda. They were both too tired, too anxious, too comfortable to resurrect the tireless performances of their early days together, reaching an implicit and unwanted end to their physical relationship. Once in a while, after a night out or if they had the house to themselves on a Sunday afternoon, they might indulge, but these were brief and rare occasions. Caroline was saddened by it, but didn't know how to put it right; it was just a fact of life. Now Anthony had awakened those memories, and it confused her, all the more because she was nowhere near to recovering from the shock of Guy's murder.

Guy – he haunted her by his absence, and by the manner in which he had been taken from her. Her life had been subsumed so totally into his that her loss was like a vital organ removed for ever, without hope of a satisfactory replacement. It made her lose her balance and stumble awkwardly, a disability she had no way of redressing. Even talking about him, as she had to Anthony, was no real therapy; in a way, she was simply trying to delay the effect of life without him by pretending he was still around, denying the facts until she was strong enough to deal with them. And when would that be? Would she wake up one morning and discover that the nausea had gone, that the impulse to carry on had finally returned and her first thought was not of him? She longed for and dreaded that moment: she wished to be free of the misery but never wanted to forget him or to see him become merely a bland and distant memory. The pain she endured was, perhaps, a small enough price to pay for keeping him close to the front of her mind.

Of course, the children were always there to remind her of his legacy. She should and would channel her love for him into them; they would become fitting monuments and he would be proud of them and her for the way in which they developed. But she was having problems with this, too: she appeared to have lost the touch of a mother, never quite certain of her relationship with them now that Guy wasn't there. Even though she had always run the family, she now lacked the poise to deal with it as effectively as she had when he was part of it. Everything had changed, and nothing for the better.

Some of this she had confided to Anthony. He was a good listener, though it wouldn't have mattered much if he weren't. She had learnt little about him and his life, and had probably told him much more than she'd wanted to about her own. Perhaps that was what had inspired him to act so boldly; perhaps he thought, in his muddled and drunken way, that she was crying out for attention – as indeed she was – and craved the strength of a man's embrace to soften the aches. If this were the case, she couldn't blame him for it. He was a man and they always got the wrong end of the stick, never engaging their brains before they made their decisions. A man's natural reaction to any woman in distress or turmoil was to say: 'What she needs is a damned good rogering,' or words to that effect. She'd heard Guy himself say it about other women, and he'd only been half joking.

That was not what she needed. The problem for her was that she didn't know what she did need, or whether anyone could deliver it even if she discovered what it was. A nice cup of tea; a holiday away from it all; a night out with the girls; a weekend at a health spa; all these temporal solutions were routinely offered as palliatives, designed to soothe but never to cure. She didn't need an escape from grim reality, she needed a way to live with it before it consumed her. Loss was like inoperable cancer: sometimes you won remission, but ultimately it would conquer you, corroding all parts until there was nothing left.

It might have been easier, she told herself, if Guy had not been brutally murdered. How could you adjust to the loss when it was so arbitrary, so violent and unexpected, so inexplicable? The thought that someone wanted him dead creased her in half;

someone had decided to kill him without apparent motive, hating him enough to go that far. It was so far beyond her imagination that she had no way of coping with it. Even long after the crime was solved and the criminal put away, she would never be able to accept that someone could do this to her Guy.

Once dressed, Caroline prepared herself for the meeting. She had arranged to see Peter Verity at eleven o'clock in his office. On the phone he had been courteous but guarded: he obviously had no wish to see her and tried to put her off, claiming that things were very fraught, but she insisted. Anthony had suggested she go alone to put them at their ease; he would only intervene once she'd established her own position and had worked out how things stood. She had to agree with this, much as she doubted her own ability to negotiate.

She travelled up on the underground, Mira having taken the car to do some shopping after dropping the boys at school. She was dressed in what she hoped was an appropriate black suit with dark tights and no jewellery other than on her wedding finger. She was greeted at reception by a spotty girl who displayed no interest or recognition when she announced her name, and she sat and flicked through a magazine as she waited for Verity. When he came out he assumed the look of sympathy with which she had become so familiar, an insincere frown that was annoying and immediately transparent. No one really cared. Death was treated as a highly contagious disease and people didn't want to get too close to it.

They walked together to Verity's office and a tray of coffee and chocolate biscuits was brought in by his secretary. 'I don't need to tell you how sorry we all are about Guy,' he began. 'He was an inspirational leader and will be sorely missed.' Caroline wondered how long it had taken him to practise this speech, so stilted and unnatural did it sound.

'Thank you,' she said quietly.

'How can I help you?' he continued.

'Well, it looks as if I'm about to become a shareholder in Asset Management Strategies. Now I have to admit that I've never taken much of an interest in the business – never needed to, frankly – but it seems I have no option. So I've come to you for some help.'

'And I'll be delighted to give it, if I can,' he replied, rather too unctuously for her liking. 'What specifically did you have in mind?'

Tilt had helped her prepare a list of demands and she now recited these. 'First; I need to know who the other shareholders are. I will also want to meet them as soon as possible. I'll need to see the latest management accounts and any other relevant papers, including the memorandum and articles of association. I expect you have a business plan and budget projections, and I'd like a copy of those.' She surprised herself with the confidence she invested in this, in spite of her faltering nerve.

Verity wrote something on a pad and nodded when he had finished. 'No problems there, as far as I can see. We could have all that couriered to your house in the next couple of days. You're in luck because the majority shareholder is actually here in the office at the moment. As you can imagine, they're quite keen to make sure the firm continues to run smoothly during this difficult time. Business is business, after all.' He gave her a little condescending smile which she hated but ignored.

'And who is the majority shareholder?'

'Investment Logistics. They control seventy-five per cent of the issued share capital. As you know, twenty per cent was owned by your husband, with the balance put in trust for employees.'

'What is Investment Logistics? Who are they?'

'Investment Logistics is a Chicago-based company which controls about five billion dollars in private funds. They invest venture capital in new businesses and take major equity stakes in those companies where they think there's a better than even chance of significant capital gain. Well, that's what it says in their brochure. They've been with Guy from the start – but you probably know that already.'

The conversation she'd had with Guy all those years ago in the restaurant now came back to her. She also recalled the launch party where she'd met some of the Americans who'd agreed to back him. She remembered Guy's boyish enthusiasm for the deal, and how happy she was that he'd finally found something he could really get excited about – his own firm with his unique character stamped all over it.

'Yes, that rings a bell,' she said. 'And you say they're here?'

'They are, and I know they'd be very happy to meet you. I can set something up, if you'd like.'

'I can't see them now – after we've finished?'

'They're going to be tied up all day in meetings with our biggest clients. But I'll arrange a meeting for later this week – they're going to be here some time, I'd guess.'

Caroline drank a little coffee and looked longingly at the plate of biscuits. Chocolate Hob Nobs were a particular favourite of hers, and three called out to her from the table. She sipped some more coffee to quell the urge. 'That will be fine. I'll probably need to bring my adviser, if that's all right with you.'

'Adviser?' Verity said, obviously taken aback.

'Yes. I don't think it's very sensible to go into all this without some professional help, do you? It's a long time since I worked in the City.' It certainly was: Caroline had been PA to a senior manager at a moribund British merchant bank, where she had met Guy. She'd gone out for drinks to the local pub and he'd come along as one of the bank's network of contacts. That was a wonderful evening. He'd immediately detached himself from the crowd when he spotted her and had taken her to dinner; there was no sex that night, but she knew they both wanted it and it was only a matter of time. He called her the next day to set up a date and they'd never looked back.

'I'm sure that won't be a problem,' Verity said, jolting her back to reality. 'Was there anything else?'

'No, I don't think so. If you'll send me all those documents that would be great. I'll give you my number and you can call me to let me know about the meeting.'

He was nodding in consent when his secretary knocked on the door and came in without waiting for his signal. She looked at Caroline apologetically before speaking. 'Sorry, Peter, but you have a call from Chicago.'

'Chicago?' he said incredulously, looking at his watch. 'God, it must be four o'clock in the morning there.' He raised his eyebrows at Caroline. 'Sorry, but I'd better take this call. It must be urgent. Would you mind?'

'No, we're finished anyway. Thanks for your time, Peter. You'll be in touch?'

'As soon as I can arrange things.' His secretary led her to the lifts and Caroline exhaled a hugh sigh of relief.

Linda Betts got a lift back from the police station in an unmarked car. She had agreed to go to the station to give a statement; that gave her an opportunity to think, and she was pleased with how things had turned out. Jane's boss was hard, but he treated her like a bimbo, and she played the part well. They swallowed her story without too much questioning and let her go as soon as the statement was signed.

It was dark by the time she opened the front door of the house, but she didn't bother to switch on the lights. She could climb the stairs in her sleep and needed no guidance. As she reached her own front door a hand grabbed her roughly from behind and clutched her face tightly, stopping her from screaming.

'You little bitch,' the man said, still out of her sight. She tried to turn her head but his grip was too strong. 'Open the door. We've got some unfinished business, remember?' She knew who it was, and she knew resistance was not an option. Things were not going quite as well as she'd thought.

ELEVEN

By eight o'clock that evening, Caroline was sufficiently worried that she seriously considered calling the police. Mira had never done this before. She was, unlike so many others, reliable if nothing else, and she would never have left the children at school. Caroline had gone to pick them up herself in a taxi after a call from the deputy head, spending the rest of the afternoon and evening in a state of distraction and anger. She'd gone round Mira's room a dozen times, half expecting to find her hiding in the wardrobe or under the duvet.

When Caroline had first mentioned the possibility of having an *au pair* to Guy he was quietly horrified; he couldn't understand why she would need one, and why she would want someone strange living in the house and having an influence, however benign, on their children. But the exhaustion in her face, and her constant weariness, eventually persuaded him that it was necessary; as he succumbed, he had visions of a seventeen-year-old Scandinavian beauty who would frequently walk about the house in the flimsiest of robes and would be strongly attracted to older men.

Caroline beat him to the punch, discovering a local EFL school in Hammersmith which specialised in girls from Eastern

Europe, strong, sturdy types who stood no nonsense from children or parents. Mira was the third in the series, and had been by far the most successful, spending more time with the boys than she did in the bathroom. She cooked for Hugh and George and ate with them, did their laundry and kept them out of the way when that seemed the best thing to do. She was almost one of the family, and had shared their grief over Guy's death. Caroline knew she still wept over it, privately and discreetly, although she was too immature to find a way to articulate her own sadness. After Jane Fox's visit, Mira was distraught and anxious, concerned not only for herself but for Caroline and the boys – what must they think? But, to Caroline, Mira was a godsend, and she was now entirely dependent on her. So what the bloody hell was she playing at?

All was revealed when she answered a knock at the front door. Two uniformed police officers, both young men, were waiting anxiously. 'Mrs Mercer?' one said as she stood before them. 'Mrs Caroline Mercer?'

She was momentarily dazed by their appearance. Thoughts of Guy came rushing back, and she felt a strong sense of *déjà vu*. 'Yes,' she mumbled.

'Could we come in for a moment?'

'What's this about?' she asked as they all went into the kitchen. She collapsed on to a chair without thinking to offer them anything to drink.

'Are you the owner of a blue Volvo estate, registration number N335 OBY?'

'That sounds right. Why?'

One policeman was doing all the talking whilst the other stood behind him, as if he was only there to corroborate everything that was said. 'Do you know a Mira Gavrilovic?'

'Yes. She's my *au pair*. God, has something happened to her?'

'I'm afraid so, Mrs Mercer. Miss Gavrilovic was involved in a serious incident this afternoon in your car. She didn't recover from her injuries.'

'You mean . . . she's dead?' Caroline swallowed hard and tried to breathe deeply.

'Yes. I'm sorry. Can I get you glass of water?' Caroline didn't reply, and the silent policeman went to find a clean glass from the cupboard. The scene assumed a surreal air for Caroline, who felt as if she were floating above it. Her ears roared and she struggled to hear what the policeman was now saying. 'Would you like us to come back later?'

She took the glass of water from the other man and sipped it. 'No. I'll be fine in a moment,' she said weakly.

There was another long moment of inactivity, the three of them unnaturally quiet and uncertain as to how to proceed. Eventually Caroline pulled herself together. 'How did it happen?'

'We're still trying to work that out. It seems as if the car just exploded and she was caught inside. No other vehicle was involved. Our forensics team are looking at it now.'

Caroline shook her head slowly in a vain effort to push it all away. Out of the corner of her eye she saw Hugh standing by the door, unsure of whether to come in or go away. 'Come here, sweetheart,' she said, and held her arms out. He walked over to her, glancing suspiciously at the policemen, and stood close to her as she wrapped an arm round his waist.

'I'm sorry to have to ask you this, but we will need some

further assistance,' the talkative constable said. 'Shall we call you tomorrow?'

'That'd be fine,' she replied.

They left, and she tried to explain to Hugh what had happened. He asked perceptive questions, understanding all too well the concept of death and how it might affect his mother more than anyone. For himself he seemed sorry but no more, as if he was no longer a stranger to tragedy and was hardened by the familiarity. She worried about him, not just in the ordinary maternal way but with a deeper anxiety about his tender thought processes. Sometimes he was too old for his years, and the strain this must cause would surely take its toll at some later stage.

He was reluctant to go back to his room, so he sat with her in the kitchen and ate a bowl of popcorn. As Caroline scribbled notes for herself the phone rang.

'Mrs Mercer?'

'Who is this?'

'I'm sorry to hear about your *au pair*. Such a terrible accident. Please accept my condolences. One can never be too careful, can one? I mean, that could have been you.'

'Who the bloody hell is this?' she screamed as her face flushed and tears welled up.

'Let's just say I'm a friend. I'm interested in making sure that no further harm comes to your family. And I want you to know that I can help. If you'll just return the money – the money that belongs to my associates – nothing else will happen. Do you understand that, Mrs Mercer?' Caroline's pulse raced as she realised what he was saying. Her throat dried up and she struggled to reply, but he didn't give her time. 'I know you do. Think about it. We'll speak again soon, I'm sure.'

The line went dead and Caroline was left holding the receiver by her side as she turned to face Hugh, who was looking at her with a puzzled expression. 'Some crank,' she said, trying to disguise the ripple of fear that had passed across her face. 'Nothing to worry about.'

In the bathroom, with the door locked and the laundry basket wedged against it, Linda inspected herself. Bruises blossomed like dark pansies across her ribs. She ran her tongue gingerly against her teeth to check for looseness and could feel the hardening lumps in her lips. Her mouth was so swollen that she could hardly keep the cigarette in place as she used both hands to feel for further wounds down her legs. It had been a calculated beating, cleverly designed to cause only superficial damage and yet still frighten her out of her wits. She had finally managed to control her sobbing and now sat slumped naked on the floor, her back jammed against the side of the bath as she assessed the severity of her injuries.

She laughed: it hurt her chest badly, but she was relieved and she didn't mind the pain. For all his bullying, he had not beaten the spirit out of her; if anything, it had merely strengthened her resolve, her determination to survive bolstered with each blow he had rained upon her. A long hot soak in the bath, an application of talc and twenty-four hours of sleep would wash away the throbbing aches. She'd already popped two arnica pills, a homeopathic remedy for bruising that she'd long ago learnt about from the necessity of experience. He was a bastard, but she knew all about them, and she was no closer to submission now than she had been when the first punch had landed on the side of her head. She looked at her fingernails and expected to see swatches of his skin hanging from them, so deeply had she scratched in her defence.

Nothing had changed. She was still alive and kicking, still ahead of the game. Sure, Guy was dead and that would hurt but, like the bruises, the agony wouldn't last for ever. She was already recovering, making different plans and calculating the odds until they fell in her favour. She told herself that her real motivation had always been the same, that Guy was only a means to an end, and she began to convince herself that this was true.

She carefully pulled herself up and stood shakily. The adrenalin rush had long since abated and now she was in shock, her legs quivering with the effort of staying upright, but she forced herself to drag the basket away from the door and leave the bathroom, going to the kitchen where she poured a large measure of Bacardi into an unwashed glass. Steadying herself against the draining board, she swigged the drink, letting out as big a sigh as she could manage without disturbing her ribs. The flat was dark, the only light coming in from the windows. Normally she liked it like this, leaving the curtains open in the evenings and sitting alone in the gloom, but she went to switch on a small lamp in the living area beyond the kitchen. She had to set it straight; it must have been knocked over in the fight.

Linda wanted to lie down and sleep on the couch, but her mind told her to stay awake, fearful that inactivity would bring its own problems. She stumbled around the flat with the glass in her hand and a cigarette hanging from her lips. Her chestnut hair hung in tangled strands over her face, but she couldn't make the effort to brush them away.

The physical pain was nothing compared to what she felt in her heart. Much as she tried to dismiss Guy's death, she knew how deeply it had wounded her. She could no longer pretend to be invulnerable, impervious to emotion and desire. He had captured her. She was trapped by her feelings for him and, now that he had gone, she was too weak to fight them. She needed to find a way out; she needed release from all this longing. She had to think, but her mind let her down. It was all too dark to contemplate.

Anthony Tilt was feeling pretty excellent. He was not hung-over and he was not drunk. His salary was in the bank and his back pocket had a thin wedge of twenty-pound notes in it. He had decided, after much debate with himself, that Caroline Mercer had not taken his clumsy advance too badly and might even yield in time – and time was about the only commodity he had in abundance. Work interfered occasionally, but he was a free agent and the firm allowed him much leeway. He had engineered this by befriending their most important client, a sports agent called Bernard Teller with a reputation for dodgy deals and suitcases full of cash; Tilt and he had hit it off after a long evening of drinking, and now Teller insisted that Tilt handle all his affairs. The other partners were envious but relieved: Teller was too colourful for their taste, and they liked his money more than they liked him. Anthony didn't share their feelings and saw Teller simply as a good opportunity, which he gratefully took.

Caroline was on his mind a lot. She was soft – that was the perfect word for her. She had no hard edges, either in physique or personality, with an aura that encouraged and enticed without threat or malice. Her losses and misfortunes hadn't affected her femininity: if anything, he felt that they merely added a sensual vulnerability. She was what he would have wanted to marry, but instead he got Angela. He tried not to think about her or the life they had briefly shared; he tried not to think about his own contribution to this continuing war of bitterness, preferring to blame her for everything. His infidelities were a symptom, not a cause; Angela was the true reason for his unhappiness.

Life, he reasoned, could only improve. For the first time in many years he felt confident, optimistic, even cheerful. He sipped his coffee and settled down to the day's work. He was halfway through a complicated letter about estate planning when his secretary, Deirdre, came in.

'I'm sorry Anthony, but Mrs Mercer is here to see you and she's quite insistent.' She shrugged to show her disapproval, but Tilt was calm.

'No problem. Show her in.'

Caroline had obviously not enjoyed a peaceful night of uninterrupted sleep. She looked drawn and tired, drained of colour with her shoulders hunched as if to protect herself from injury. 'I apologise, Anthony. This is out of order, I know, but I'm not thinking too straight.'

'Sit down. Would you like a coffee?' Deirdre was hovering and watched Caroline nod faintly. 'And one for me too, please,' Tilt added as she was leaving. He sat down at his desk and tried on his best sympathetic look. 'Tell me.'

'I'm scared shitless, to be frank. I can't stop shaking.'

'What's happened?'

'It's Mira, the *au pair*. She's dead. They say the car just exploded.'

'Exploded? What do you mean?'

'That's what the police told me. It just went bang.'

'Jesus, that's horrible. It must be awful for you.'

'It's not that so much. She was a lovely girl and I am upset. But it's what happened afterwards that really frightened me. I got a call. Some man – I have no idea who – called me to say how sorry he was about it. A strange foreign accent – I don't know, maybe German? But I'd only just found out myself. The police had come round to tell me. And I cannot see how this guy could have known about it unless . . .' She tailed off, clearly not strong enough to finish the thought.

'Unless he had something to do with it?' Tilt asked, unsure if this was what she meant. She confirmed it with another weak nod. Deirdre arrived with the coffee and set the tray down on a table next to Caroline. Tilt got up, poured two cups and then sat in the other visitor's chair, pulling it nearer to Caroline. 'You really believe that?'

'It wasn't just what he said, Anthony – it was the way he said it. He told me that you can never be too careful, that it could have been me. He wasn't just passing the time of day. He was threatening me, for Christ's sake. And he knows about the money. He said that it belonged to his associates.' She sobbed, but caught it before it turned into anything more. 'I told you they'd get to me next.'

'Have you discussed this with the police?'

'Not yet. I thought I'd speak to you first.' She looked at him imploringly, hoping he would have some perfect response which would set her mind at rest, but he could find nothing intelligent to say.

'You've got to go to them now,' he finally managed. 'You've got to come clean. It's too bloody dangerous otherwise.'

'I've been thinking about that all night. Something keeps on

117

nagging at me, though. Guy left us with nothing. He wouldn't have done that. He wouldn't have walked away from us unless he was sure we were going to be taken care of. The cash – well, after all the debts are paid off and I've put money aside for school fees, we'll have very little left. If he really knew that his life was in danger – and that's what the note suggests – then I'm convinced he would have tried to do more for us. There's got to be some clue, some sign that I'm supposed to recognise, but I can't work out what it is.'

Tilt thrashed around for an answer, and drank some coffee for inspiration. 'Do you remember the will?'

'Vaguely, but it hasn't done much good. The life policies had expired and both houses are heavily mortgaged. Why?'

'Going on what I remember, there were two mysterious trusts, weren't there? Something like Hartmann and Shadowlake? Does that ring a bell?'

Caroline screwed her face up like a child considering a tricky exam question. 'Shadowlawn,' she said, almost shouting. 'Shadowlawn, for God's sake! That's it. I have been *so* stupid. It's there, it's got to be.'

'What are you talking about?'

Caroline stood up abruptly. 'Do you have a car?' she asked, her eyes gleaming.

'No, but I can get my hands on one.'

'How do you fancy a drive out into the country?'

'I . . . what, now?'

'Yes. Now.'

'I'm really busy. I don't think . . .' His prevarication cut no ice with her.

'Come on, sort things out and let's go. You're brilliant, you know that?' Tilt shook his head in bemusement, but could see no way out. 'Don't worry, I'll explain everything on the way down.'

TWELVE

The inevitability of it did not make his dismissal any easier. Peter Verity had started to enjoy the power he had assumed almost by stealth, and was certain that he could repair any damage which Guy – and his death – might have caused to the firm. But the men from Chicago had been decisive in their actions; they had offered him a severance package that could not be refused, tied to a confidentiality agreement that he signed but had little intention of honouring.

There was information that he had withheld from them, data that might prove useful at a later date, but he wasn't really thinking about that now. What mattered was that he was losing his position, the fleeting chance he'd had to make his mark and show his worth, and that was hurting more than he would ever have imagined it would. The fact that they clearly didn't trust him was almost a secondary pain. They were snatching away his opportunity, and their money wouldn't ease the agony.

He'd seen Nancy with them, seen the way she'd forced herself to smile at them when it looked as if her face might crack apart from the effort, and he knew she was pushing her nose so far up their backsides that she'd need a snorkel and flippers to escape. She came out of her meeting looking flushed but confident, and

121

the way she darted an anxious glance in his direction confirmed what he feared most; she had told them about the account, AMS666, which had all the mysterious trades on it, and how Peter planned to cover it up. She would do that, he was sure; that was her style.

He didn't argue; he didn't cry; he didn't try to defend himself; he didn't react in any way that they might have expected. He went to his office and wondered what there was that he could possibly want to take home with him. There was nothing here that he needed, just as he was no longer needed. He picked up a photo of himself with other senior managers and customers in Scottsdale, Arizona, all dressed in tropical golfing kit with white knees peeping out beneath their shorts, Guy in the centre of them grinning hugely before they set off for their morning's round. Peter had enjoyed that trip, even though he couldn't play golf and didn't have the first idea of how to deal with clients. But he'd learnt fast, and by the end of the long weekend he was relaxed and happy, sore from the sun but feeling he was amongst friends.

No longer; now he was the stranger again, the man whose face didn't fit and whose motives were being questioned. He was back where he had been for most of his life, on the margin and about to be pushed off altogether, an irrelevance to be ignored or avoided. He had nothing to fall back on, no family to which he could return and share his frustrations; he was utterly alone and, with their decision to jettison him, completely dislocated from order and routine.

Numbed by this, Peter sat in his chair for a long time and stared at the golf photo. He had liked Guy, even though he had lived and worked under his shadow and had never received any credit for what AMS had become. Peter knew the private Guy, the Guy who was kind and generous and was always available in time of need, and he was able to discount the public image and bluster. This was the first occasion he'd had an opportunity to think about Guy and what his death meant to him, and he was shocked to realise it: he'd been so occupied with the business, so tied up with his swelling importance that he'd barely given a thought to Guy. Even when he'd fended off Caroline – and how he regretted that now, the cold manner he'd used and the lack of true sympathy he'd extended – it hadn't registered with him. Now it did.

But his reaction was not to break down and weep, not to feel anger or remorse. Peter, to his own great surprise, had only one thought in mind: what would Guy have done now? How would he have dealt with this? For possibly the first time in his life, Peter was sufficiently wounded that he wanted revenge, though he would never have used so strong a word. He needed to redress the balance, and he needed to pay his respects to Guy. There was, he knew, one way to achieve both, and the thought warmed him.

Deirdre, in her own quiet way, was fuming. One minute he was there, the next he was off with that woman without so much as a decent explanation. He really was the limit. She, of course, was left to pick up the pieces and cover for him. Meetings had to be rescheduled, calls intercepted, partners diverted, and all this on account of some woman who didn't even appear to be a client of the firm. Sometimes she thought that his brains were in his trousers; much as she loved him, Mr Anthony Tilt caused her more aggravation than was strictly acceptable by her lights.

Another call came through and she sighed before picking up the receiver. 'Mr Tilt's office,' she said, bracing herself for another round of apologies and excuses.

'Is he there, please?'

'I'm afraid Mr Tilt's out at a meeting. Can I help at all, or take a message for him?'

'If you would. Tell him that Linda Betts rang, will you?'

'I certainly will. And this is in connection with what?'

'Guy Mercer. He'll understand.'

'Guy Mercer. All right, I'll tell him. Is there somewhere he can contact you?'

'I'll try and reach him later.'

Deirdre was about to finish the conversation, to warn her that she had no idea when Anthony might return, when the line went dead. More mystery; another unknown woman looking for Anthony. Deirdre tried to put it all to the back of her mind as she started work on the filing.

The drive took no more than an hour. They got lost once, turning off the A3 too early, but Caroline had eventually got them back on course and they made it to Chiddingfold with no further detours.

'Just here,' she said as Tilt drove slowly round the village green. He stopped the car outside a large house on the edge of the north-east corner of the green. The front garden, overgrown and neglected, was about one hundred foot long and wide, with a drive running up the left side; the house was clearly unoccupied, with paint flaking off the window frames and several tiles loose on the roof and the upper parts. But even Tilt could see how beautiful it had been, and could be again, and they both sat in the car and admired it. 'This is it,' Caroline said. 'Welcome to Shadowlawn.' She opened her door and got out, and he followed.

The front gate was falling off its hinges and covered in lichen. Caroline carefully pushed it open and walked up a brick path, aubrietia and mint growing between the cracks and softening their footsteps. Flanking the path were flower beds that had once boasted fine rose bushes, now mostly withered through a lack of pruning and care. The lawns were nothing more than vast areas of dandelions, bramble and ground elder. Up both sides of the house there grew clematis and honeysuckle, still bravely clinging to wooden trellises, and a wisteria had been trained out of the out of the end of a barrel to fight its way up to the first floor. Someone who had lived here had been an enthusiastic gardener, and would doubtless have been horrified to see the decay.

Caroline tried the bell but nothing happened. She used the door knocker, once painted black gloss but now mainly rusted, and the raps on the door seemed as dead as the rest of the house. It was hot and bright outside, in stark contrast to the cold darkness they could see through the windows. 'Let's go round the back,' she said.

They walked along a gravel path that took them down the west side of the house. There was a wooden-framed greenhouse attached to the whole length of the side wall: all the glass was smashed and the wood was rotten. Inside they could see terracotta pots and propagation trays where seedlings had once been nurtured and geraniums brought on. Past the greenhouse they reached the rear garden, which extended for about two hundred yards down to a copse. The garden was full of specimen trees and shrubs, all carefully planted and planned to draw the eye effortlessly from one spectacle to another. There wasn't much grass: the area had been devoted mainly to a show of horticultural expertise that Tilt had never witnessed before.

'This is amazing,' he said.

'There's more. Come with me.' They went down the garden towards the copse, following a path of York stone that snaked its way through the shrubs and brushing against huge conifer bushes. Once at the end of the formal part of the garden Tilt saw what she was talking about: a large octagonal summer house sat on the border between the garden and the copse. Inside there was a wrought-iron table with eight chairs set around it, and there was still plenty of room to move. 'Quite something, isn't it?'

'I'll say. Who owns it?'

'Well, we wanted to. We found it quite by chance. We were meeting some friends for lunch at The Crown, and we were early so we had a walk around the green. It was in a state then, and that must have been about five years ago. We asked at the pub and they told us that on old man was living there, almost like a hermit. Guy, typically, got all excited and decided that we must buy it, and I humoured him. But he did get in touch with some local estate agents and told them that if it ever came on the market he'd be very interested. Nothing happened – then, out of the blue, an agent called about a year ago and said the old man had finally popped his clogs and it would be up for sale. We dashed down and looked around the place, but there was no way we could have afforded to renovate it. Everything needed doing – heating, wiring, plumbing, kitchen, bathroom, roof – you name it, it needed money spent on it. So we came back to London and that was that.'

'I'd love to see inside,' Tilt said.

'Maybe the back door's open.' Anthony looked at Caroline and could see she was flushed with excitement; he wondered how much this meant to her, and thought about her and Guy as they had wandered through the grounds, hand in hand, sharing their dreams, and he found himself a little envious. He had never had dreams like this, and had never had anyone with which to share them in any event. Angela would have laughed in his face and told him to grow up. But Caroline had been a willing partner in the adventure; he liked her for that.

At the back of the house there was a brick outbuilding to one side and the walls were covered in variegated ivy and a climbing hydrangea. The back door had two glass panels and they peered through to look inside; there was a large lobby area and they could see a sad pair of black wellington boots standing neatly against a wall. Caroline reached for the door handle and turned it, but it was locked. She sighed. 'Fancy a spot of breaking and entering?'

'No thanks,' he said. 'I have a nasty feeling we're already breaking the law, as it is. I'll just use my imagination.' They stood waiting, as if they didn't know what to do next. 'So, if I can just get us back to reality,' he continued, 'what does all this have to do with the will?'

'I have absolutely no idea,' Caroline said. 'But Guy obviously thought I would, the little devil. Come on, you're my adviser. What does it mean?'

'Can you think of anything special about the house, anything the two of you particularly discussed that might give you a clue?'

She thought for a long time about this, and then she went very red and put her hands to her cheeks. 'Oh my God,' she said, almost laughing. 'Yes, I can.'

'What?'

'You have to come with me, back down to the summer house.' She was off and he followed obediently. They reached the building and she went in. 'Come on, there's nothing to be afraid of – only a few spiders.' He came in uncertainly, his face brushing against a large cobweb that hung across the door frame.

'OK. What's the deal?' he asked.

'Privileged conversation?' she said teasingly.

'Of course.'

'Guy and I . . . well, you know, in here, we . . .' She tailed off and began to giggle, her cheeks flushing again as her eyes began to water at the memory.

'You . . . what, here? You're winding me up.' Anthony was surprised at his reaction: he felt both outraged and a little excited by the thought of it.

'It was uncomfortable, I have to say,' Caroline said, now in better control, 'but it was very . . . passionate.'

'You are a real enigma, Mrs Mercer.'

'I've had my moments,' she said rather proudly.

'I'm shocked. But what does that moment of madness have to do with anything?'

'We need to look for something, Anthony. Whatever it is, it's here, I'm sure.'

They both looked round the room but there was nothing obvious in sight. Caroline walked around the perimeter, her head bent down to see the floor better, while Anthony merely stood still. Then he stared at a spot under the table. 'There!' he shouted. 'Under the table. It's a door or something.'

They both dragged the heavy table to one side and he knelt

128

down and ran his fingers over the surface of the floor. He could feel the faint ridges of a trapdoor. 'How the hell does this open?' he said, still feeling his way through the dust. His fingertips found a catch set into the wood and he managed to lever up the little handle. He pulled gently and the door started to move. Caroline joined him on her knees and they looked inside.

There was a package sitting in the small space revealed by the open door. It was covered in thick plastic sheeting, held together with silver insulating tape. Anthony pulled it out very carefully and a spider ran across his hand, making him jump and drop the package.

'Cissy!' she shouted, and retrieved it. Resting it on her thighs, she pulled at the tape until it gave, tearing away parts of the sheeting to reveal an old briefcase of Guy's, still bearing his red initials on either side of the handle. She clicked the two catches of the case and opened it.

It was a two-part case. The lid had several pockets attached to its inside, and she put her hands into each of them, but there was nothing there. The lower half of the case was covered by a fabric partition, and now she lifted this. The first thing that caught their eyes was the note: on a single sheet of A4 paper was a message, written in large black capitals:

YOU REMEMBERED! WELL DONE!

Even without moving the sheet of paper, they could both see what was beneath it. The sight was enough to silence them, to stop their breathing completely for a long moment. Once again, Caroline was looking into a case which contained more cash than she'd ever seen in her life.

THIRTEEN

Jane knew where he'd be. She was trained to know these things, after all, and the training was very important to her. She used it all the time. She waited until she was sure, and then she went in. At first she couldn't see him, and she had to walk up to the bar and order a drink – white wine spritzer – and look around over the top of her glass. Then she spotted him, sitting with a group of people in the corner, his jacket off and a pint in his hand.

As casually as she could she walked towards him, as if she might almost be going to a different table, before stopping and looking directly at him. She smiled, a good smile that promised a lot. He was caught full in its blast. 'Hallo,' she said. 'It's Alan Apostle, right?'

'Yeah,' he replied, a little uncertain of himself but unwilling to pass up the chance. His mates around him stopped their chatter to follow the exchange.

'You don't remember me, do you? I'm Jane – Jane Fox. I came to see you at your office about Guy Mercer. Ring a bell now?'

'Oh, of course, yes, right,' Alan said. He remembered her legs, but she hadn't looked as tasty as this when she was in his office. She was made up now, dressed to kill, looking like she was dying for it. Clumsily he squeezed himself out from the table and came across to her. 'Let me buy you a drink.'

'That'd be nice. I'll have another spritzer, please.' They walked together to the bar and he fumbled with his money in his excitement.

'Are you here . . . professionally?' he asked as he waited for the barman to come back with the drinks.

'Not really,' Jane said. 'I just happened to be in the area and I thought I'd pop in on my way home.'

'So, have you found out who murdered Guy yet?'

'We're getting there.' She shrugged as if to show that she didn't want to talk about it.

The drinks arrived and Alan seemed reluctant to go back to his friends. 'Do you . . . would you like to sit somewhere else?' he asked her. 'Those guys can get a bit out of hand, if you know what I mean.'

'Whatever,' she said sweetly. She followed him to a free table at the other end of the room and they sat down. He was every bit as repulsive as she remembered him, with his stained teeth and puffy pink flesh, but this was work and she gritted her teeth. 'So, how are you getting on? Last time I saw you, the firm seemed to be in a state of turmoil.'

'Things have calmed down a bit,' Alan said. 'We've got new management in, and they've taken control and no mistake. They fired Guy's right-hand man, Peter Verity.'

'Did they?' she said, trying not to sound too surprised. 'When did that happen?'

'Just today.' He swigged at his beer. 'I could well be next.'

'I'm sorry to hear that.'

'Well, it's pretty inevitable, isn't it? They don't like the look of anyone who might know what the bloody hell they're doing. But I'll be all right. I've got other plans, don't you worry.'

'I guess morale must be pretty low in the office.'

'You can say that again. And, no offence intended, but it doesn't help having your people round there all times of day and night.'

'What do you mean?'

'Well, like your boss, that Grass fellow, he's been in and out so many times I had to give him his own security pass. He's seen all the top brass – don't ask me why, because they know bugger all about bugger all.'

'Oh, I see what you mean,' Jane said, although she didn't at all.

'Yeah, he's been a regular pain the *derrière*. Still, that's life. And we don't want to talk about work all evening, do we?' Alan leered at Jane and she smiled back at him.

'Certainly not. Would you just excuse me while I make a call, and then I'll be straight back?'

'I'll be waiting,' he said. Alan waited for one hour before realising she wasn't coming back.

The silence in the car had not been easy. It had sprung from the knowledge that Anthony had too many questions and Caroline too few answers, and they were both so acutely aware of this that they kept quiet to avoid any further embarrassment. Anthony had put the case in the boot and had checked the lock before setting off, as if it might leap out and scatter its contents across the Surrey countryside in a wilful act of retribution.

'Turn left here,' she said suddenly, surprising him by breaking the spell. Without question he followed her instructions, his stare firmly fixed on the road ahead. 'There's a pub along here. We're going to have a drink.' He nodded in a small way, apparently unwilling to move his head too much in case the action aroused too many thoughts. He saw the pub and pulled into the car park at its side; when the car was at a standstill he looked at his watch. It was two o'clock in the afternoon. He wanted to ask her about the children, to find out who would look after them, but it seemed such a mundane question that he refrained.

Caroline got out first and did not wait for him. She was strange; she was almost behaving as if he were the one who had done something wrong and she didn't want to be too near him. He followed her into the saloon bar, a pretty village room that had somehow escaped the attentions of the brewery's marketing suits. There were the inevitable horse brasses and blackboards with the day's menu, but there were also fresh flowers and genuine antique prints. A young girl with a skirt no larger than a modest curtain pelmet stood behind the bar and smiled at him as he joined Caroline.

'What will you have?' he asked.

'A large gin and tonic.' Caroline went and sat down at a polished table in the corner while he was served. When he walked over she would not make eye contact but looked out towards the French windows that led to a small beer garden full of nasturtiums and hypericum. He set the glasses down and took his seat opposite her. They both needed to take some immediate action, she by drinking, he by lighting a cigarette.

After she had finished half her drink Caroline looked at him and he could see the fear in her eyes. He had no clue of what to

134

say and, unusually, he did not try to find the right words. He simply waited.

'I don't have an explanation, if that's what you're waiting for,' she said defiantly.

He shook his head. 'No, I'm not waiting for that. I'm waiting to see if this is all a dream and I'm going to wake up soon.' He tried to make it sound humorous, but he failed.

'It's no good, Anthony. I can't go on like this. We'll finish our drinks and go straight to the police. It's over.'

'What's over?'

'The uncertainty. I can't face any more surprises. It's gone too far, and it's time for someone else to work out what the hell Guy was up to.'

'Tell me about him. Tell me everything you know.' He couldn't believe he had asked her this; he had no right, and he had no real interest, but he thought it was the best thing he could say.

'Guy wasn't complicated,' Caroline started, after taking another large sip of her drink. 'He wasn't difficult to fathom, an enigma that couldn't be cracked and all that crap. He didn't have dark secrets. What you saw was what you got. That's why none of this makes any sense – this bloody treasure hunt and all the rest of it.'

'What do you mean, the rest of it?'

She sighed heavily. 'Get me another drink.' He hurried to do as he was told and returned quickly to the table with two fresh glasses. 'Not long after all this blew up, a very nice policewoman came to see me. She suggested – she implied – that Guy might have been having an affair with a woman in his office, Linda Betts. I dismissed it at the time, as you do, but it nagged away. The more I think about it, though, the more likely it becomes.'

'Let me tell you something for free,' Anthony said. 'From the little you've told me about Guy, I think you're letting your imagination run too wild. If you look at the facts – and that's my job as your solicitor – your suppositions don't add up. He loved you, you loved him. He had a great family and his own business. Running away from all that doesn't seem logical. Yes, I'll grant you that all men are bastards and we can be fairly irrational, but you're taking it a bit too far. And I speak from experience.'

'Meaning?'

'Meaning that the only good thing that ever happened to me was when I met my wife and we had our daughter, Sophie. Everything since then has been total, unmitigated shit.'

'I'm sorry. I had no idea.'

'No reason why you should. But even a sad case like me can see that Guy would have had to have been completely mad to throw up everything he had with you and the children. Nothing else matters. That's how it is.' Then he lit another cigarette and tried to hide the ache his face was clearly showing.

'Anthony,' she said softly. 'Thanks.'

'For what?'

'Just thanks. That's all.'

They sat there together, looking to the barmaid like two middle-aged lovers at a secret tryst. Caroline put her hand over his and stroked it gently. It was hard to know who was more injured, and she could see the irony. 'What a pair we are,' she said. He nodded and smiled weakly. He had no idea what to do next, but it didn't matter so much any more.

FOURTEEN

It never changed, that feeling when it was over and she handed
him a bunch of tissues to clean himself up. Gerry Grass would
lie there feeling stupid and ashamed, promising that this
wouldn't happen again because the illusory excitement wasn't
worth the dreadful aftermath when they had nothing to say to
each other, and she was climbing back into her cheap knickers
and trying to pretend that nothing had happened. He would
look around the room as he wiped himself and wonder what the
hell he was doing there; the tacky video would play on for a
while until she stopped the machine and pulled out the tape,
and then she'd look at him and put on a watery, professional
smile and say: 'I'll see you in a little while.' She would spray
the room and take out the ashtray, tottering on her ridiculously
high heels as she left, and he would remain here, stark naked
on the dirty bed, desperate and empty and foolish with nothing
to show for his money but a sticky groin and a churning stomach.

This time was no different; the slut was new, that was all,
but everything else was the same. They all called him darling,
and they all did the business with that look of bored distraction,
and sometimes they said, 'That was nice', as he rolled off them
and they were holding the condom carefully to prevent any

leakage. He wanted to ask them: 'What do you like? What turns you on?' But that wasn't part of the deal: he paid enough to use them, but nothing more, nothing too personal or passionate, and yet that was what he longed for, to find some tart who wanted it, wanted him, and who wasn't afraid to enjoy it and say so. He kept coming back in the hope that, just once, a woman would be there who understood him and what he needed, so that it wouldn't turn out like this again.

He got up from the bed and caught sight of himself in the mirror. His body was white and hairless and every part of him looked tired and feeble. His erection had rapidly subsided and his penis now hung sadly between his legs; he looked away, unable to deal with his feelings of inadequacy and regret. It was always like this. He dressed quickly and left the room, the smell of stale cigarettes and manufactured *pot-pourri* lingering unpleasantly in his nostrils. He nodded at the maid on his way out and slammed the door behind him, out into the street with a quick look around to make sure there was no one who knew him within sight.

He walked along in the sunshine and wondered what to do. He could go back to the office, deal with the paperwork, have a few beers with the lads; or he could go home and call in from there. He was undecided, and that summed up his life. Trapped in a lacuna like some boat on a windless lake, he appeared unable to shift direction or change the course of events. He knew that what lay ahead was to be wonderful, a new life with no worries and all this grief behind him, but he had no way of stepping on the accelerator to get there more quickly. He had to wait: that was in the contract. Nothing could be done in haste, nothing could be pushed. The door would magically open when the time was right and he would disappear through it, leaving no traces and clean as a whistle.

There were things he would miss, of course: he knew the food would be awful, and he'd never get good beer out there, but he'd make new friends and the money would certainly help in that department. It was the right thing to do, he continually told himself. He was going nowhere and he deserved a break. Others hadn't been as smart as him, had they? They hadn't taken their chances – he had. That was the difference: he'd seen what was on offer and he'd liked what he'd seen. Nobody got anywhere unless they looked after *numero uno*, right? With this endorsement of his own actions still clattering in his head he began to feel better about things, and he found himself grinning with the anticipation of it all. He was on the up, and nothing would stop him.

After Deirdre had frostily briefed him on what he had missed the day before, the queue of calls he needed to return, the letters he must sign and the documents he must read, Anthony sat alone in his office and did nothing. The previous evening he had driven Caroline home and dropped her off, getting a light but welcome peck on the cheek for his troubles, but they had not gone anywhere near the police station. She would sleep on it, they had agreed, and come to a decision soon. When he left her he had gone back to his flat and, finding nothing there to amuse him, he'd gone down to the local pub to drink five pints of Fuller's ESB, then on to the local curry shop for a steaming meat tandoori.

He felt better than he deserved to, and was grateful for it. The briefcase was in his private safe in the office, the cash untouched and Guy's note still inside. He tried to think of it as just another deposit of client assets: the firm offered safe-keeping facilities to many customers, holding valuable and cherished property, legal documents, plain brown envelopes with unidentified contents, share certificates and other items too sensitive or precious to be kept at their owners' homes. This was simply another item on the inventory, duly tagged and recorded; he had no other involvement, no lien on the property and no interest in it. He should forget about it and attack his professional work with an uncluttered mind.

Some chance: the money worried him, not because it wasn't safe, but because of its unknown provenance and its owner. Was it hot? Was Caroline, perhaps, using him, knowing exactly what was going on? Why was he still involved? This could all be an elaborate plan, designed to compromise him and satisfy the requirements of some evil mastermind. He shook his head vigorously in an effort to dispel such stupid thoughts. Surely Caroline could be trusted, surely he was only doing what any other man would do in his position, helping the widow of a client who was down on her luck?

That was part of it; but there was a deeper fear, overriding these other worries, a concern that he was falling for Caroline in such a major way that his judgement, which was never his strongest suit, was deserting him altogether when he needed it most. When they had stood together in the summer house, and she had blushed as she remembered past indiscretions, he was overwhelmed with a pumping passion for her, an urgent desire to caress her and be inside her, as close as their skin would allow. Even now, sitting quietly in the sanctuary of his office, that urgency had not entirely dissipated and he shifted uncomfortably in his chair to try and fight it.

Work was the cure, as effective as a strategically placed cold spoon. He shuffled through his phone messages and binned the ones that needed no action. Finally he came across one, written in Deirdre's hand, which caught and held his attention: *Linda Betts rang* re *Guy Mercer at 10.35. She will call you again.* He stared at the note as if it might be hiding some more information, or he had missed something. Nothing came to him, and he set it down carefully in the middle of his desk. He rubbed his face and waited, willing the phone to ring. It was too quiet, and he got up and went out of his office to see Deirdre.

'There was a call yesterday from Linda Betts,' he said. 'Did she say where I could get in touch with her?'

'No. If she had, I'd have put it on the message, wouldn't I?'

'Of course. It's just that I'm rather anxious to speak to her.'

'Is she a client?' Deirdre didn't want to be helpful this morning, but he was used to that.

'Not exactly. But she has some connection to one, and it might be very important.'

'Well, if she rings again, I'll put her straight through.'

'Thanks. Is there any coffee made?'

'I'll see.'

He was waiting for the coffee when Deirdre opened his door, rather more tentatively than usual. 'Anthony,' she said, 'there are two people outside wanting to see you. They're from the police.'

'The police?' he said. 'You'd better show them in.' He stood up as Gerry Grass and Jane Fox came in, showed their IDs and introduced themselves. He motioned for them to sit down in the two visitors' chairs on the opposite side of his desk, then sat down himself. 'So – how can I help you?' He tried to sound professionally disinterested.

Grass took charge of the meeting. 'Mr Tilt, I understand that you were Guy Mercer's solicitor.'

'That's right.'

'You know, of course, that Guy Mercer was murdered. We are now investigating that murder, and we need your help.'

'You want to see the will, I suppose. I don't have a problem with that – but I'd like to check with Mrs Mercer first, if it's all right with you.'

'What's your relationship with Mrs Mercer?' Grass asked. 'Are you her solicitor as well?'

Anthony was beginning to feel hot; this should have been a routine visit, but it didn't seem to be entirely routine. 'Not exactly. I'm advising her on a couple of issues, that's all.'

'Such as?'

'Following her husband's death, she's now a shareholder in his company. She's asked for my help with that. And the will itself is a little . . . opaque, as you'll discover.'

'What do you mean by that?'

'I mean that certain beneficiaries are not clearly identifiable.'

'Didn't you draft the will for him?'

Anthony wasn't enjoying this. 'Yes, but under my client's instructions. Within the law, I'll do whatever my clients tell me. That's how we operate.'

'So you're saying you don't know to whom he left his money? Surely that can't be right?'

'I'm saying there are certain sections of his will that are probably understood by those beneficiaries – and no one else.'

'Is this for tax avoidance, or what?' Grass asked, clearly angered by Anthony's tone.

'Please, I really can't answer these questions. I'm not an accountant, I'm a solicitor. I suggest you have a look at the will for yourselves, and see what you make of it.'

'We'll do that. You must have a copy here – can we see it?'

'As I say, I'd prefer to speak to Mrs Mercer before allowing you to do that. I think that's only right.'

'Mr Tilt,' Grass said aggressively, 'you're not being very helpful. All we want to do is see the will and, as you say, we'll draw our own conclusions from it. Now, why don't you just get it for us and stop worrying about Mrs Mercer? She'll understand, I'm sure. She's very keen for us to find out who murdered her husband, so she's hardly likely to say no, is she?'

'I suppose not,' Anthony said meekly. He got up and walked round his desk, going past them to the door. 'Deirdre,' he said as he opened it, 'can you dig out a copy of the Mercer will?'

'I have it right here,' she replied, and handed it to him. He knew she'd been listening to the entire conversation.

They were both standing when he turned back into the office. 'You've been very helpful,' Grass said as he took the photocopy. 'Thanks for your time.' They left and Anthony collapsed in his chair. He was still shaking when a call came through, crisply announced by Deirdre. 'It's Linda Betts for you,' she said, then connected him. He sat up and rolled his shoulders.

'Miss Betts, how can I help you? I gather you want to talk about Guy Mercer.'

'That's right, but I don't want to speak on the phone. There's a pub across the road from your office. Is it possible you could meet me there in half an hour?'

143

'But—'

'Don't worry. I promise it won't take long.'

'All right. But how will I recognise you?'

'You won't need to. I know you.' She hung up immediately, and Anthony was left to wonder about this latest twist.

Anthony went straight over to the pub and positioned himself at a corner table away from the bar. He watched the office workers drift in and form little groups which would reshape themselves as allegiances shifted and interests changed, a ritual he knew only too well from long personal experience. He watched the clock drag the minute hand across its face, fretting that it was inaccurate. He really must buy a new watch; the old one was smashed when he fell over one night after a particularly heavy session.

He was lighting his third cigarette when a woman appeared from nowhere in front of his table. His eyes were at the level of her waist, and he knew almost before he looked up that he was going to fancy her. She was slim and pretty, her thick chestnut hair tied back so that it fell across her shoulders. She had deep brown eyes, difficult to look into without feeling intimidated, and her face was lightly made-up. She wore a crisp white blouse with a smart chocolate brown suit and matching shoes.

'Miss Betts?' he said through his smoke.

She nodded and held out her hand. 'Please call me Linda,' she said.

'Can I get you a drink?' As he looked more closely at her, he noticed that her face and lips were bruised, but he was not brave enough to comment on this.

'No thanks. As I said, I hope this isn't going to take too long. I'll come straight to the point. I worked for Guy Mercer. He was a very dear friend of mine, and I was absolutely devastated to hear about his murder. I expect you were too. Anyway, shortly before he died, Guy told me that, in view of our special relationship, he was going to remember me in his will. He gave me your details – said you were the executor? Naturally, I didn't think very much about it, because none of us expected him to die, did we? But, well, now we find ourselves in these unhappy circumstances, and I thought I'd better check in with you just to let you know who I am.' She smiled winningly at him.

'I see,' he said, warming to her to the extent that he could almost forget his recent encounter with the police. In spite of this, he did not forget his agreement with Caroline, and the loyalty he felt towards her, so he played for time. 'It's perfectly proper that you should do this, Linda, and thanks for helping me. I'm having to sort out one or two little . . . issues with the will – nothing major, you understand, just some wrinkles, but it might take a few more days to sort it all out. Shall I call you when it's all done?'

'The thing is, I'm a bit elusive at the moment, not easily reached. It's probably better if I call you – say in a week?'

'You're sure I can't get in touch? I mean, I might need to speak to you sooner than that.'

'Whatever you have will keep, Mr Tilt.' She smiled again and her brown eyes sparkled. She really was very attractive, Anthony thought.

'Well, that's fine then,' he said. 'I look forward to hearing from you. Was there anything else I could do for you?'

'Sadly not,' she replied. 'I have to deal with Guy's death by myself.' Then she got up, shook his hand and left. He was shivering and he needed another drink.

FIFTEEN

Through the grapevine Jane had heard about the accident with the *au pair*. Grass would never have told her; it wouldn't have made sense if he had. He had suddenly and inexplicably started to freeze her out, leaving her to amuse herself with peripheral matters in which he had no interest. He drafted in other officers to help on the case, and they seemed to be under instructions to avoid her.

She had tried to react with dignity and silence to this treatment, not allowing herself any behaviour which he might ultimately use against her. Perversely she worried about this, the way in which, almost unchecked, she was weathering the misfortunes and slights of her life. She didn't want to be hard; she didn't want to be known as hard. The lads would soon mark her down as bitter and insensitive until they regarded her as little more than a bloke with a skirt on. A woman first, then a copper: that was her credo, but she was finding it increasingly difficult to adapt this to her own circumstances.

Jane chewed at a jam doughnut as she flicked through a file and made some notes on a pad. Grass was out; officially he was doing some fieldwork, although everyone knew he was recovering from a heavy night in the pub, a privilege that his junior officers were not afforded. They had to stagger through the day with only coffee and painkillers to sustain them. There were benefits to Jane from this collective hangover: the office was quiet and she could work without interruption in the certainty that no one would interfere. All they wanted was to die quietly in a corner.

The Mercer case; she came back to it whenever her concentration lapsed. At school she had been good at maths – she especially liked algebra – and her teachers would commend her on the way in which she could look at the same problem in ten different ways. That technique was what she needed now if she was going to unravel the story. Nothing added up as it should; there were too many unknown factors, too much assumption and too little analysis.

Grass had told her two things to set her on edge. He had said that he had visited the self-storage unit and had thoroughly searched it, but had turned up nothing of any interest. Whilst she was inclined to believe him, she couldn't help wondering who had accompanied him. No one else knew anything about it; had he really gone on his own? Not only was this uncharacteristic, it was also against regulations. He should have had another officer with him, but she couldn't find anyone who'd been there.

More disturbingly, he now seemed very interested in Anthony Tilt. Several times on the journey back from Tilt's office he had said that he didn't trust him. When Jane suggested he was merely doing his job as a lawyer, Grass snorted. 'They're all the same,' he spat. 'They're all a bunch of tossers.' She asked if she should do some background work on Tilt, but he merely shook his head and said he'd deal with it.

148

But this was not what troubled her most. The investigation was veering away from the obvious focus – Mercer's business connections – and centering instead on his personal life. Admittedly, her visit to see Peter Verity had been unsuccessful: he had given her nothing new to work on, no fresh lines of inquiry to pursue, but she continued to believe that AMS and its employees were keeping something from her. She was confused by Grass's decision to steer his resources away from the business: how could that be happening at the same time as Alan Apostle had told her that Grass was in the AMS offices at all times of day and night, and even had a security pass? It didn't make any sense to her, unless . . . Jane wouldn't allow herself to think the unthinkable, so she avoided it. Instead, she concentrated on devising a way to keep the investigation alive, and rapidly reached another dead end. There was nowhere she could go, no one to whom she could speak, without rattling cages and arousing fear. She finished the doughnut and licked the sugar from her fingertips. Still distracted, she jumped a little when the phone on her desk rang. With sticky fingers she picked it up.

'Jane Fox.'

'Oh,' a woman said. 'I was looking for Mr Grass.'

'I'm afraid he's not here. Can I help?'

'Could you leave a message for him? It's Fiona from Alhambra Property Services. If you could tell him that the papers are now ready for signing. Is that OK?'

'That's fine. He'll know what to do?'

'Yes. Thanks.'

Jane tore off the message slip from a small yellow pad and took it into Grass's office. She placed it on top of a pile of other messages in the centre of his desk and her gaze switched from that to his in-tray. The Mercer file was sitting there, and she flinched before casually reaching towards it and picking it up. She left his office slowly, trying to behave innocently, and managed to make it to the Ladies without passing anyone. She locked herself in a cubicle, sat down and began to read.

The formalities of Mira's death were complex and intensive. Her parents spoke no English, and the police seemed uninterested in finding someone who could break the news to them. Legally, they told her, Caroline was responsible for all the arrangements; she, in turn, contacted the English school where Mira was studying in a bizarre and distasteful parody of pass the parcel. She was lucky: a close friend of Mira's at the school agreed to call the parents and organise the shipment of Mira's charred remains back to Belgrade.

Mira's death was a devastating blow to Caroline. She missed her, and not just because she was so good with the boys. Having another woman in the house, and one as sensible as Mira, was a major comfort as Caroline tried to reorganise her life. That she should be killed so heartlessly was the final torment: there was no protection, no security, no place of safety left.

She wanted to run, to scoop the boys up and disappear, but every plan she had she instantly dismissed as hopeless. She felt she was being watched, that all her movements were monitored and that even her deepest thoughts were transparent and visible; snared by this sensation, Caroline was overwhelmed with inertia. It was all she could do to worry about the care of the boys now that Mira was dead.

In her search for Mira's replacement, Caroline revisited an

old idea. Instead of enlisting the services of another girl, she found an agency that specialised in male *au pairs*. Bereft as she was of female company in the house, she still thought that it would be more useful and constructive to have a man in close attendance. The boys, she reasoned, might also value him more highly now that the dominating presence of Guy was gone for ever. She wasn't ready yet to talk to Hugh and George about it, because she needed to find an outstanding man – preferably with a World Cup winner's medal round his neck – before she had enough ammunition for an assault. In the interim, she hired a stern Irish lady from a temporary agency who was expensive, unsmiling and formal. The boys did as they were told, wisely recognising that they had met their match.

Caroline was reading through the biographies of potential incumbents when she was struck by the full force of her situation. Like a malignant cancer the feeling spread from her stomach in all directions, its power debilitating and pervasive: she was crippled by the waves of dread, grief and weariness as they broke remorselessly over her. She didn't have enough strength to combat this, nor the presence of mind to try and break down her overwhelming sadness into more manageable constituents. Guy was gone, and from that moment everything else had disintegrated and re-formed in a new and hopeless shape; the things she had known, the beliefs she had held, all seemed to have disappeared, her former certainties now in ruins as she struggled to cope with the most basic tasks of living, of carrying on and bearing up.

Two little lives depended on her entirely, just as they had when they were within her womb and would live or die according to her actions. She had never felt so inadequate, so totally incapable of offering them what they needed; it was hard enough to keep herself together, so frightened had she become by what had happened to Guy and now to Mira, let alone provide the nourishment and guidance the boys needed, and her desperate solitude resounded loudly, an insistent backbeat to the rising nausea. Tears dropped to the table and on to her hands as she hung her head in defeat, yielding to the agony as it throbbed in a ceaseless crescendo.

As Caroline sobbed she felt herself defeated also by the insignificant parts of her life, the details that had previously meant nothing – school runs, laundry and ironing, shopping, cooking, paying bills – but which now assumed immense proportions in her confusion. Every small function, from the time she sat at her dressing table and wearily put on her make-up to the time she rubbed it off again at night, daunted her. She couldn't see where it was all taking her, where the end might be that would justify the means, an objective to which she could aim her energies in hopeful anticipation of future serenity. With Guy that hadn't been an issue; she was happy to be led by him along a path, any path he chose, making her quiet contribution as he cut a swathe through the tangled maze for all of them to follow.

She waited, expecting that her natural defences would finally kick in and fight back against this onslaught, but relief was neither quick nor decisive. Normally she would cry and that would purge her, at least temporarily, of all the demons haunting her, but this time the malaise was so deep-seated that she couldn't find the usual compound of emotional antibodies. It was as if each battle in the continuing war against despair was depleting her reserves of will, until she would reach the stage where nothing could rally her. Even in the darkest moments, when she felt as if she had been condemned to a living death, she could find some comfort to cling to, some flickering light that would sustain her, like George's smile or the unquestioning cuddles she could rely on from both of them. She could even take comfort from Hugh and his mannish boyhood: shortly before Guy had died, Hugh had made her promise that she would never kiss him or hold his hand in public, especially at or near school. He would relent only on special occasions, and had set a tariff of bribes that ranged from fifty pence for hand-holding to two pounds for a peck on both cheeks. After Guy's death, however, he imposed a unilateral suspension of this fee schedule, and was even willing to be kissed at the school gates.

Now, however, none of these little joys was enough to bring her round. The tears didn't dry up, the sinews didn't stiffen with fresh purpose, and she remained hunched and broken, battered into a submissive torpor and incapable of escape. There was no remission; her anticipated resurgence of hope did not arrive; the horror of what had gone before, and of what was yet to come, was finally suffocating her, and she was left to choke in anguish.

By nine o'clock that evening, with the boys efficiently despatched to bed with scrubbed, clipped fingernails and ears that were burnished from vigorous excavations with cotton buds, Caroline had gone beyond despair and was in a state of shock. The Irish matron had departed – she had refused to sleep at the house, claiming that she disapproved of such a practice – and Caroline sat alone once again, oblivious now to the tasks that should be done, no longer feeling guilt or lethargy but merely concentrating all her efforts on breathing.

In the sitting room, that supposed haven where Guy and she were to spend their quality time, she was surrounded by memories of another life – not her life, but theirs, the one they had shared and had planned to keep going for ever. She had never been prepared for another life, one where she was independent and managed by herself, and the slow realisation that this was now her world had affected her in much the same way as some major accident, when all the body's defences club together to protect the mind and deflect it from too much thought or analysis. She gazed into empty space without focus, as if there had been a dislocation of her eyes from her brain.

She barely noticed when Hugh pushed his face uncertainly round the door, ready to retreat if he got the wrong signal from her. He held himself still, half in and half out, until she looked up and smiled weakly at him.

'Sorry, Mum,' he said.

'Come in. There's nothing to be sorry about.'

Hugh padded over to her on the sofa and arranged himself next to her, leaning against her much as he might have done only a few years before. He was lean, his limbs no longer soft and pliant – when he was a baby, they had always described his legs as Marks & Spencer's medium chicken quarters – and he was beginning to acquire the smells of a grown man, his sweat no longer sweet but tinged with a distinctly vinegary edge.

He was silent, relishing this snatched moment of privacy but also fearful of articulating his own fears and doubts lest they upset her too much.

'Can't sleep?' she asked.

'I'm not tired. There are too many things going round in my head.'

'Lucky you. I'm so whacked I could sleep on a clothes line.' That was pure Guy: they would all laugh about Guy's ability to drop off anywhere, at any time, and this had become a family expression.

'I'm thinking about Dad a lot,' Hugh said, picking up on this. He wanted to talk but, just as importantly, he wanted to be listened to.

'So am I,' she replied, not yet in tune with him.

'It's just . . . there are lots of things I want to tell him, and lots of things I need to ask him about. I know that sounds really stupid, but . . .' He shifted against her, squirming a little in embarrassment at this confession. He wanted to be strong and tough, and had hidden his stormiest weeping from her and his brother, but now he instinctively needed to prove the depth of his own loss.

'I think we all feel like that. It's nothing to be frightened of, though. It's going to take a long time before we get back to normal.' She was still only partially with him, as if a crucial part of her brain had ceased functioning.

'Why did they kill him, Mum?'

It was the question she dreaded, the one without an answer. She settled for honesty. 'No one knows. That's what the police are trying to work out.'

'I don't understand. Who could want to do that to him? He was the best dad ever,' Hugh said firmly, struggling to control the crack in his voice.

'And you'll always have that, Hugh. No one can take that memory away from you.'

'Talk to me about him.'

This plea finally roused her, and she closed her eyes and drew in a large breath through her nose, steadying herself before thinking of what to say, of how to describe the man she had loved so completely and yet who had, possibly, led another life about which she knew nothing.

'Well,' she began cautiously, 'he was a big man. Not just physically, but in a lot of other ways too. Everything about him was larger than life. But it was his appetite – not just for food and drink, although heaven knows that was enormous – that was really huge. When he found something that interested him he became totally obsessed by it, wanted to know everything about it. He was like that with people, too. He always behaved as if he really wanted to know about the person he was talking to. He could make people feel really special, really important. Not many of us can do that, you know. Most of us are just worried about ourselves, and we only pretend to show an interest for good form's sake. But with him, it was genuine.'

'I know. Whenever he came home from work and I was still up, and I knew he was tired and worried by all that office stuff, he'd still ask me about what I'd done at school and I always felt he was listening to me.'

'He was very special like that. Everyone thought they were his best friend.'

'But you were his best friend, weren't you, Mum?'

'I think I was. I think he'd always have come to me first if he had anything he wanted to talk about, even it if was business and I didn't really understand everything he was saying. Yes, I was his best friend. But you and George ran me pretty close. He used to say to me that it was my responsibility to punish you if you'd been naughty, because he didn't want to upset you in case you wouldn't be friends with him any more.'

Hugh thought about this. 'But he did punish us once. Don't you remember? When we were all going to Chessington, and George and I wouldn't stop fighting in the car, and he got really agitated and drove us home. I've never forgotten that. It was totally unfair.'

'But he told you that, didn't he? He came to your room and apologised to you.'

'Yes, and he really meant it. I knew he was upset about it.'

'He felt guilty for days afterwards. And, if you remember, he bought you both special presents.'

'He got me a new tennis racquet, one I'd been wanting for ages. I thought I was going to have to wait for my birthday.'

'That was another thing about him. He knew how to say sorry. When he'd done something wrong, he wouldn't just ignore it and hope it would all get forgotten. He'd sort it out. That's another thing not many people can bring themselves to do. Your dad was unique in a number of ways.'

They fell silent as they both recalled private memories; then Hugh spoke. 'I don't think I'm ever going to get married.'

'What makes you say that?'

'I don't want all the aggravation. I want to keep my freedom, and do what I want to do.'

'I understand what you're saying, but I think you'll find that life isn't quite as simple as that. Marriage isn't about doing what your wife wants you to do. It's about wanting to share things together with someone you love, the person you want to be with all the time. It isn't a question of giving up your freedom. It doesn't work like that. When you find the right girl you'll know what I'm talking about.'

He grimaced at the thought of it. In Hugh's list of priorities, girls came some way below washing and Latin homework. 'It's not fair,' he said, and began to sniff as his thoughts refocused on his father.

'I know,' she said softly, pulling him closer to her. 'I know. We just have to do the best we can. That's what he would have wanted.' Caroline tried to imagine how Guy would have counselled and comforted them, how he might have reacted were he in her position. She yearned for his strength and ached at the lack of it. She had never felt so utterly hopeless.

SIXTEEN

When Gerry Grass went out for a drink he took it seriously. His body sang with anticipation and he became slightly intoxicated before he'd taken his first sip. He would drag along a few cronies, those men with broken home lives or no life at all outside work, men who appreciated the need for each other's company and who also relished the chance to submerge themselves in the meaningless chatter that alcohol released. They would stand at the bar and order beer and whisky, smoking and drinking frantically until they could stand straight no longer, at which point they'd stagger to the nearest curry shop and challenge each other to ever hotter dishes. The pattern never changed, even if the players did.

Grass was in full flight when Jane came into the pub. She hated these sessions, not so much because they intimidated her but more because she saw them as so pointless, grown men behaving like children and making themselves violently ill in the process. She knew that her disapproval was mocked by them, and that they viewed her with deep suspicion as a result, but she couldn't bring herself to become one of the lads. If this was to be the price of getting on, she thought, then maybe it was too much to pay.

'Hallo,' Grass shouted at her as she approached the group. 'What'll you have?'

Jane looked from face to face as they waited for her reply. 'If you're buying, I'll have a large Scotch, please,' she said, and the men all cheered. Grass smiled and shook his head as he waved a fiver at the barman. Jane wasn't mad about whisky, but she'd enjoy this one.

When she had the glass in her hand Grass detached himself from the crowd and took her to one side. His face was flushed and his eyes bright, but he was still in control: give him another hour, she guessed, and he'd be over the edge. The Scotch burned its way down to her stomach and she took very small, careful sips.

'Listen, I don't want you to hear this from anyone else,' he said. 'You know how quickly rumours get around. I wanted to tell you first.'

'What?'

'The Mercer case. There've been some developments and I need to explain them to you.' He shrugged, drained his glass and held it out where the other men could see it. 'I've been thinking. We've been looking in all the wrong places – and I'm as guilty as you on that one, let me tell you – and it just doesn't add up. That's why I brought some fresh eyes in, to get a different perspective on the thing. And I think it may have worked. All this time we've had a suspect under our noses and we've done bugger all about it.'

'Who?'

Grass was handed a pint of beer by one of his colleagues and he took a large swig before answering. 'The solicitor, of course – Anthony Tilt. I got the lads to do a bit of research, and suddenly it's all falling into place.'

'Is it?' Jane could hardly believe what she was hearing, and she sipped a little of her drink to cover her confusion. 'How so?'

'Look at him. He's a waster. He's a smarmy git who's down on his luck. He's broke and he's got a wife giving him constant earache about his payments. Then one day Guy Mercer walks into his office and Tilt sees the main chance staring him in the face. He does his bit with the will, so he knows there's plenty of money. Mercer tells him about those two trusts, what they represent, and gives him all the information he needs. Tilt can't resist the temptation. He bumps Mercer off and waits, putting us – and, no doubt, Mrs Mercer – off the scent by saying he was just acting on client instructions and has no idea about the trusts. It's perfect.' Grass grinned, as if he thought she'd share his elation at this information.

'Oh,' Jane said. 'So what about the money? I mean, did Guy Mercer leave a lot? I got the impression from his wife that she was still pretty broke.'

'Perhaps he didn't tell her about it. You know, all this bullshit about them being skint, it doesn't exactly ring true, does it? For all we know he had plenty to spare.'

'Not according to his bank accounts. I've checked.'

'Guys like Mercer are smart enough to know where to hide it, to keep it out of sight of the taxman. That's why he used Tilt – to set up these trusts which nobody would understand.'

'I see,' Jane said. 'Have you questioned Tilt yet?'

'We're going to wait a bit. We want to keep watching him, see if he slips up. He doesn't know we're on to him, and we'd like to keep it that way.'

'So where does that leave the investigation? Is there anything you want me to do?'

'No. My advice is to have a few drinks and celebrate. We've cracked it. Let's enjoy it. Cheers.' He drank almost the entire contents of his glass in one, then sighed loudly. 'Bloody marvellous, isn't it?'

Jane didn't know how to react, but she realised that any argument would be pointless. She raised her eyebrows in resignation and held her glass up in a small salute. 'Well done. That's great news,' she said quietly.

'The best. And now, if I'm not very much mistaken, it's your round.' He winked at her and moved back towards the bar. Jane weighed her options and decided to acquiesce, at least for now. The row could come later.

It had been a stupid thing to do, coming straight back to the flat from Heathrow, and Linda wasn't stupid. Her mum had always told her that – 'You've got brains, my girl, and you should bloody well use them' – and she hadn't forgotten that advice. Up until the moment when she realised Guy wasn't coming, she had been rational, prudent and wise, considering every alternative and covering her tracks with immense care. They had nothing to go on. The office records were clean and no one could pin a thing on her. It had been brilliant, and she was proud of herself for it.

But that was then. Things were different now. Too many people knew she was back in circulation, and they all wanted to ask her questions she wasn't too keen on answering. The sooner she dropped out of sight, the sooner she'd be out of mind. She was getting used to living like a nomad; a few more days wouldn't hurt. There was nothing in the flat to pack: everything she wanted to keep had been put into two new suitcases in preparation for her flight to Corsica. They'd been a present from Guy – part of a set of six – a sign that he was committed to the travel plans they'd made together. 'Look after those,' he'd said. 'They're worth more than you could possibly imagine.' She could tell that just by the look of them, and she did treat them well; she reckoned she'd never had anything quite as expensive given to her before.

The meeting with Mr Tilt had been difficult, draining, like appearing on stage without knowing her lines; he was not as she'd expected, and she found his odd mixture of formality and friendliness tricky to deal with. He was not aggressive, but neither was he submissive – just a guy doing his job and trying his hardest to be fair. She could see that, even through the haze of her own anger and bitterness, and she didn't want to frighten him. She'd set out to charm him and it had worked.

Linda could be a mean bitch if she wanted; she had realised early on in her career that being a nice girl wouldn't always get her where she wanted to be. At first it was tough, treating colleagues so roughly, but they soon complied and she grew to do it by habit. She knew what they said about her, and some of it hurt. In her eyes, those who claimed that they felt no pain when verbally assaulted by others were merely liars of a different kind. At least she was honest: she wanted to be liked, but she wanted other things more, and sometimes those other things won.

What Linda wanted most was justice. She had been denied what she considered was hers by right. Guy was her property; to have him taken away, and all that he would have brought

163

with him, was an injury she could not ignore. She knew that she faced a difficult task, especially as she only had fragments of information to work with, but that would not deter her. Guy had intended to share everything with her, and she would still take it, her reward for all the crap she had endured. Nothing else mattered now; if she couldn't have Guy, she would accept second best.

Caroline cursed the unwanted intrusion; no one who came to the front door ever had any good news for her – unless you counted the God-botherers who frequently arrived on her doorstep with glad tidings and messages of imminent salvation. She got two pound coins from her purse in anticipation of just such a visitor and opened the door, prepared for a cheesy smile and a sincere look of concern from her caller. But the man on the doorstep was recognisable, though she struggled to place him at once.

'Caroline? Hallo. You probably don't remember me – I'm Peter Verity.'

'Yes, of course you are,' she said rather stupidly.

'Could I . . . would it be convenient if I came in for just a few moments? I have something I need to discuss with you.'

She looked at her watch and then at him. He was rather a sad man, she thought, devoid of threat or malice as he stood there in his khaki slacks and polo shirt, clutching a briefcase and blinking nervously. She decided to give him the benefit of the doubt. 'I'm just on my way out, so you'll have to be quick.'

'I won't take long, I promise.'

They went to the kitchen and sat at the table. Caroline didn't offer him anything to drink; she didn't want him to get too comfortable. 'So, what do you want to tell me?' she asked impatiently.

'First of all, you should know that I've been fired. They paid me off a few days ago – a very generous settlement, and now I'm supposed to be happy about it all.'

'But you're not?'

'I have some doubts – some real concerns – about AMS and its shareholders. I used to warn Guy, tell him that he'd better keep on making a lot of money or else they'd put concrete boots on him and drop him in the Thames. He'd just laugh and say that was typical me, always worrying about the downside of things, and that everything was working out fine and he'd got the measure of them. And I have to say, he really did a superb job of keeping them sweet. The numbers were always good, and he would put on a good show when they came to town to check on their investment. I never found cause to complain, and I never discovered anything that he couldn't explain away.'

'So what's your problem?'

'When Guy died, I had to put in a lot of work straightening out the books and getting the records in order. I found some things that didn't make any sense at all. But I persevered. I may have my faults, but I'm very determined when I need to be. I went through practically every transaction the firm has done over the last three years. And I found some things that I don't think I was meant to find.'

Caroline could feel the hairs rise on the back of her neck. 'I don't know what you're talking about, Peter.'

'I'm not going to beat about the bush. Based on what I've found, it looks to me as if Guy was engaged in a massive sting. What he was doing was clever, and practically indiscernible to the untrained eye, but all the evidence is there if you look hard enough. He was using the shareholders' money to generate cash which he then siphoned out of the company. At first the amounts weren't big – at least, not in the overall scheme of things – but they were large enough to make a difference to him without them noticing. I think he used these deals to see if he could pull it off. When he realised he could, he went for the big one.'

'The big one?'

'Yes. Guy engineered a deal. I think it was meant to be the last one. It was for twenty-five million dollars. The money was transferred from an account held by Investment Logistics, and it came into AMS. But where it went is still a mystery. It certainly never arrived at the destination suggested by our internal records. I'm positive Guy took that cash and parked it somewhere safe, somewhere where no one could find it, let alone get their hands on it.'

'You've lost me.'

'OK. Let's take a step back. It doesn't take a genius to work out that the shareholders in AMS are villains. They have always been paranoid about anonymity and confidentiality – now why would that be, unless they were up to no good? My guess is that their money was dirty and they needed to find a place to park it and launder it. AMS was the perfect vehicle. The whole business is based on non-disclosure so that the counterparties to a deal don't know who's on the other side. They only see AMS – good old Guy, we can trust him, that kind of thing. And, to be perfectly frank, most of the big traders don't care where the money's coming from, in spite of all the rules and regulations. They just want to do deals and make a big profit. Nothing else matters to them.'

Caroline sighed, though even she couldn't have said whether this was from sadness or frustration. There was nothing to say to him, no way to rebut what he had told her. She shook her head and he took this as a sign to go on.

'What you have to understand is that this veil of secrecy is a dangerous weapon. They thought they could trust Guy, so they gave him the discretion to manage their money without too much interference. That's a big temptation for anyone, however strong-willed you think you are. If you could find a way of making a little bit on the side for yourself, with no risk, you'd have to be very straight to say no to it. Don't get me wrong – in all the time I knew him, Guy was as straight as an arrow – but this must have been too difficult to resist.' Peter waited to gauge her reaction before making his final comment. 'Especially if he had pressures in his home life.'

'What the hell is that supposed to mean?' Caroline asked, now animated.

'Come on, let's be honest with each other. Guy was up to his neck in debt. Everyone knew that. What with the school fees, and the three houses . . .' He knew immediately he had said something wrong. A series of emotions flashed across Caroline's face – defiance, bewilderment, shock – as she reddened and moved forward in her chair.

'No. Two houses. This, and the one in Minster Lovell.'

Peter realised before she did. 'What about that one in Chiddingfold? I thought—'

'Shadowlawn? You think we bought Shadowlawn?'

'Well, maybe I'm wrong. Anyway, that's hardly important, is it? The point I'm trying to make is that he was pretty committed financially, You knew that, at least?'

'Better than you'd imagine.'

'So he had a motive, if he was trying to ... well, you know.' Having seen that she knew less than he'd assumed, Peter had lost confidence and didn't know how to continue. They sat opposite each other, both struggling to deal with the importance of his information.

'Peter,' she said at last, 'forgive me for being stupid, but why are you telling me this?'

He put his hands up to show that he was her friend. 'Don't worry. There's no love lost between me and the shareholders, and I couldn't care less about their money. What concerns me is that they might decide to come after you, especially if they think there's a chance that you can lead them to the cash. I just wanted to warn you. These guys can be pretty unpleasant when they need to be.'

'I already know that.' Caroline didn't want to elaborate about Mira; it opened too many wounds that he wouldn't know how to begin to heal.

'I want you – and your family – to be safe from them. You have to know what you're dealing with.'

'That's very kind,' she said, meaning it. 'And it's time that I was honest with you. I know Guy was up to something. I didn't at first – at least, not whilst he was alive. But a lot of things have happened since then and I'm much wiser now. I think I'm almost beyond shocking, whatever I'm told. I've gone into a kind of trance where I'm almost immune to pain. So what you've told me doesn't surprise me.'

'But I'm not telling you this to shock you, or to show Guy in a bad light. I'm telling you this because I think you're in significant danger. Whether you know anything or not, these people are going to assume you do. They're not going to give up. I came here to offer my advice. Get away while you can. That's what I'm going to do. I'm not planning to join the Foreign Legion, but I want to try and forget everything that's happened and make myself invisible. You should do the same.'

Caroline wanted to agree with him; she desperately needed reassurance that her fear and exhaustion and resignation were entirely understandable, but she wasn't yet ready to give in without going through the motions. Her reticence was heightened by practical matters, such as what she would do about schools for the boys and where they would live. For him it was easy; for her it was not. 'I know I should, but it's not as simple as that. There are too many unanswered questions, and I'm not sure I can leave them like that.'

'Isn't that what the police should be doing? You and the boys need to get out of harm's way. That would be my first priority.'

She liked his affirmation, but didn't know how to say so. 'What will you do?'

'I'm putting some contingency arrangements in place. I want to make sure that other people know about the AMS shareholders and what they've been doing. I have information that I'm going to use as health insurance.'

'I see.' Caroline started to understand what this might mean. 'I hate to ask this, but will it affect me?'

'I hope not,' Peter replied. 'That's not the intention, far from it. If anything, what I'm going to do will protect you and the boys. And, if you get away now, I'm sure you'll be all right.' He was a kind man, a good man, and she could see that he had been deeply hurt. She would have liked to know more about him, but he looked at his watch abruptly as if he had anticipated her thought. 'Well, I said I wouldn't take too long and I have to go anyway. I just want to say one more thing. I admired Guy. I was truly fond of him. What happened to him defies belief, and I'd hate to see you and the boys suffer the same fate. Please look after yourselves.'

'That's very sweet,' she said. 'And don't worry, I'm going to take your advice. I have no intention of hanging around here any longer than is absolutely necessary. We'll be fine, you'll see.' As she walked him to the door she wondered if she had convinced him; she certainly hadn't convinced herself.

SEVENTEEN

Something had changed about him – of that much Jane was certain – but she couldn't quite put her finger on what it was. He no longer looked so . . . deflated, that was it, so weighed down by the pressures of the job and his personal inadequacies. He was carrying himself differently, almost as if he might have attended a course on body language and deportment, with the overall effect that he seemed lighter on his feet and less prone to the violent arm-swinging and head-shaking to which she had become so accustomed.

She'd always thought she could read Gerry Grass like a book, but now he was showing her another facet of his character, a side that didn't ring true and which irritated her simply because it didn't fit in with her perception of him. He wasn't meant to behave like this; he was a regular bastard with few saving graces and, as long as he remained so, she would have little difficulty in dealing with him. But this was altogether a new situation, and her immediate reaction was to ascribe his changed mood to the love of a good woman. No sooner had she had this thought than she discounted it: his pattern of life hadn't changed – which, in her opinion, it most certainly would have done were he seeing someone. He wore the same stained taupe suit and polyester tie which Jane classified as instant passion killers. He drank no less, and never had to run off early from an evening session in the pub. And, to her knowledge, he had not been receiving mysterious phone calls which would make him close his door as his cheeks reddened.

But that wasn't quite true, either. There had been that odd call from the woman at Alhambra Property Services, the one she had taken when Grass was out on one of his regular and unexplained absences. Her questions about that had never been resolved, her natural, professionally honed nosiness unsatisfied. There were papers ready to be signed by him; was that some kind of coded message? Who the hell were Alhambra Property Services? It was no good at all, having these mysteries about a boss who had previously been so transparent.

Equally frustrating was the fact that there was no one with whom she could share these observations. Her male colleagues were, by and large, uninterested in each other's personal details; they might work together for weeks at a time on a case, close enough to recognise each other just by their smell, but they rarely shared intimacies other than the usual tales of grief from wives and girlfriends, accompanied by gentle teasing and the ritual masculine banter. Jane was a spectator, never truly part of the circus around her, and she found it impossible to relate to their mannerisms and behaviour. She even doubted if they experienced the same feelings as she did about their work, whether they believed that what they were doing was a valuable and necessary contribution to society. Sometimes she suspected that it was just a job for most of them; they might as easily have been working at the benefits agency or the supermarket for all the fervour they showed. Without doubt they were brave and worked hard, but that was not enough for her. She needed to be driven by zeal, by an unambiguous cause that demanded total loyalty and commitment.

Grass was in his office and she was watching him. Ever since she had illicitly read the Mercer file she had been paying him much more attention, not so much because of what she had seen in the file but more because of what had been left out. Several of her memos and notes were missing: this could be explained away by poor filing, but she didn't like that excuse. Jane preferred to be suspicious; that's what she'd been trained for. Her curiosity, like the proverbial cat, might lead her into trouble: but, even though she had no idea of how to broach the subject with him, her mind wouldn't rest until she was satisfied that the Mercer case had been properly handled, and she needed to find a way of achieving this.

The worst possible thoughts had flashed through her mind and, try as she might, she could not reject them. Grass was a plodder, a guy with no inspiration and no special insight into the criminal mind. He pursued each case energetically, and had a good clear-up record, but he was not a gifted policeman. He liked the obvious, preferred evidence to supposition and theory, and used muscle when brains might have been more appropriate. Anthony Tilt was the perfect suspect for Grass: he was flat broke – a good enough motive – an adviser to both Mercer and his wife, and he had the opportunity. Above all, Jane suspected, Grass had him in the frame because he was a solicitor. If necessary, Jane knew that Grass would happily try and intimidate Tilt until he got a confession out of him if he felt that was the only way to do it. That was his method when all else failed, and it was hard to argue against it.

But the facts of the Mercer case suggested that this was not the line they should be pursuing, and Grass's own dramatic shift of direction hinted that something major had happened to which she had not been a party. He had lost interest in Caroline Mercer and her unexplained fears, and the story of Linda Betts was similarly discarded as peripheral to the investigation. More sinister to Jane was the whole question of the self-storage unit. As she thrashed around for inspiration, she had driven to Battersea to take a look at unit 327A for herself. She had flashed her warrant card and gained access, but she was disappointed to find it completely empty. Grass had told her that he'd thoroughly searched it, but what could he have searched? It didn't add up, and her visit merely confirmed her doubts. Grass was clearly maintaining the line that this was a routine killing, motivated by greed. His own file notes carefully avoided any references to the convoluted trail left by Mercer himself. Why, Jane wondered, were there so many loose ends?

There were two possible answers, and neither tasted good to Jane. She might have completely misread the case, seeing evidence that wasn't there and picking up signals that were nothing more than white noise. She was young and inexperienced, and the case was complicated, perhaps too complex for her to cut through to the essential details. It would damage her confidence to accept this, but she had to entertain the possibility.

The alternative explanation was substantially more unpalatable. Everyone in the office knew that Grass was up for promotion. Whenever this happened there was frantic activity as outstanding crimes were miraculously solved and files were closed. It was human nature and they all played the game, knowing that at some stage they would need the same support. Were they to charge Tilt, it wouldn't be the first time that such action had been initiated on the basis of incomplete evidence; if Grass were determined enough, and sufficiently sure of his own position, he could get Tilt into court, even if he had to bend the facts to support the charges.

The idea sickened her, and she wanted to disprove it. Much as she disliked him, she couldn't bring herself to believe that Grass would do this; beneath the veneer of bravado and bullshit, she liked to hope that there was a core of decency, a set of basic values that would deter him from actual wrongdoing. He had never given her any reason to suspect otherwise, and her professional judgement was that she could trust him: that when the going was tough he would respond as a policeman and stay true to that code, rather than be driven by any distorted personal motivations.

If this were so, what was he up to? It was a question to which she could find no easy solution, and she knew she had to. She was still working on that when a call came through for her.

'Miss Fox? It's Peter Verity. We need to talk.'

Caroline was spurred into action by her conversation with Peter Verity. She had seen too much, flown too close to tragedy, to let herself ignore the futility of what she was trying to achieve. Peter had clarified her thinking with his calm, measured advice. She knew that things couldn't go on as before; the status quo had become unsustainable and she needed to make a clean break.

His revelation about the extent of Guy's dishonesty – twenty-five million dollars' worth of it – could not be absorbed. It was such a fantastic number that Caroline reeled in the face of it.

How could he have been so stupid, to believe that he could get away with it? Guy had been many things, but she was unable to accept that he was so totally amoral that he would attempt such an enormous fraud. Try as she might, however, she could come up with no more plausible explanation. She wasted little time in considering his motives, shaken as she was by the additional terror she now felt. If that was the cause of all this, she must fly: anyone who had lost that amount of money would be extremely anxious to have it returned, whatever methods were used.

In the back of her mind, too, was the thought that she didn't have to pursue the same agenda she'd shared with Guy. Because everything had been so changed by his death, she found the idea that she should carry on as before untenable. She agonised over whether she had a duty to do what Guy would have wanted – but who could tell what that was? How could she know what was best for her and the boys, now that he was no longer there to give direction? She was further confused by what she had subsequently discovered about his life: he had kept too much from her and his murder had served only to draw her into a terrifying maelstrom. She had never considered herself as being driven by Guy, submitting to his will, but he had imposed a natural order which only now did she truly appreciate in its absence.

Without noticing it, Caroline was reaching a stark conclusion. It was her life now, and she had to live it to the best of her own abilities. She alone could reset the compass and follow its new direction without the reassurance of another guiding hand. Although the prospect scared her, she avoided too much speculation on how it would all turn out. She had an overwhelming priority to get herself and the boys to a place of safety and calm where they could start the process of reconstruction.

She began her tasks by calling Jane Fox, leaving a message that she needed to see her urgently. It was important to get this resolved, and there wasn't much time in which to do it. Then she sat down and wrote a letter to Anthony.

Anthony –

You have been kinder to me than I can possibly have deserved, and I will never be able to tell you how grateful I am. I've dragged you into a bad situation that doesn't concern you – and I'm sorry for it.

Will you forgive me if I tell you that I now bitterly regret what I've done, and that I've decided to give up my stupid and stubborn pursuit of whatever it is I thought was so important? I've come to understand that the only thing which matters is the well-being of my boys – and that can best be guaranteed by leaving the past behind and starting afresh.

By the time you get this letter we will have gone. I realise that I'm leaving many things unresolved, but I need to get away and clear my head before I can tackle all of them. Until I know what I can expect from life without Guy, there's nothing more I can do.

Sorry to be so obscure, but that's the best I can do for now. I'll be in touch, I promise.

All love –

Caroline.

Feeling stronger from her deliberate actions, Caroline set about packing clothes for all of them. She was rigorous, taking only what she felt was absolutely necessary. Nothing was irreplaceable; nothing, that was, except her memories, and she had already secured them.

Grass never met them in the same place, or at the same time. It was two o'clock in the morning, and he could still taste the large whisky he'd swallowed down in one when he left his house two hours before. They made him wait – it was part of the deal, he realised – and he was always early, left to sit in his car and chew his lip.

He saw the approaching headlights and stiffened. This was the moment; the interim settlement was due and all he needed to see was the proof. He wasn't nervous in case they had stitched him up because, ironically, they had always behaved honourably. He was more agitated by his own position, which was so severely compromised that he had begun to mistrust his own motivations and actions.

Once he was out of his car the meeting followed the usual routine. Two men got out of their car; one came over to him whilst the other hung back. There was no handshake, but a nod of mutual recognition. The man looked round, as if anyone else would want to be here in the dead of night, then returned his attention to the business in hand. He pulled an envelope from his inside pocket and handed it over. The remittance advice had been produced by a computer on a pre-printed form. It told him all he needed to know; he looked for the beneficiary account number, the amount and the value date of the transaction, finding they were all exactly as he had expected. He couldn't help grinning as he nodded repeatedly in affirmation.

'Cheers, then.' That was it. Before he could move they were gone, the tail-lights of their car glowing like dying coals. He stood there for a long time, clutching the slip and trying to get it all straight in his head. The stupid thing was, there wasn't anyone to tell about it, and that's what he wanted to do more than anything else.

EIGHTEEN

Caroline had posted the letter to Anthony and was walking to the front door when a car pulled into the drive behind her. She braced herself, hardly able to move, let alone turn round and see who it was; the engine was cut and Caroline could hear nothing else, as if all sound had been deleted at this moment of truth.

'Mrs Mercer,' a voice said. 'You asked to see me?' It was Jane Fox. Caroline managed to exhale, then turned round.

'Thank God it's you,' she said with heavy relief.

They went inside and Caroline made tea in the kitchen. Jane remained standing, surveying the muddles on every available surface. 'Going somewhere?' she asked.

Caroline dropped a teaspoon noisily against a saucer, her hands shaking as she worked. 'That's why I wanted to see you. We're leaving, going away for a bit. I can't stay here any more.' She turned to face Jane and her eyes were red and moist. 'I need a break.'

Jane nodded. 'Where will you go?'

'Do I have to tell you that?'

'I suppose not. It would help, but I can't force you.' Caroline cleared a space on the table and set the teacups down. She sat heavily and Jane moved over to sit opposite her. 'What's the problem, Caroline? I can't help you if I don't know what it is you're frightened of.'

'I'm frightened of what I don't know. Guy's been murdered, the *au pair* has been blown up, and you don't know who did these things so they're still out there. Every time the doorbell rings or the phone goes I think the worst. I don't want to let the children out of my sight but they've got to go to school and have their routine, otherwise they'll be as screwed up as I am. This can't go on. I must have some security.'

Jane drank some tea as she considered how to deal with this. 'Running away isn't going to solve anything. It's just going to delay it.'

'What would you do in my situation?'

'I don't know what your situation is. You won't let us in on the secret, will you? I know you're keeping something from us, and if you'd only tell us, tell me, then we could sort this whole mess out a lot quicker. Why won't you trust us?'

Caroline ignored the bait. 'I want you to find my husband's killer,' she said. 'I want you to make us safe. Isn't that all there is to it?'

'But you're putting yourself in more danger by doing this, by holding back information.'

'I am not holding back information,' Caroline said firmly.

'Have it your way. It's nothing to do with me anyway. The case has been taken off my desk. I'm only here as a friend.'

Caroline reacted to this as Jane hoped. 'Why? What's happened?'

'We have a prime suspect, and now there's a special observation team watching him. I'm not involved in that.'

182

'Who is it?'

'Listen. He's just a suspect, and maybe we'll eliminate him from our inquiries. I don't really want to say anything more about it.' Jane tried but failed to sound convincing.

'You don't believe it, do you? Whoever it is, you've got your doubts.'

'Let's just say it seems a bit far-fetched, but what I think doesn't matter. Let's get back to you. If you won't tell me where you're going, who else knows? How can I get a message to you?'

'You can't. But I'll call you. I have to control that part of it, at least.'

'OK. But it's probably better if you call me at home. The number's on the back of my card.' They sat silently for a few moments as they drank their tea. 'Look, I have to ask you this, and I don't want you to take offence,' Jane said. 'What is your relationship with Anthony Tilt?'

In spite of herself, Caroline twitched at the mention of his name and felt herself redden. 'Anthony? Well, he's been helping me out on the legal side of things. He was Guy's solicitor and he's the executor of the will. But . . . why do you ask?'

'Just be careful, OK? He may not be all that he seems,' Jane shrugged apologetically.

'Is he . . . are you trying to tell me that he's your suspect? This is a joke, isn't it? You can't be serious.'

'I'm just saying you need to take care, that's all.'

Caroline stared into her empty cup, bewildered to the point of anger. 'You want me to trust you, and then you tell me not to trust him. For God's sake, what sort of game do you think this is?'

'I don't think it's a game at all. It's deadly serious. That's why I've told you to watch your back. The bad guys don't always wear black hats.'

Caroline calmed down a little. 'Well, it's completely irrelevant anyway. Anthony and I have a business relationship and that's it.' She thought of the cash in his safe, the pass he had made, the interest he was showing in the beneficiaries of the will; internally she shuddered but tried not to show it.

'Good,' Jane said. 'Keep it that way. If you want my advice, I wouldn't tell him where you're going, just to be on the safe side.'

'Tell me one thing – off the record. Do you have any idea of what happened?'

Jane sighed loudly. 'Every time I think I've got close to an answer, I find something in the way, or something that doesn't make sense. I'm seeing someone tonight who might be able to put a different spin on it, although I don't hold out much hope. But officially I'm off the case. There's not much else I can do.'

'Why don't you talk to your boss?'

'That's one of my problems. I shouldn't be saying this, but I've been frozen out. It doesn't add up.'

'So what will you do?'

'Everything I can, although I'm not sure that's going to be enough. But there are so many loose ends that I've got to do something. I know you don't believe this, but I'm on your side, I really am.'

'Yes, I think you are,' Caroline said. 'And I appreciate it.'

When they were at the front door Jane took Caroline's hand. 'Take care of yourself and those boys,' Jane said. 'And call me. I need to hear from you.'

'I'll do that,' Caroline replied. She watched Jane's car as it slipped through the gates, and she wondered who was fooling whom.

Anthony lay on the bed and groaned. He was sick – flu, he said to himself, though he knew much better – and was now shaking violently as he tried to light a cigarette. Pressure: he had avoided it for so long that its reappearance took him by surprise. In his shrinking world of insignificant deals and petty squabbles with Angela he had forgotten how badly pressure affected him. The immediate remedy was alcohol, but it could only delay the symptoms. He was succumbing to the onset of all its effects and he had no way to evade them. He waited for relief, but none came.

This time he had no need to call Deirdre and make his pathetic excuses for another day off. The senior partner of his firm had already intervened, sending a letter by courier that had arrived first thing. The partnership, it said, had been kind and considerate, patient and understanding, but they could no longer cover his workload for him during his increasingly frequent absences. They were proposing that he be put on the firm's long-term disability plan, with the proviso that he seek professional help; they had worked out the details and a personalised schedule of benefits was enclosed. The letter was all written like that, in strange, stilted management jargon which bore no resemblance to the way people spoke to one another. But he got the message: he was no longer considered suitable as a partner, his private problems enough reason to jettison him. The money would ensure he didn't starve and make them look bad, but it was not enough to keep Angela at bay; she'd have him back in court at the drop of a hat, pressing to have his visiting rights withdrawn because he was unable to provide for her and Sophie.

It was an interesting symmetry, the way his career and his life had both collapsed under pressure. He thought about that as he held the letter in a shaking hand, the trembling not so much from illness as from fear. When it subsided, he summoned up the energy to make it from the bed to the kitchen where he hoped to find something both healthy and appetising to eat, preferably already prepared. He looked in the fridge at a ripped carton of milk, two eggs and half a loaf of stale white bread. He shook his head slowly and shuffled back towards the bedroom.

He could not escape from thoughts about Caroline. He recalled the meeting with Linda, and the visit from the police: these were incidents that had conspired to bring him to this state, weakened to an exhaustion that no amount of sleep could allay. Every organ in his body screamed painfully for remission, but he could not rest while his business with Caroline was unfinished. She held a key for him, an exit from all this agony that would expedite his recovery. He needed her, and she must need him; he had tried to make himself useful without intimidating her, insinuating himself into her life with stealth and tact. She must respond, he told himself; it had to happen.

Something had stopped him from telling Caroline about the latest developments: he wanted to retain some information for himself, to be divulged only when he was sure it would be of value. He had so little with which to trade, but what he had he would use to its greatest benefit. She was lonely and so was he, a perfect match if only he could make her see it.

The visit from Grass and his silent colleague had frightened him. It was routine, he said a hundred times, and yet it did not appear that way. There was an undertone of suspicion, an implicit hostility to unsettle him, and it had worked. It now became even more important to have Caroline's trust, to convince her that his motives were honourable: the police would waste no time in undermining that with her.

And Linda Betts: what a surprise she had turned out to be. He had seen immediately what Guy would have seen in her, both victims of the same charms and looks. Caroline wouldn't have known about that, wouldn't have any idea about the potency of Linda's allure; she could deny this whilst ignorant of it, and Anthony reasoned that it was better to keep this from her, at least until she was strong enough to bear it.

The phone rang and he jumped, so rare had the noise become. He staggered to it and caught it on the eighth ring. 'Hello,' he said weakly.

'Mr Tilt? It's Linda – Linda Betts.' God, was she telepathic too?

'Oh. Hallo there.'

'Sorry to bother you at home,' she said gently. 'Your secretary said you were a bit under the weather, so I'm calling to see how you are.'

'That's very kind,' he said, bemused. 'I think I'm coming down with the flu.'

'I feel terrible disturbing you. I'll be as quick as I can and then you can get back to bed. Have you got anywhere with the will?'

'Sadly not, but I'll be working on it again as soon as I'm recovered.'

'I quite understand. I'll give you a few days and then call you – would that be all right?'

'No problem.'

'Well, get better soon. Thanks a lot.' She hung up and he stood there for a long time with the receiver still in his hand. Something wasn't right, but he couldn't tell what it was.

NINETEEN

'I don't trust your boss. In fact, I don't trust anybody a great deal, but you're all I have. I hope you won't let me down.' Peter Verity was sitting in the passenger seat of Jane's car; as arranged, she had parked in a lay-by near the M25 at nine o'clock in the evening and, ten minutes later, he had arrived from nowhere. He was calm, seemingly forcing himself to stay settled whilst he executed this commission. Clutching a shopping bag to his stomach, he twisted round in his seat to face her, to study her reactions in the light of passing cars.

'You've got my full attention,' she replied, not wishing to deter him by letting on that she had little control of the situation.

'Do you know what's going on – I mean, do you know the real story?'

'About Guy Mercer? I doubt it. Everything about the case smells bad. That's why I'm here.'

'Sometimes I think I must be paranoid,' Peter said. 'I'm seeing shadows which don't exist. This whole thing must have made me a little crazy, I expect. But now I'm giving you the problem, and you can sort it out. You will do that, won't you?'

'If I can. It depends on what you tell me.'

'It's really a very simple story. It's about greed. Guy Mercer

was a greedy man. He was a good man, but greed got the better
of him. He watched too much money travelling under his nose,
and decided to take some of it. It was a risk he thought he
understood. In the light of all that's happened, I'd say that was
a bad judgement, wouldn't you?'

'I don't know. You tell me.'

'Yes. It's all in the details, like the devil. But tell me first,
why haven't your people shown any interest in AMS? What's
holding you back?'

'I don't know what you mean. My boss has been to the AMS
office, and so have I. There's nothing there, is there?'

'There is if you know where to look. And your man Grass –
well, he hasn't exactly tried very hard. In fact, I'd say precisely
the opposite. You should think about that.'

Jane deliberately ignored this remark; what she thought about
Grass and his behaviour was not yet for public consumption.
'Go on.'

'The shareholders of AMS are an unsavoury bunch. I don't
know precisely where their money comes from, but it's tainted,
of that I have no doubt. They financed Guy on very favourable
terms when he started up. They let him trade with their money,
but exerted minimal influence and control. Why would they
want to do that – unless there was something which they didn't
want to draw attention to? AMS was a perfect vehicle for them,
and Guy was the driver. He knew what was going on – not at
first, maybe, but Guy wasn't stupid. He worked it out, and that's
why he decided to rip them off. He knew they'd have a hard
time getting it back because they certainly weren't prepared to
go to the police and report him.'

'Rip them off? How did he do that?'

'There's a deal. It's one transaction among the hundreds that are done every month. It's there, but it's well disguised. It's for twenty-five million dollars. It was very simple. They gave the money to Guy to invest in a reverse repo – they lend the money, they get collateral as security, they earn a nice bit of interest and AMS takes some of that as commission. He'd done reverses for them before, and this was no different, except the amount was larger. He'd played around with other deals for them, adjusting his commission so that he could skim some money and see what happened. If they raised it, he could always say it was a systems error and he'd correct it. But they never complained – they seemed perfectly happy with what he was doing. So he knew they weren't paying enough attention. They trusted him.'

'I'm still not with you.'

Peter patted the shopping bag. 'It's all in here. I've made notes to help you. Guy created a dummy transaction on the system. Effectively, he pretended to do the trade and lend the twenty-five million dollars, but in reality that cash went straight to him. The deal was never done. He sent the shareholders a confirmation of the trade which looked entirely plausible, and he passed bogus entries across the AMS books. Bingo! He's twenty-five million dollars to the good, and no one even knows about it. The beauty of the whole thing is its simplicity. When I discovered it, even I had to admit I was impressed.'

'So what went wrong?'

'That's what you've got to work out. It's obvious that someone found out about it and got to him before he had a chance to do anything. I'd put my money on the shareholders. Perhaps they suspected something all along. There's one guy in particular –

a very unpleasant gentleman called Christian Lemmerich. He's
been looking after AMS since Guy died, and he's the man who
fired me. You might want to talk to him.'

Jane was silent as she took all this in. It was beginning to
come together in her head, but she needed to have everything
completely straight before another confrontation with Grass.
'Is that all there is?'

'No. There's one more thing you should know. I was in charge
of controls at AMS. I had to make sure that all our procedures
followed City regulations. One of the most basic controls is to
ensure that no one person can initiate, approve and execute a
transaction. There has to be separation of duties to minimise
the risk of fraud. If a trader strikes a deal, someone else has to
settle it. There are different reporting lines and managers, all
sorts of checks and balances on the computer to make sure that
happens. There is absolutely no way Guy could have done this
alone. Someone else was in on it with him – someone within
AMS.' Peter waited for a reaction.

'Do you know who?'

'There's only one person who could have done it. Linda
Betts.'

'Linda,' Jane said in a whisper.

He let her think about that; then he handed her the shopping
bag. 'I haven't told anyone else about this. It's yours and yours
alone. You've got everything you need in there,' he said. 'Just
promise me you'll do something with it.'

'I will, Peter.'

'You should know that you'll never see or hear from me
again. I'm giving you this in the strictest confidence. This is
dynamite. Handle it carefully or it could blow up in your face. I

192

have no plans to be anywhere close when it explodes.'

'But what if—'

He cut her off. 'No. I'm out of this now. I'm trusting you. Don't let me down.' He was out of the car and gone in a single movement, leaving Jane to wrestle with the problem.

Caroline was pleasantly surprised by how well the journey went. As planned, the boys slept for most of it, curled up in unnatural positions with pillows jammed against the car doors. The car was hired, provided by the insurance company whilst they sorted out her claim for the burnt-out Volvo. She had needed to battle with them over this, as the Volvo was registered as an AMS company car, but they relented after she came close to tears on the phone.

She got there at five-thirty in the morning. The sun was already starting to lighten the sky and her mood lifted with it. This was a part of the country she had never visited, though she and Guy had often promised themselves a holiday here, and she felt a childish excitement as she pulled the car through narrow lanes towards their destination. Laurel Cottage was set back from the road which bisected the tiny village of Holme-next-the-Sea. In the early light she could see the flint elevation of the house, a detached building with a long back garden which ran down to a meadow, beyond which was the sea.

The car tyres crunched on the loose gravel chippings of the drive and, once she had switched off the engine, Caroline sat there and waited. Inside the car she felt safe and warm; she had no desire to get out and get started, to kick off their new routine, unpack the bags and the shopping, feed the boys and straighten out their little lives. She liked the comfort of the car and the peace inside it as the children continued to slumber. Reluctantly she opened the door and caught her first full breath of the Norfolk sea air, crisp and clean and refreshing, stinging her eyes with its salty tang. She walked to the front door and put her hand into the letter box, pulling out the string from inside to which the key was attached. She opened the door and waited, ready to be disappointed but still hoping it might be as the brochure had described it. After all, she told herself, she was lucky to get anything at all at such short notice, so she shouldn't expect too much.

It was clean and functional, and that was all she truly wanted. The kitchen was large, if a bit old-fashioned, and the sitting room had a big television and three sofas covered in a ghastly maroon material. There was a separate dining room, for which she would have no need, and upstairs there were three good-sized bedrooms and a bathroom with a brown suite. All the carpets were worn but recently vacuumed. She came back downstairs and went to the car, unlocking the boot and hauling two large tote bags to the entrance hall. Deciding to leave the boys as they were, she spent half an hour ferrying bags and boxes into the house and getting her bearings. She put the kettle on and made a large mug of strong coffee, wandering out of the French windows to the garden. The lawn was immaculate, surrounded by borders of shrubs, and a stand of tall fir trees at the far end effectively screened the garden from the meadow. Above all, however, she noticed the tranquillity: all she could hear was birdsong.

By nine o'clock Hugh and George were up and doing, wolfing down toast, boiled eggs, cereal and orange juice before bursting into the garden with a football and exploring hidden corners of the house. With all this activity Caroline was almost able to forget why they were here and discard the legacy of Guy's death, but the memory kept coming back to chill her blood. They were on the run, but she didn't know from what; she felt guilt, but couldn't say about what; and she was frightened, but couldn't be sure by what. So many doubts and fears threatened her, and she was incapable of building any defence against them.

She had put the briefcase of money in her bedroom, and now she went up there to shower and change. The case lay on the bed, inert but still exuding that fearsome power which had so concerned her when she had first brought it back from the storage facility. She undressed and padded to the bathroom, taking a cool, slow shower, carefully soaping and rinsing herself until she felt completely clean. Once out and dried, she walked back still naked to the bedroom and caught a glimpse of herself in the full-length mirror on the wall. She was thinner, much thinner than she imagined herself to be: instead of a roll of fat around her midriff there was just loose skin, and her breasts seemed to have shrunk, even to be – God, please, she thought – a little tighter and firmer. Her thighs and buttocks also looked slimmer, and she turned round in small circles to appreciate the effect. She knew that it was worry rather than control which had caused this change, but that didn't diminish her pleasure.

She turned away from the mirror and looked at the case. For the first time it no longer exerted such a gut-wrenching potency, and she strolled over to the bed and took it by the handle, pulling it towards her as she sat down. She clicked open the catches and slowly raised the lid. The cash was still there, carefully batched in bundles, and she took one out, flicking the notes with her thumb so that they made a little breeze against her face. They smelt no different from honest money, giving off the same intoxicating, seductive aroma. She put the bundle back neatly in the case and ran her fingers across the surface of the notes. Nothing happened; she didn't feel guilty, or dirty, and she began to believe that she might be able to control this monster, that her power was greater and her will stronger. She stared into the case as if trying to intimidate what lay within. Satisfied, she gently closed the lid and snapped the catches back into place. When she got up from the bed she caught sight of herself in the mirror again, and saw that her face, for the first time in many weeks, looked flushed and healthy; she also saw that she was wearing a small but satisfied smile.

It couldn't have been easier, and it couldn't have been more convenient. Rain fell heavily as he walked up Castelnau, and he welcomed it. There were few people on the pavement in this weather and he knew it would be simple to slip undetected into the front of the house. His coat collar was turned up around his jaw and a large hat concealed the rest of his face.

Once in the drive, where no car was parked, and standing opposite the house, Christian Lemmerich picked up a stone and threw it hard against a downstairs window. The crash of glass was muffled by the rain and wind; he waited, counting to thirty before doing the same to another pane. There was no response: no alarm, no lights going on, nothing. He nodded to himself, then moved swiftly to the front door. The locks were straightforward and he was soon inside.

He had, he reckoned, about thirty seconds before the alarm would go off. He watched the flashing red motion sensor in the hall as he reached the control panel, pulling off one glove before punching in the four-digit code. It was a gamble, but a calculated one: the vast majority of London householders used the last four digits of their phone number as the burglar-alarm security code. He held his breath and counted again, this time reaching ninety before he was satisfied it had worked. He checked the console, and a small green light appeared showing that the alarm had been reset to standby – he was free and clear.

He pulled out his torch from his coat pocket and went into the kitchen. It was tidy, with no sign of any recent activity. He pulled open a few drawers without much interest; then, having withdrawn a carving knife from a block on the work surface, moved to the front sitting room where the curtains were drawn. There was nothing to be searched in here, but he pulled cushions off sofas and chairs and took down some antique prints in the vague hope that there might be a safe behind one. He realised that his venture would, in all probability, turn out to be fruitless, but he couldn't prevent himself from making sure: that was his nature.

When he went upstairs he briefly looked in each room before arriving at the master bedroom. He pulled the covers off the bed and dragged the mattress on to the floor, slitting it open with the knife. He did the same to the duvet and pillows before opening all the cupboards and tossing the clothes into a pile behind him. He tapped on the back of the cupboards to see if there was any space behind them, but without success. He tipped the contents of the bedside table drawers on to the bed and scrabbled through them, now more desperate to find something. Sighing with frustration he eventually gave up and walked back down to the kitchen.

He flashed his torch round the room once more and its beam

fell on a cork noticeboard by the telephone. He went over to it and looked at all the papers and cards pinned to it, pulling them off and throwing them on the floor. He was just about to scrumple up one piece of paper without really reading it when he understood its significance:

CONFIRMATION

Thank you for booking your holiday with Norfolk Coastal.
Here are the details of your accommodation:

Dates: Saturday 5 July – Saturday 19 July inclusive
Laurel Cottage
High Street
Holme-next-the-Sea
Norfolk
Directions: From Fakenham take the B1355 to Burnham Market, turning west on to the A149 signposted to Hunstanton. Drive through Holme-next-the-Sea until you reach the end of the speed limit and turn immediately right opposite the village signpost. Laurel Cottage is at the end of this road at the junction with the High Street.

He read and reread the note, hardly able to believe his luck. He neatly folded the letter and put it in his pocket. He was so pleased with himself that he decided not to start the fire he had planned. There was no point now; he had what he needed.

TWENTY

Jane heard it first in the canteen; in fact, she was asked to verify the rumour by one of the two men who were discussing it. She knew him quite well, Detective Sergeant Tim Canbury, a reasonably pleasant guy who had never given her any aggravation – knew him well enough to sit at his table when she'd bought her coffee and toast. Canbury was with someone she didn't know at all, and they were deep in conversation; she merely nodded at them and smiled as she sat down.

Canbury looked at her and then at his mate. 'Hallo, Jane,' he said. 'How's it going?'

'I think the technical expression is same old shit,' she said.

'Yeah, that's one thing you can't polish,' he replied, obviously pleased to be able to give such an eloquent riposte. His friend snorted in appreciation. 'We were just saying, there's a lot of changes going on, isn't there? I hear your boss is on his way.' He darted another quick look at his still unidentified friend, then slurped his tea.

Jane didn't know how to respond: she didn't have the faintest idea what he was talking about, but didn't like to say as much. 'Is that the latest rumour? It's a wonder we have time to do any detecting with all the gossip in this place.'

Canbury was not deterred by her evasion. 'Is it true, then? Is Grass going?'

She chewed on a slice of toast to give herself more time to formulate a reply. Jane knew, like everyone else, that Gerry Grass was up for promotion, but that didn't mean he was leaving. She'd heard nothing about a move or a transfer, and needed to discover exactly what was being sent up and down the grapevine. 'Who told you?' she asked.

'It's common knowledge, Jane,' he replied, sensing her confusion. 'Grass is taking early retirement. From what I've heard he just walked into his first interview and told them there and then that he didn't want to be considered and that he was jacking it all in.' Canbury waited, looking back and forth between Jane and his friend, clearly relishing this small moment of triumph when he had the premium on information.

'Maybe,' she said, trying to look and sound inscrutable.

'So you haven't heard anything.'

'Tim, let me tell you something for free. I've heard so many things about my illustrious boss that have turned out to be untrue that I no longer give the rumours any credence. He is a force within the force, a law unto himself. Does he strike you as the type who'd take early retirement? He has no life outside work, and no interests apart from villains and boozing with his mates. He put concrete over the garden, so he's not about to go home and tend the roses all day. That may make him sound like a very sad person, but it's the truth. Believe me, Grass would die of boredom within a month if he was pensioned off. So whatever you've heard, I'd treat it with a major pinch of salt. It doesn't sound very likely to me.' She returned to her toast to demonstrate that she was no longer either interested or concerned by what she'd been told.

'So you won't want to hear the other rumour, then?' Jane tried not to flinch as she finished her toast and wiped her fingers with a paper napkin. Canbury persisted.

'About his lady friend.'

She stared at him over the top of her coffee, sipped a little, then smiled. 'Go on, I'm enjoying this. It beats working any day.'

'Word is, Grass is madly in love with some rich widow and is running off with her. That's what's behind all of this.'

'Now I've heard everything. That is so much bullshit it's not even worth discussing. Grass is about as attractive as a dose of herpes. He smells bad, his personal habits defy description and he's a chauvinist pig. Who in their right mind would want to spend the rest of their life with him?'

'Perhaps she likes a bit of rough. Some women go for that, you know.'

'In your dreams, Tim. No, sorry, but I don't buy that one either.'

'Well, maybe not, but I'm only telling you what I've heard.'

'And I'm grateful for it.' She looked at her watch. 'Must be going. Lovely talking to you.' She got up and left the canteen, taking the stairs up to her office and stopping in the Ladies on the way. She washed her hands and studied her reflection in the grimy mirror, unable to discount what Canbury had said. She didn't understand the new Gerry Grass, she admitted, but it all seemed too fanciful for her to believe.

Once again, the spectre of something much more sinister came back to nag at her: all the little signals – the Mercer file and its missing contents, the chat she'd had with Alan Apostle, the focus on Anthony Tilt, Caroline's naked terror, the change in Grass's attitude – prompted darker conclusions, much as she would have liked to dismiss them. None of these could be viewed as hard evidence, yet still she found herself adding them up and reaching a figure that exceeded the sum of the parts.

That equation had been further complicated by her meeting the previous night with Peter Verity. After he had gone she had raced home with the papers, studying every word and figure until she was sure she understood. She drew flow charts on a pad and scrumpled them up when they didn't make sense, starting again and adding in all the protagonists to try and arrive at a reasoned, and reasonable, conclusion.

Now, in the relative calm of the Ladies' room, she dried her hands slowly and ran her tongue around the inside of her mouth. She wanted to confront Grass head on, present him with her fears and conclusions and have them strongly rebutted; she wanted to get things sorted, and go back to a monochrome life where right and wrong were where you expected them to be. But . . . there were too many ifs, buts and maybes, and she hated them all. She might achieve nothing but further confusion, not to mention the damage she could inflict on herself, were she to open both barrels on Grass and then discover that she had missed the target. Better, she concluded, to leave well alone and just get on with her own affairs.

All day, as she tried to fulfil this objective, what came back to her most frequently was one little phrase, one aphorism which she'd never before had the need to entertain: Beware the enemy within.

Peter Verity was ready to leave, but he had one last task – the morning walk of his dog, Elfie. It was a ritual that nothing – not even the loss of his job and his dignity – would change. Elfie knew the time and would come and bother him if he was late. He would put her on the back seat of the car and they would drive together to Wimbledon Common, up past the clubhouse of the golf course and into a small car park at the end of the road. She would get increasingly excited as they approached and would burst out of the car as he opened the door for her, streaking off and then tearing back to make sure he was coming.

He would talk to her as they walked and she would look up at him with those sad Labrador eyes as if she understood everything. He would throw sticks which she retrieved and he would tell her when he saw squirrels that she could chase. He would shout at her when she got close to the pond but she would pay no attention and would plunge into the water with a spectacular bellyflop, coming back to dry land and shaking herself close to him.

Often he met no one on these walks. Needing the peace and a break from human contact, he had devised a circuit that was not popular with other walkers and, if he did pass anyone, he would lower his eyes and give them a wide berth. He was happiest in the company of Elfie, her devotion to him unequivocal.

On this last walk she disappeared, as usual, into a small wood which ran beside one of the fairways of the golf course. It was a tough hole, as the tee and the green were on opposite sides of a wide and deep gully with a muddy stream cutting across the bottom of it. He often stumbled over lost golf balls here, but he left them in their final resting place rather than

203

pick them up and sell them back to the players, as others did.

He crossed the gully and reached the woods on the other side, Elfie still sniffing and tracking out of sight behind him. He didn't need to worry about her: she could do this walk blindfold. He was deep into the woods before he turned round to see if she was catching him up, and he must have had time to catch a brief glimpse of his attacker before he was brought to his knees by the blow to his head which knocked all the sense out of him. He would not have seen anything else, would probably not have felt the knife delve under his ribcage and pierce his heart in a single swift motion, would not have tasted the blood as it flowed from his mouth. He was beyond revival when Elfie arrived and licked at his battered face, and her whining fell on his deaf, dead ears.

Linda sucked on her cigarette and let the smoke trail out from her nostrils. The flat she had rented – at the top of a house in Camberwell – was grubby and functional, but she didn't care: she was so angry, so consumed by her feeling of betrayal, that she barely thought about more temporal issues like health and hygiene. Dressed only in her underwear, she sat by the open window and looked out towards the railway line that ran behind the house – eight trains an hour trundled past in a rattling, clattering cacophony – lost to her plans for revenge but unable to identify the guilty parties.

Linda planned to visit Caroline Mercer. She had no clear idea of what such action would achieve, but she knew that it had to be done: she would present herself, catching the woman off guard and maybe, just maybe, getting the result she craved. In the absence of Guy the money would have to compensate as second prize; she was even prepared to share it, if that was what it took, but she was determined not to come away empty-handed. Linda was not accustomed to losing, gracefully or otherwise, and she had the weapons to win the battle.

Though she struggled to accept it and deal with it, Linda did know that she needed a man. She had known that from an early age, had already made the mistake of trying to bend the reality to fit her dream. But the experience had not sufficiently deterred her from the search for that elusive paradigm of partnership, where her man would look after her and honour her, and she in turn would deliver in full her love and attention to him. It was a silly girlish fantasy, more appropriate to the pages of romantic novels than the harsh life she had endured, but it still existed within her as a flickering pilot light. She resented the emptiness she felt, hating her inability to do more than survive by herself. Every time she met a man she liked she was possessed by involuntary and contradictory forces: on the one hand she wanted him badly whilst, on the other, she tried to push him away to protect her fragile independence. This conundrum invariably led to disaster and misery – until, that is, she met Guy.

So close but, ultimately, so far away: like gold dust running between her fingers, Linda had been unable to control and retain what she had acquired with Guy. She was blameless, and it had still gone wrong for her. That was what needled her most, that life was just so unfair. Everywhere she looked she could see others getting the breaks she so obviously deserved, losers who became winners without lifting a finger. Take Caroline Mercer: there she was, sitting on a pile of cash so high it would give her vertigo, and all she'd had to do to get it was lounge about in her interior-designer house in Castelnau and supervise the nanny. I can change that, Linda thought: that money is mine, I worked for it and I won't let some dried-up old witch take it away from under my nose.

As the bile rose within her, Linda jumped out of her chair and went over to an open suitcase on the floor. She pulled clothes out and evaluated their suitability, discarding those which looked too dull or dowdy and setting more promising items to one side. She remembered a day – was it the first day when she knew for sure? – when Guy came into the office and looked at her strangely, more engaged and engaging than was necessary for mere politeness, and had told her quietly that she looked like a million dollars. She had never forgotten what she was wearing that day. She had on a perfectly cut plain pink dress, with short sleeves and a round neck, the colour offsetting the light tan from her summer holiday. It was a good dress, neat enough for work but not interfering with the message that she was a woman in great shape. She searched for it now, but to no avail.

Disappointed, she settled for a powder-blue dress which hugged her in all the right places. She washed, made herself up and eased on new tights. Once she had wriggled into the dress, she brushed and re-brushed her hair until she was satisfied with her appearance. She put on a pair of black court shoes and poured herself a neat Bacardi, swigging it quickly and waiting for the buzz. After a liberal spray of breath freshener she had one last check in the mirror and then left the room, clothes still scattered across the floor.

She walked out of the gloomy house into brilliant sunshine, so dazzling that she had to stop to delve into her bag and pull out her sunglasses. As she was putting them on she felt a hand grasp her upper arm tightly from behind. She froze.

'Miss Betts,' a man said, but not with the voice she had half-expected. She knew it vaguely, but couldn't put a name or face to it. 'You don't know how pleased I am to see you.' She jerked her arm free and turned round to look at him. His face was blank, as if all emotion had been leached out of it. 'You remember me, don't you?'

She recovered quickly from the shock. 'No I don't, and I'm in a hurry.'

'That is a pity.'

'Can this wait? I really don't have time just now.'

He ignored her request and continued to stare fixedly at her. 'You see, I thought you and I could go on a little trip together. Wouldn't that be fun?'

'What are you talking about?'

'We can talk about old times – you know, at AMS?'

Then it dawned on her. 'Oh, I do know you. Chris Lemmerich, right?'

'I'm so glad you remember. Come on, let's take a drive in my car.' Before she had a chance to move away he had grabbed her arm again and her pushed her roughly towards a smart green Mercedes with black windows parked at the kerb. With his free hand he opened the rear door and bundled her in behind the front passenger seat; as he held her down he produced a set of handcuffs from his jacket pocket and snapped one manacle round her wrist, swiftly attaching the other end to the grab handle on the ceiling of the car. 'I hope you won't be too uncomfortable,' he said with a grim smile.

As Linda let rip with a torrent of abuse, Lemmerich went round to the driver's door and got in. He started the engine and drove off. Realising that she was helpless, Linda concentrated on the back of his head and went silent, desperately rehearsing her story.

'So what do you want?' she asked.

'You and I have a lot to catch up on,' he replied. 'Fortunately, we have plenty of time to do so.'

'Where are we going?'

'To the seaside.'

TWENTY-ONE

Somewhere in the near distance Caroline could hear a peacock calling. There was no other noise as she stood in the garden, barefoot and still in her dressing gown. Bathed in the soothing silence, she sipped her coffee and closed her eyes, using the breathing pattern she had learnt from antenatal classes. Nothing had felt as good as this for a long time, and she didn't want to break the spell. She knew the boys would soon wake and clamour for her attention, and she was ready for that, but this short time alone was precious to her and she savoured it. She smiled as she thought about Guy, how much he would have hated it here for exactly the reason she liked it. Guy needed action and noise: he would have made friends with the locals in the pub and learnt all their secrets within a day of arriving. That was his way, completely natural and unforced.

Caroline had slept for eight hours uninterrupted, the first time she'd had an unbroken night since Guy's death. She had woken at seven and drawn back the curtains to gaze out at the lush green vista, drinking in the peace. Her body was refreshed and, more importantly, her mind was cleared of doubt and anxiety. At last she had attained some sense of order and was ready to face up to whatever lay ahead; in a wilful act of determination she had taken eight fifty-pound notes from the case and tucked them into her purse, no longer intimidated by their provenance. They were part of Guy's legacy, and she was fully entitled to them – why else would he have left them for her?

She had reassessed the value of what Peter Verity had told her. If he wanted to insure his own health, he was most likely to set the police on the trail of the AMS shareholders. According to him, they were laundering money through the business: with that knowledge, she had become slightly bolder about her own position. The cash she already held was not hers, but they'd find that difficult to prove and its owners might be very unwilling to raise it as an issue. She felt she might be inching towards greater safety, just as long as Peter did what he'd said he would: *If anything, what I'm going to do will protect you and the boys.*

Two weeks here would sufficiently repair her so that she could begin to plan and set them all on a new course. She already had some notion of moving permanently to Minster Lovell, an option that she and Guy had discussed so often it became a standing joke: whenever they came back from a break there they would pull out all the school prospectuses and indulge in harmless but pointless fantasies. Caroline knew he would never do it, that the magnetic force of London exerted far too strong a pull on him for the idea to become anything more than idle chat over a bottle of wine. Guy was too big for country living, his metabolism too demanding for the simple pleasures of a bucolic existence; he needed stimuli that couldn't be found in the middle of fallow pastures and rolling hills.

When they went down for a weekend he would behave impeccably for about thirty-six hours. He would go on adventures in the woods with the boys and take them all to the pub on Saturday evening, and Caroline could just about believe that he might eventually get used to the different beat of life. On Sunday morning he would get up early and put on his approximation of the country gentleman's outfit – check shirt, green woollen trousers, brown brogues – and sit in the garden to read the newspapers. But, by lunchtime, he was already starting to twitch and he liked to pack the car as soon as pudding was finished. He would herd up the boys and deter them from going too far from the house in the early afternoon, and by three-thirty he was ready to go. Only once had they stayed at the house on Sunday night, and she vowed never to repeat the experiment: he was surly all evening and was up at four-thirty on Monday morning, crashing about downstairs so that they wouldn't oversleep. The drive back seemed to resemble nothing more to her than the last qualifying session for a Grand Prix, and their hands all ached after the trip, so strongly had they gripped their seats.

As she stood in the garden and waited for the warning sounds of a rampant George with a grumbling belly, Caroline was prepared for what she now considered to be the first day of the rest of her life. She had been living in a vacuum since Guy's death, anaesthetised by the distorted reality it had caused; it was as if she had finally woken up from a tortured sleep and was beginning to dispel the lingering memories of bad nightmares. She curled her toes into the damp grass, searching for greater purchase on *terra firma*. Oh Guy, she thought, if only you could see us now: would you be proud of what I've done?

* * *

211

'All right, all right, shut up and listen, will you?' Thirty people went silent as Grass called them to order. He grinned broadly and took his time preparing himself, making eye contact with each of them as he looked around the room. Satisfied that he had their undivided attention, he drew a deep breath. 'You really are a bunch of bastards, aren't you? You spend all day spreading rumours and all night pissing it up.' There was laughter and a few cries of 'Hear, hear!' Jane sat towards the back of the room, perched on the edge of her desk, as keen as anyone to hear what Grass had to say.

'Look, I'm not going to give a big speech or anything,' he continued. 'But now it's official, I thought you'd better know.' He paused and snorted. 'I've decided that it's time to get out while I've still got a bit of life in me.' There was a shout of 'Too late!' from the back, and heads turned as the laughter erupted again. 'Yeah, thanks for that,' Grass responded. 'Anyway, I've put in for early retirement, and it's been accepted. So you can all breathe a huge sigh of relief, knowing that I'm not going to be around much longer to make your lives hell.'

'When's the piss-up, Gerry?' some wag called out.

'I was just about to get on to that. As of midday, I shall be in residence at The Goat in Boots. All are welcome – except of course the Chief Super – and the drinks are on me. That's all I've got to say. No, hang on, there was something else.' They went quiet again and waited. 'You're a good bunch of coppers – the best, if you want my opinion – and I'll miss you all like buggery. There we are, I've said it. Now, get your drinking boots on and let's get hammered.'

There was a huge cheer and a round of applause, then the meeting broke up as smaller groups convened, eagerly discussing

212

what Grass had told them. Jane remained on the desk, her hands folded across her lap as she evaluated the ramifications of his news. Grass walked past her on his way out of the room and shot her a big wink. 'Well done, guv,' she said half-heartedly, but he probably didn't hear her in his hurry to get to the pub.

Once the room had calmed down Jane moved round the desk and sat down. She had come in very early that morning and had done some further, unofficial work on the Mercer case. There was one discovery in particular that she wanted to follow up, something they seemed to have overlooked in their rush to get a result. She wanted to talk to Linda about it – but Linda, hardly surprisingly, had disappeared, so she had no alternative but to take the direct route and go to the source. That required a little more research and some fieldwork: with Grass engaged in a major drinking session she would have more than enough time to do this before calling into The Goat in Boots later in the afternoon.

Jane had never behaved like this before. She had never stepped out of the box of routine and procedure, always careful to play by the rules and get her results honestly and openly. She was nervous but determined. This had to be done, and she justified her actions with her belief that an innocent man might be accused of a murder he would never have committed. If for no other reason, she had to help Anthony Tilt – whatever else came out of her inquiries would just have to be dealt with. Grass, she was sure, was running away from something, something that might well have a connection with Guy Mercer's death.

She drove to Norbiton, a small built-up area to the north of Kingston, and parked the car in a side road near the railway station. On one side of the road there were several shabby office buildings; on the other was a terrace of small Victorian houses – two-up, two-down and a pocket handkerchief for a garden – and her focus rested on Number 3. All the curtains were drawn and in the front was a large untended elder tree, hanging sadly over the crumbling wall. It was hot in the car and she didn't want to sit and stew; she got out, adjusted her skirt and ran her fingers through her hair. Steeling herself, she crossed the road and went up the short path to the front door of the house. She pushed the buzzer and waited, looking up to see if anyone was watching her from the first floor.

After thirty seconds she rang again and she could hear activity behind the door. Chains rattled and eventually the door opened. The man standing in front of her was dishevelled and unshaven, suggesting he had just got out of bed. His face was covered in scratches. He looked more resigned than surprised to see her, and he held one arm back to invite her in. 'I wondered how long it would take you,' he said as they went back to the sitting room.

If it hadn't hurt so much, Anthony might have laughed. This was the first time in living memory that he had fallen over while stone-cold sober, an irony that didn't escape him. Recovery was proving elusive. Anthony was so weak that he found every movement an enormous effort: he was shocked by how feeble he had become, how quickly the despair had wasted his muscles. After too many years of neglect and abuse, his body had finally rebelled and he was suffering from a physical breakdown against which he had no defence. He lay on the floor, Caroline's letter still in his hand, while his body convulsed.

So she had found him out: she had seen through his game

and was getting away before he had a chance to put his side of the story. It was all too familiar, this circle of hope and disappointment. He had thought, briefly, that this time it would work, that he could steer the outcome his way and manage the consequences of his actions. Once again he had been proved wrong; once again, he had reckoned without the Fates, which were always against him. He was doomed to fail before he had even begun.

At night he would lie in bed, eyes wide open in the dark, and worry about his future. After he had split up with Angie his own future became very unimportant, to him at least, and he faced each day with the sole intention of getting through it and making it to bed in one piece. The furthest milestone in his life was always pay day; nothing, save for the brief occasions he spent with Sophie, mattered very much. This immediacy, a sort of bastard existentialism, was all that saw him through; had he stopped to consider what lay ahead he might well have collapsed completely.

Now, with hard evidence of how pathetic he was, he appreciated the need to think ahead, even though he was incapable of doing it rationally. The partners, his colleagues, had chopped him out like a branch infected with fire blight. He would have to sell his grotty little flat and move to Bury St Edmunds to join a local practice concerned with births, deaths and marriages. He would never see Sophie again and, eventually, she wouldn't care. Angie would poison her mind if she hadn't already done so.

Without work, without Sophie, what was left? He had put his faith in a result with Caroline, a stupid, irrational dream that had never been encouraged by her and which only existed when he'd had too much to drink. What had happened, he asked himself, to the bright young man with his whole life ahead of him and the opportunities spread before him like a glorious feast? How had he come to this, that he now built his dreams on foundations of quicksand?

Even as he shivered on the floor, his senses shot, Anthony knew that there was a choice. He could lie there and die – who the hell would care, one way or another? – or he could pull himself out of this selfish torpor and start to rebuild. He needed to roll the dice one last time, to remember what had been his before and might be again, if he could only drag himself back from the brink. He had been sharp, intelligent, witty; there had been a time, so far back it was almost antediluvian, when he had mattered, when he made a difference, when he was a contender. Could he not, even now, rescue some of that from the wreckage of his current existence? He might be a sprawling mess on his own carpet, but he could still do it. As he rearranged his limbs he made the decision: it was this or nothing.

'I need to pee. Either you stop or I ruin your lovely upholstery.' Linda's arm had gone completely dead, past the point of pain, and she felt faint and very nauseous.

Lemmerich quickly looked round at her and then turned his head back to concentrate on the road. 'We'll stop at the next petrol station,' he said.

'Your risk.'

Fortunately for both of them, a garage soon appeared and Lemmerich pulled in. He parked the car away from the pumps and the shop, and climbed into the back next to Linda. He was, she noticed, holding a black gun in his hand, resting it on his thigh as he pointed it at her. 'No tricks,' he said as he leant across and unchained her hand. Her arm collapsed on to her lap and she tried to shake some life back into it.

'You coming with me?'

'What do you think?'

They got out of the Mercedes and walked together to the lavatories, Christian tucked in so close that he was touching her back. When they got to the door of the Ladies, he grabbed her wrist and pulled her in with him. He shoved her towards a cubicle and made no effort to move away as she closed the door and locked it. She took her time, knowing how infuriating it would be and hoping that someone else might come in and see him standing there. But she was unlucky. Having spent a good five minutes on her own, she pulled up her knickers and reluctantly opened the door.

'You'll never get away with this, you know that?' she said as she washed her hands.

'You and I need to talk. There's no more time for fooling around.' He grasped her wrist again and marched her out to the forecourt.

'Can I have a drink?' she asked.

'No. Get in the car.' He bundled her in and reattached her wrist to the grab handle. He sat jammed against the opposite door, twisted so that he could face her. 'You've wasted a lot of my time, and that makes me very angry. You have information that I need, and you're going to give it to me. Do you understand?'

Linda tried to stay calm and reasonable. 'I don't know what you're talking about. If only you'd tell me, I might be able to help you.'

217

Lemmerich produced the gun again and jerked it towards her. 'How brave and how stupid. I know all about you. I know about your little scheme with Guy Mercer. Did you really think you could get away with it? Did you think you could fool us? You've very naive if you did. Now, think hard before you answer this next question. Where's the money, Linda?'

Linda did think hard but couldn't come up with a good answer. 'What money?'

'Oh dear.' She thought she saw a flicker of a smile on his face as he raised the gun and swung it against her head. So it was true – you did see stars when you got hit like that, she thought as the pain flashed up and down her body. She could feel a bump developing instantly on the side of her head and tears formed in her eyes. Even though she couldn't see straight, let alone think clearly, she came to a rapid conclusion.

'If I tell you everything, will you let me go?'

'Possibly. It depends on what you tell me.'

'What do you want to know?' Tears of pain now streamed down her cheeks.

'Just that one thing – where's the money?'

'I swear I don't know anything about any money,' she said desperately. 'Don't you think, if I knew where it was, I'd be long gone by now? I don't have a bloody clue, and that's the honest truth. He never told me.'

Now he looked at her with real menace, his face etched with evil. 'You expect me to believe that? You were going to run off with him without even knowing what had happened to the cash? I don't buy it. Let me jog your memory – see if this helps.'

He raised the gun again and she screamed 'No!' but it made no difference. This time the blow was much harder and she slumped against the door, her head hanging as far as it could. She threw up all over herself but could do nothing to stop it.

Lemmerich opened his door and got out, slamming it behind him. He got back into the driver's seat and started the engine. 'Think about it. We don't have much more time.' But Linda wasn't thinking about anything. She had sunk into a stupor and wasn't fit to communicate. Lemmerich didn't seem to care. 'You know, I could be your best friend or your worst enemy. Only you can decide which it's to be. We'll stop again in an hour and talk it through, shall we?'

Linda retched but there was nothing more in her stomach. Even moving her eyes was painful, but she forced herself to look up at the back of his head and silently promised she'd make him regret this. Then she lurched forward again, suspended by the handcuffs, and passed out.

TWENTY-TWO

When Jane walked into the pub she could see that several of her colleagues had been there all afternoon; half a dozen of them stood in a semicircle near the bar, with Grass leaning against it facing them. He was pissed, of course, and they were just as bad. Dreading the next hour or so, Jane walked over to them with as genuine a smile as she could muster and waited for the comments.

'So you finally made it,' Grass said. 'Nice of you to turn up.'

'Sorry, guv, I was busy.'

'What the hell. No harm done. What'll you have?' She ordered a gin and tonic and slid into position between two burly men who were both having difficulty standing up. When Grass gave her the drink he put his hand on her forearm. 'I'm glad you're here, actually. I wanted a quick word.' He pulled her away from the group and stood close to her, his breath strong enough to knock over a weightlifter.

'What is it?'

'You're a good copper, Fox. You know I think that. But you've got to lighten up. You walk around as if you've got a cucumber up your arse and you always look as if there's a bad smell under your nose. These other blokes, I know they can be a bit laddish, but their heart's in the right place. That's what matters. Get to know them, go out for a few drinks now and again, just to show willing, eh? Otherwise you'll never get on.'

'I appreciate the advice. Was there anything else?' Jane saw no reason now to conceal her contempt for him: as a policeman he might have been fine, but as a human being he was a disaster, and she no longer minded him knowing.

'There is, yes. A little bird tells me you're still sniffing round the Mercer files. Now, I'm sure you're just being diligent and all that crap, but it no longer concerns you, right? Leave it alone. If you haven't got enough to do, I'm sure they can find something else for you. Do you get the picture?'

'Completely. And while we're on the subject, is there any reason why you didn't follow up on Linda Betts? I mean, you must have known she'd been married before, and I was wondering why you didn't speak to her ex.'

He was angered by this and made no attempt to hide it. 'If it's any business of yours – which it isn't – there was absolutely no reason to interview him. Sure, we knew about him. So what? He hasn't featured in the investigation because he doesn't have to. That's all there is to it.'

'I see. You'll forgive me if I choose to disagree with you – sir – and I hope you won't mind if I mention it to Chief Super Watts, but it could be quite important, especially when you bear in mind who the man is. I think he should at least know about that, don't you?'

'Listen, Fox, you're going way out of your depth here. We've got nearly everything we need on Tilt, and the rest is just bollocks. Whatever you think you've got is bullshit, you hear? Poke your nose into this one and you're likely to get it blown off. Now, what I suggest is your drink your drink, have another and loosen up. Forget all about Guy Mercer. It's history.'

She smiled at him and raised her glass. 'I'll do that.' She swallowed down the rest of her drink in one, then handed him the glass. 'I'll have the same again, only this time make it a large one.'

'That's a girl,' he said, and winked at her. At that precise moment Jane knew what she needed to know, and she realised that she'd have to get smashed to dull the pain of it.

She was inside her flat, but it wasn't her flat and it annoyed her that she couldn't sort that out while there was so much banging on the door. Her head was swimming and she was finding it very hard to concentrate on anything as the banging got louder and a man's voice kept on shouting: 'Linda! Linda! Open the door!' She knew that she was in serious trouble and she couldn't think of what to do or how to defend herself, and the door looked as if it might cave in at any moment and suddenly there was Guy, sitting in an armchair by the window, and he was smiling at her and saying quietly: 'Trust me'. She couldn't reach him, couldn't move towards him at all, her legs having completely seized up, and all the time the man outside was getting more and more agitated as he tried to break in until, with a splintering crash, a fist clutching a gun broke through one panel and shots rang out in the room.

Linda woke with a start as the car pulled to a halt. The relief she felt at breaking the dream quickly dissipated as she came back to reality: she stank like a dog's blanket and her left arm was frozen with agony, the wrist now raw and bleeding where the manacle had rubbed the skin off. She could see little out of her darkened window, and she was too stiff to turn her head to look around. Lemmerich sat still in the front seat. He adjusted the rear-view mirror so that they could see each other's eyes.

'Where are we?' she croaked.

'Very close. Another two miles and we'll be there. This is your last chance. I've been very patient but I really can't wait any longer. Have you thought about what I said?'

'That and nothing else. But I can't get you what I don't have.'

'Quite tough, aren't you? Come on, Linda. Where's the money?'

'I don't know anything about this money you're on about. I can't say more than that. I don't know.'

In a sudden swift movement, Lemmerich was out of the car and round to her side, pulling open the door and thrusting his face close to hers. 'You stupid bitch,' he said as he landed a punch on the bridge of her nose. He unlocked the handcuffs and climbed into the car, knocking her across the seat and kneeling on her arms. He pulled out a roll of insulating tape from his pocket and unwound a strip which he bit off and then stuck across her mouth. He rolled her over on to her stomach and grabbed her wrists, pulling them behind her back and handcuffing them as he pressed his knees into her kidneys. He wound more tape around her ankles before getting out of the car; her feet stuck out of the door and he pulled off her shoes before he dragged her out and dropped her to the ground. Having opened the boot he came back to her, picked her up and threw her into it.

'I'm disappointed in you,' he said. 'I didn't want to have to do this, but you've given me no choice.'

Face downwards, twisted unnaturally and hurting beyond

understanding, Linda heard the boot lid shut and was enveloped in darkness. She could feel the blood stream from her nose and she desperately wanted to wipe it away. She tried to concentrate on this to take her mind away from her claustrophobia. She heard the engine start and felt the car move – backwards or forwards she couldn't say – and she wanted to cry.

Caroline felt all the maternal instincts rushing back. She wanted to look after Hugh and George, to smother them with her love so that they could be left in no doubt about her feelings for them. They needed the security of her comforting cuddles, she reasoned, and she wanted them to feel as normal as the circumstances would allow. In her struggle to deal with everything she'd confronted, she had neglected them for too long when they needed her most, and she was determined to redress the balance.

Perversely, Hugh had other ideas. For him, it was important that Mum was given time and space. He could be very helpful when he wanted. He had days when, unasked, he would undertake many of the domestic chores which Caroline hated, but his biggest contribution so far on this holiday had been to keep his brother amused. In this he was both effective and patient, and would even ignore the scratches and punches laid on him in the cause of harmony.

They had spent most of the day on the beach, and Hugh had been a star, playing ball games with George and taking him for a walk while Caroline sat under an umbrella and read her book or prepared the picnic she'd brought. It was Hugh who had insisted George was regularly smothered with cream, Hugh who found his hat, Hugh who helped him with tricky sections on the

Game Boy. Occasionally he would look long-sufferingly at his mother, murder in his eyes, but he would carry on his duties with the air of a martyr and Caroline secretly accumulated the Brownie points on his behalf.

Tired, sticky and wilting from the surprisingly fierce sun, they left the beach at four o'clock and bought ice creams for the short journey back to the house. Once home, they had baths and showers and got dressed and ready for the evening. As a special treat they went down to the local pub, The White Horse: they sat in the garden, Hugh and George with their Cokes and crisps whilst Caroline drank white wine spritzers and wondered what she'd give them for supper.

'What about fish and chips?' she suggested. There was general enthusiasm, even though she knew they would enjoy the anticipation more than the reality. After they'd finished their drinks they drove to Hunstanton and bought three portions of cod and chips, doused with vinegar and salt, and took them home. It was only when she looked in the fridge that she realised they'd run out of ketchup: she rummaged in her purse and gave a five-pound note to Hugh.

'Go down to the shop, would you, and get another bottle of ketchup?'

'All right, but I'm keeping the change.'

Hugh left the house and set off for the shop, which was less than four hundred yards away. As he walked along the dusty road a large green Mercedes swept past him, almost knocking him against a drystone wall. He uttered a choice obscenity – one which would have horrified his mother – and continued to the shop. Hugh did not see the Mercedes pull into the drive of Laurel Cottage.

* * *

Christian Lemmerich got out of the car and closed the door. He walked up to the front door and knocked three times, one hand in his pocket. He could hear a child's laughter from within, so he knew they were home. The door opened and Caroline was smiling, but her face immediately changed when she saw him. She tried to slam the door shut but he was too quick, jamming his leg and arm into the gap and prising it open again.

'Mrs Mercer,' he said flatly, 'there's no point in fighting.'

'Who are you?' she shouted. 'What do you want?'

'Let me in and we can talk. It's better that way.'

Aware of her own impotence she relented and took her weight off the door. He walked in and closed it behind him. He pushed her back through the hall and into the kitchen at the rear of the house. 'Call the children,' he said as he pulled the gun out of his pocket and waved it in front of her.

'George!' she shouted. He came in from the sitting room and Lemmerich looked round at him, dropping his arm so that the gun rested against his thigh.

'Where's the other one?' Lemmerich asked.

'He's away for the night,' Caroline said swiftly. 'Sailing.'

Lemmerich seemed satisfied, a merciful if small relief. 'Upstairs,' he said, and Caroline put her arms out to shepherd George towards the stairs. He followed them up and looked into all the bedrooms before choosing hers. 'In here.' They all went in, George looking puzzled and frightened and keeping close to Caroline. Lemmerich went to the window and strapped up the catches with his insulating tape, then drew the curtains. He turned round to face the boy. 'Your mother and I have some business to discuss. You are to stay here, and not make any

227

noise. Do you understand?' The little head nodded as Caroline's eyes moistened.

Lemmerich took the key from the lock, the only bedroom door which had one, and guided Caroline out. He closed the door and locked it. 'Any trouble, and he will suffer, believe me.'

They walked downstairs and back to the kitchen. 'Sit down,' he said. He remained standing, the gun still in his right hand. 'I have to tell you that I'm not happy. You and your husband have caused me a great deal of personal aggravation.'

'You still haven't told me who you are,' Caroline said defiantly.

'How rude of me. I'm Christian Lemmerich. We have met, but you probably don't remember. I represent Investment Logistics who, as I'm sure you're aware, are major shareholders in your late husband's firm. Now do you understand?'

'No, and I wish you'd put that gun away. What do you think I'm going to do?'

'Who knows, Mrs Mercer? You're a very resourceful woman. I'm sure we can settle this matter amicably, and I mean you no harm if you'll just cooperate. Tell me where the money is and we can finish this very quickly. If not . . .' He shrugged and gently moved the gun.

'What money would that be?' she asked, still determined to remain brave.

'The money your husband stole from us – twenty-five million dollars. You know all this, so let's stop playing games.' He moved closer to her until he was standing right behind her chair. He leant down and spoke into her ear. 'I will kill the boy if I have to.'

Caroline's throat had closed up and she was finding it difficult
to swallow, let alone concentrate on what he was telling her.
'OK,' she managed to say. 'The money's yours. You can have
it. Just please, please, don't harm the children.'

'No one's going to get hurt if we all stay calm and do what's
right. Where is the money? Do you have it here?'

'Some of it, yes. The rest is in London.' Her head was
throbbing with terror and her vision had almost completely
deserted her.

'Where in London?'

'In a safe. I can get it for you, if you give me time.'

'There's no time left. Write down the address.' He nodded to
a drawing pad and some crayons that George had left on the
table, and she scribbled Anthony's office address on it, her script
shaky and uneven. He ripped off the piece of paper and stuffed
it in his pocket. 'Where's the rest?'

It was now or never. Caroline had to decide, in that split
second, whether she fought or gave in. She could be brave and
stupid or cautious and wise. But her normal faculties of reason
and logic were way beyond her reach and she didn't have the
power to recall them. She looked round at Lemmerich as her
head shook with fear, her neck muscles twitching as she tried to
hold herself steady. She thought of little George upstairs, crying
and petrified, and nothing else seemed to matter, not even a
madman with a gun in his hand.

'It's in the car. In the compartment for the spare wheel.'

He jerked his gun upwards to show her that she should get
up. 'Let's see it. If you're fooling me you'll regret it.'

'I'm not.' She picked up the car keys from the side table in
the hall as he marched her outside, gun muzzle in the small of

229

her back. They reached the back of the Volvo estate.

'Open it.'

She pressed the remote-control button on the key and heard the click of the locks. She pushed the catch on the boot door but he brushed her to one side, taking the lip of the door and raising it so that it was fully open. He pulled a blanket away from the floor of the boot to reveal a handle that was sunk into it. He looked around at her as she stood three paces away from him. 'Stay right where you are,' he said. He grabbed the handle and pulled up the flap. There was a spare tyre and, next to it, a dirty brown canvas holdall stuffed down the side. He leant further into the boot and yanked the holdall free.

As he turned his head to check her again Caroline leapt forward and upwards, catching the top of the boot door and pushing all her weight down on to it so that she was off her feet as it began to close. He had no time to move or react before the combined mass of Caroline and the door crashed into his hip, the door lock piercing the skin and reaching the bone. He shouted something, she wasn't sure what, and the gun span out of his hand and into the tyre well. Knowing he was wounded but not beaten, she managed to bring the door up again and get in a shorter blow with it, even though his hand came up against the window to protect himself. This time the force of it knocked him on to his side so that his legs now stuck out of the opening; with frantic, smaller repetitions of the action she slammed the door against his legs until he was no longer putting up any resistance. He was groaning and there was blood seeping through the rips in his trousers; Caroline opened the door enough to reach the jack in the well and pull it out. Without thought she opened the door fully and leant into the boot, swinging the jack as Lemmerich raised his head and striking him on the temple. The force of the blow whipped his head backwards so that it hit the supporting arch on the side window hard; as he slumped down she could see a broad smear of blood on the glass. She struck him once more as he lay on the floor and then dropped the jack to the ground.

She was startled by the sound of feet on the gravel drive and looked round to see Hugh walking towards her with a bottle of ketchup in his hand. 'Sorry I took so long,' he said brightly. 'The shop was closed so I had to get this from the pub.' Caroline ran towards him and hugged him tightly, tears streaming down her face.

'Jesus Christ,' Hugh exclaimed as he looked round her at the car. 'What's happened?'

'It's all right, we're all all right, don't worry,' she said in a rush through her sobs. 'Just go and call the police – now!' Hugh did exactly as he was told, running to the house but unable to take his eyes off the car.

Caroline went back to the car and looked at Lemmerich. He was inert and blood oozed from various wounds. She found the gun and took it out before clasping his ankles and pushing him right into the boot. She closed the door and then looked for the car keys which were lying on the drive. Having found them she pressed the remove control; the rear doors had child locks – she'd specially asked for them when she was negotiating with the insurance company – and she felt better with him locked in there than in the house. She went across to the Mercedes and pulled the keys out of the ignition. Then she went into the house and rescued George, tearful and shaking.

* * *

231

Two police cars arrived within seven minutes. An ambulance arrived three minutes later. After half an hour there were eight uniformed officers and a detective inspector at the house. Several neighbours were stationed on the other side of the road and watched attentively as the paramedics treated Lemmerich in the drive and then loaded him into the ambulance.

Caroline was already in the first phase of shock and was incoherent. The boys were looked after by a policeman who amused them with his radio and showed them round his car. The detective sat with Caroline but asked no questions, simply telling her to take her time and ordering one of the men to make tea.

As they sat in the kitchen a uniformed officer came in. 'Sorry, sir. Can I have a word?' They went into the hall. 'There's a woman in the car – the Merc. She's pretty groggy but she's alive.'

'What next?' the detective asked, amazed and pleased by so much excitement in Holme-next-the-Sea.

TWENTY-THREE

Detective Chief Superintendent Dennis Watts was a man who could no longer be surprised or disappointed by life. He would sit in his office and survey the reports that drifted across his desk; he would make and receive phone calls with a weariness that was only overcome by his sense of duty; and he would listen to the complaints of his officers as they sat stiffly in front of him and tried to convince him of the merits of their arguments.

He was tired, and the tiredness often presented itself as cynicism: he could seem as if he had no interest whatsoever in policing, and that he was merely waiting for his pension as he sat at his desk. But he was not a cynic by nature: he was a man who had begun his career by believing in the power of good over evil, yet his eyes had been cruelly opened to the real world, and he felt defeated in the face of so much crime. Saddened by his personal inability to change society he had become wary of life, to such an extent that he could not greet any news without considering its blacker side. He tried to remain optimistic but the brutality of his profession made it a hard act, leaving him with little more than a shallow smile and watery eyes.

Watts was in the act of sharpening his arsenal of pencils

when Jane Fox walked in. 'Hallo, Jane,' he said warmly, as if he was actually pleased to see her.

'Hallo, sir. Have you got a couple of minutes?'

'Take a pew,' Watts said, pointing at a chair with the tips of six pencils that he clutched in his hand. 'So, what can I do for you?'

'It's about the Mercer case. I'm not happy about all the details, and I thought I'd better tell you my concerns.'

Watts's face sagged as he realised that this was not to be a comfortable conversation; more than anything, he disliked having to mediate in disputes between officers. 'I thought the Mercer case was all but solved. Haven't we got someone in the frame?'

'Yes, we have, and that's one of my problems. I just don't buy it.'

Watts sighed; how often had he been through this routine, where a young officer came in knowing all the answers and ready to criticise vastly more experienced detectives? 'Look, Jane, before we start on all this I'd better tell you that there is very little chance of you changing my mind. Gerry's done a good job so far and I've no reason to question his judgement. So you'd probably be better off sparing your breath and using your energy more . . . constructively.' He spoke kindly, trying to divert her before she got too worked up.

'Are you saying you wouldn't be interested if I had new evidence – evidence that makes the whole case against Anthony Tilt look very flaky?'

'Do you?'

'I'm working on it,' Jane said, somewhat regretting her boldness.

'Why are you working on it? Don't you have enough else to do?'

'Because something doesn't smell right. When I was working on the case I thought there must be a strong link with Mercer's business – then suddenly Grass pulls me off that, says it's irrelevant and I should be concentrating on the murder. The next thing I know I'm off the case and Tilt is the prime suspect – and whenever I've mentioned it since Grass has got very aggressive and told me to leave it alone. There's so much that's been left undone, uninvestigated, that I can't help feeling there's more to it than is in the file.'

Watts rubbed the inner corners of his eyes with his middle fingers, then looked up at her and smiled. 'What you will find, as you progress up the ladder, is that it's not always wise to try and deal with the things you don't know about. You should stick to what you do know – the facts – and work with them. Once you start dabbling in the unknown, you can cause yourself a lot of problems. Do you read me?'

'No, I'm afraid I don't. We may be about to charge the wrong man for Mercer's murder, in spite of a lot of evidence to suggest it was nothing to do with him. That really worries me, sir.'

'But what you think, ultimately, isn't very important. Greater minds than yours have looked at the case file and have decided that Grass has done the right things. It looks to me like this fellow Tilt is our man. End of discussion.'

'What would it take to convince you to have another look?'

'A signed confession from someone else, the murder weapon with perfect fingerprints, along with two impeccable witness statements. Do you have all that?' He was smiling as he said this; it was fun to play games occasionally and relieve the misery of the job. Jane would not be deflected so easily.

'If,' she said, 'if I could prove that Grass had deliberately suppressed evidence, and that he had chosen to ignore certain facts, would you reconsider?'

'Why? To be frank, I'm more interested in the end than the means. How Grass got there is largely irrelevant, as long as he didn't break any laws and followed procedure. You know that. It would take more than a few scraps, a couple of missing memos, to make me want to do anything.'

Jane brought her hands up and then dropped them on to her thighs. 'OK. I get the message. I'll leave it be.' She smiled winningly at Watts, so beautifully that it lit up the rest of his day.

George would not sleep in his bedroom. He would not sleep with Hugh, either; he cried and shook whenever Caroline attempted to leave him alone, and she eventually relented and brought him downstairs to lie on the sofa with his duvet over him. He watched her every movement like a suspicious dog, unwilling to close his eyes for even the briefest moment. Hugh sat with him and stroked his head, but the looks he shot at his mother suggested there was a storm brewing, an argument she would do anything to avoid.

Caroline looked out of the front window and checked that the police car was still parked in the drive before sitting down opposite her boys. Since school – when she had attacked another girl with her hockey stick in a fight over something she couldn't even remember – she had not hit anyone. There were times, of course, when she would have liked to lay one on Guy, or whack one of the children on the backside, but she felt that resorting to physical punishment was an admission of failure, a breakdown of reason and logic, and she would not willingly use violence.

Today had been different, as if animal instincts had overtaken her and driven her to use force when she was under threat. Caroline had been provoked into action like the docile dog that will bite to protect its puppies. Even though she acknowledged this, and was sufficiently aware of the reasons behind it, she still felt sick and angry: he had turned her into little more than a wild beast, striking out with blind fury as human dignity dissolved. She was not proud of herself: in her own eyes she had overstepped an important boundary, and she could not resist the conclusion that the money was to blame. Had she given it to Lemmerich, or burned it, or handed it over to the police, this would not have happened. They would not now be holed up in Norfolk, terrified out of their wits, if she had simply put up her hand and said 'No'.

But that opportunity seemed so long in the past that she couldn't even relate it to what was happening to her now. When she had visited the self-storage facility in Battersea, and opened the briefcase full of money; when she had travelled with Anthony to Shadowlawn and discovered more cash; when she had failed to surrender it all to Jane Fox; those moments were too far removed for her to appear as more than fleeting pulses in another life, something that had almost happened to someone else. The money was now ingrained, like dirt ground into her flesh, so much a part of her existence that she no longer thought about it as anything other than hers by right.

That scared her. The money threatened her independence, but she had no way of breaking free from it. She was caught by its magical allure, trapped into acceptance whilst simultaneously wanting to reject it. Having fought so hard to keep it – and, she asked herself, did she really attack Lemmerich to protect her children or the cash? – she now wished it would vanish. She had thought she had it under control, that she was strong enough to use it to benefit her and the boys, but she saw now that it would always be in command and would continue to deliver trouble to her door.

She also knew, as she balled her handkerchief in her hand, that Lemmerich, or his colleagues, would be back. He had mentioned twenty-five million dollars, the same figure Peter had given her. By resisting him, she had given the clearest indication yet that she had the money, and they – whoever they were – would redouble their efforts to recover it. Safety had become her ultimate priority: where could she possibly go that would be out of reach? How would she keep the children under constant surveillance? Would they become prisoners by default, exchanging the misery of poverty for the misery of wealth? She had brought them to this; she had made the decision to accept the cash and go along with Guy's mysterious game, and now she was asking the boys to pay the price with her. She screwed her face up in agony at the thought of it and the tears began to arrive.

Linda had her own reasons for not wanting to press charges. She wanted to be out of the hospital, into a cab and back to London as soon as possible. Lying in the boot of Lemmerich's car – before she had passed out – she had reached a decision: this had all gone way beyond the original intentions, and she was best off leaving it alone. Whoever had the money was welcome to it. All Linda wanted was a warm, clean bed, a packet of Silk Cut and a big glass of Bacardi and Coke. She'd get another job, disappear into the woodwork until everything had calmed down. She was no heroine, despite the potential rewards on offer, and she was determined to avoid any further grief.

But, as she lay on a trolley in the casualty department, she had too much time to reflect on this decision. OK, so the police up here weren't too interested and looked pretty relieved when she told them she'd prefer to let the matter rest. 'A misunderstanding?' they'd repeated. 'That's right, a misunderstanding,' she'd said. 'Could happen to anyone.' She'd thought that some judicious discretion could well be her salvation at a later date, and she'd like to have that in her locker: 'Look Christian, I could have had you locked up for what you did to me – but I didn't.' The police shook their heads, made copious notes and left her to recuperate. She waited for treatment and thought again about the money; through the fog of concussion and shock she could remember that her original idea had been to confront Caroline Mercer, that she was on her way to do this when she'd been intercepted. Somewhere, floating just beyond her immediate understanding, was an impression that Lemmerich was also on his way to see the Mercer woman. What had happened? She was too groggy to work it out.

The flaws in her plan, however, were becoming more apparent. So she'd just start a new life, would she – as she had when she'd walked out of her marriage? By now everyone in the City would know about AMS and Guy and her, and the fact that she'd disappeared in a hurry. They'd also know that the police had been burning her tail and, eventually, the rest of it would come out. No employer in their right mind would offer her a job, even have her in for an interview; she was damaged property, regardless of how good she was, and she'd better start thinking about a shelf-stacker's job at the local supermarket as the most likely employment option.

There was Lemmerich to be considered as well. He wouldn't give up for the sake of a few broken bones; he'd be back soon enough, sniffing around and getting even nastier with her. If she was to have any chance of escaping from him she needed a serious amount of money – and there was only one source. Caroline Mercer had to be tapped, had to be convinced that the money was just as much Linda's as it was hers. Again, there was a misty recollection of some recent connection, some vague memory that just wouldn't focus.

She was contemplating her glorious future prospects when a nurse slipped in through the curtain and, grim-faced, looked at Linda's head injuries. The nurse grasped her wrist and timed her pulse, then sighed. 'So, how did this happen?' she asked nodding at Linda's face.

'It's a long story and you wouldn't believe it even if I told you.'

'Who was it, dear – boyfriend, husband?'

'Something like that. Now, what's the prognosis?'

'A few cuts and bruises. Nothing that won't heal. But we'll need to keep you in overnight, keep an eye on you. Is there anyone you'd like us to get in touch with, let them know you're here?'

The question took Linda by surprise. There was no one to whom she could turn, no one who would be remotely interested in her condition, save a handful of police officers and villains.

'No,' she said quietly. 'No one needs to know just yet.'

'Definitely suffering from concussion,' the nurse said to herself as she pulled the curtain closed.

TWENTY-FOUR

Caroline watched the dawn arrive with heavy eyes. She had not even tried to take herself upstairs to sleep, knowing that she would be restless and uncomfortable: the guilt she carried would ensure that. She had flitted from room to room, unable to shake off the unease that had fallen heavily upon her. She drank strong black coffee and made a dilatory effort at packing up their belongings, half-heartedly resolving to leave Norfolk at first light and head for . . . where, exactly?

This was the question she couldn't answer. She could race like the devil to the Cotswolds and hope that the folding hills would conceal them, but that was too obvious; she even speculated that the house in Minster Lovell had probably already been ransacked and vandalised by Lemmerich and his cronies. Going back to London seemed equally out of the question. There was nowhere to hide. Whatever, whoever was in pursuit would surely find her without much difficulty.

Although she had hoped that a night's contemplation would lead to great clarity of purpose, she was disappointed to see the morning sun appear without any similar enlightenment on her part. She was no further on; the doubts that had attacked her in the dark were no less powerful now, and she ached with the exhaustion of having reached no conclusions. Life was in rapid rewind, unspooling back to the time when she'd not been required to make decisions and had merely deferred to what Guy decreed. She was now incapacitated in the same way, transfixed by a dilemma from which she saw no escape.

She rummaged in her bag and found the card Jane Fox had given her. Her one remaining hope was to transfer her inertia to someone else, to present them with the problem and wait for a solution to be supplied. She was too tired, too scared, too beaten to try anything more by herself.

She called the number Jane had written on the back of the card, and waited an age before there was an answer. 'Hallo,' a sleepy voice said.

'Jane, is that you? It's Caroline Mercer.' She heard rustling at the other end of the line, as if Jane were sitting up to attention.

'Yes, what is it? Are you all OK?' She sounded concerned.

'We're fine, but there's been some trouble. It's over now. Jane . . . I just don't know what the hell I'm supposed to do now.'

'Stay calm. We'll sort this out, Caroline. Just tell me what's happened.'

'A man called Christian Lemmerich came to the house – I don't know how he found us. He threatened me and George, and he got pretty nasty. I managed to . . . well, he's in hospital now under police guard, and we're all OK, I think, just a little shaken.'

'And where did this happen? Where are you now? Can you tell me?'

'Will you come and get us?'

'I don't know if I can, but I'll try. Give me the address and phone number.' Caroline did as she was told; it was comforting to listen to someone taking charge. 'OK,' Jane continued. 'I want you to stay where you are. There's nowhere safer now. I'm working on some things down here that could get all this sorted out once and for all.'

'Jane – I can't hold out much longer. I've really had enough, and so have the boys. We need to be safe. Whatever you're working on, will it make us safe?'

'If it all comes out the way I want it to, it will. But you have to sit tight. Don't think about moving or running off somewhere else. I'll get to you as soon as I can.'

'Don't leave it too long.' The fleeting reassurance Caroline had felt disappeared as soon as the line was cut. What Jane had said was too ambiguous, and raised too many fresh concerns, for Caroline to gain any lasting confidence. She might come up, there was something that might resolve everything – these were grey statements that did little to soothe Caroline's growing fever.

She was surprisingly pleased to see George come downstairs. He had dropped off on the sofa next to Hugh: much later in the night Caroline had carefully transferred him to her bed. George was always first up, and his face was smudged from sleep and anxiety; Hugh surfaced at nine o'clock, very early for him. Caroline suspected, without really knowing, that he had stayed up into the small hours, doing whatever a young boy would do in the privacy of his room: with every month that passed he got up later and later. Eventually, she felt, they would only see each other as they passed on the stairs, one going up as the other came down.

Breakfast was a quiet affair, the only time during the day when neither of the boys wanted to talk. Caroline encouraged them now, desperate to hear their voices and be diverted from the terrors that closed around her like a fist being formed. 'So what shall we do today – go on a boat trip? We could go out and see the seals. What do you think?'

George ignored her efforts to be jolly. 'Mum,' he asked, 'where's that man gone? You know, the man with the gun.' He still sounded frightened.

'He's gone, George. The police have taken him away and locked him up.'

'And he won't get out again? He's not coming back?'

'No, he's not coming back. You've nothing to worry about.'

'I wish Dad was here,' George said, his voice now quavering.

Caroline moved to hug him. 'We all do. But we've just got to get on as best we can without him. I bet Dad's watching us now and he's so proud of us, especially you for being so brave.'

'I want him back,' George said as the tears began. Hugh watched this exchange helplessly, wanting to intervene to lighten his mother's burden but too absorbed in his own sadness to do anything but stop himself from crying.

George broke away from Caroline's embrace and ran from the kitchen. She shook her head in exasperation; there was no way to deal with this. She looked across at Hugh.

'Dad did something very bad, didn't he?' he said solemnly. 'That's why we're having all this trouble now.'

'I don't know, Hugh. I honestly don't know what he did.'

'We have to do something, Mum. We can't sit and hide here for ever. If Dad is the cause of all this, we've got to tell someone.'

'What do you mean?'

'I mean I don't want to live like this, and see you like this. It just isn't fair on George and me. You haven't thought much

246

about us, and what we want, have you?' He was angry with her, a defence against his sadness, and needed this argument.

Caroline was hurt by the accusation. 'That's so unfair,' she said. 'I'm constantly worrying about what's best for you and George. It drives everything I do.'

'Does it? So having some madman here with a gun is your way of protecting us, is it? Dad would never have let that happen.'

She reacted before she had time to think it through. 'It was your father who got us into this mess in the first place,' she barked. 'If it weren't for him we'd all be fine.' She regretted it immediately but it was too late.

'Well, at least you've finally admitted it,' he said sarcastically. 'It's all Dad's fault.' Hugh scraped his chair back and stood up. 'I don't know whether it's crossed your mind, but George and I don't want things to go on like this. I don't want to be on some crap holiday in Norfolk, playing Monopoly with George and letting him win all the time. I want to go home and do my own stuff. And George can hardly speak he's so scared – have you any idea what this has done to him? You're so bloody wrapped up in your own life, you've forgotten about us. You're being really selfish, Mum.'

She was going to reply, to try and repair the damage, but Hugh didn't want that; he had made his statement and that was enough. He walked out of the room, the slope of his shoulders accentuated as he relaxed after his tirade. Caroline watched him go without making the pointless effort to stop him; his words reverberated in her ears.

By the time they discharged her – at three minutes past nine –

Linda had smoked two cigarettes and drunk three cups of murky machine coffee. She was sore but alert. Her first priority was to go into the town centre and buy some new clothes: her dress was stained and stank to high heaven, and her shoes were too tight to bear any longer.

She walked across the car park away from the hospital and smiled at a paramedic as he came towards her. 'Hallo there,' he said. 'So they're letting you out.'

'I'm sorry?'

'You don't remember me? Well, I'm not surprised. You were pretty beaten up. I looked after you yesterday in the ambulance coming down here.'

Linda thought about this, smiling at him as she did so to encourage him to stay put. 'Right,' she said. 'Well, thanks a lot for all your help. As you can see, I'm right as rain now.'

'I don't know about that, but you certainly look a lot better than you did before.'

'Tell me something.' Linda put on her best voice for him. 'Where exactly did you pick me up? You see, I think I may have dropped something up there and it's quite valuable to me.'

'As I say, it was a place in Holme, up on the coast. Nice house, too.'

'How far is it from here?'

'From King's Lynn? About twenty miles.'

She considered this information, all the time fixing his gaze so that he'd stay interested. 'What about the man – you know, the driver of the car? Is he here?'

'Oh no, he was transferred to Norwich. He's pretty badly beaten up. She gave him a right going-over.'

'She?'

'Yeah, the woman he attacked. I don't know, it's like a Hollywood film or something. We don't get a lot of stuff like that up here.' He shook his head and smiled, clearly delighted that he'd been involved. Linda took it all in and came to a decision.

'What's the best way of getting to this place – Holme?'

'Well, you could get a cab in town, or . . .' He leant his head to one side rather bashfully.

'Or?'

'Or I could drive you up. My shift finishes in an hour. It'd be no bother – I'm going in that direction anyway.' Linda got the impression he wasn't, but didn't contest it.

'Well, that would be very kind,' she said. 'Are you sure?'

'It's all part of the after-care service,' he replied, looking very pleased with himself that his boldness had paid off.

'So where shall I meet you?'

He looked at his watch. 'Here. At ten o'clock. Is that OK?'

'That's brilliant. You're a real hero.' He beamed as if he really believed her.

By mid-morning an uneasy peace had been restored. George was dressed and reasonably clean. Caroline had warned him not to leave the garden or go beyond her sight, and he seemed to understand that her concern was genuine and should not be treated lightly. Hugh claimed to have a splitting headache and, having taken two paracetamol, dragged himself out of the kitchen, saying he was going back to bed. As he was walking to the stairs there was a knock at the front door. 'I'll get it,' he said.

'No!' Caroline roared from the kitchen. 'Stay away from the door! Go upstairs now!'

Every fear she had ever had returned in that instant. She had never actually experienced the much-described sensation of legs turning to jelly, but now she did: unable to move, she heard herself panting heavily and could feel the blood rush to her face. There was another knock, two slow raps of brass on brass.

Caroline managed to put one foot in front of the other and forced herself into the hall and towards the front door. Hugh stood on the stairs, unwilling to leave her. When she finally got near enough, she shouted: 'Who is it?'

'It's PC Sowerby, madam.' Caroline closed her eyes and her head dropped back; she had entirely forgotten about the policemen stationed outside the house. Relieved, she reached forward to open the door.

The policeman was standing there, but he was not alone. Behind him was Linda Betts.

They sat in the kitchen as the boys played in the garden.

'I need to tell you the whole story,' Linda said.

'I'd rather you didn't.' Caroline was stiff, her voice gritty with discomfort. 'I don't know why you came here, but I think you should go.'

'He always said you were a tough bitch.' She said it lightly, but it didn't work.

'A tough old bitch, actually. Get it right if you're going to quote him.'

Linda didn't want or need hostile confrontation: it was as if she'd been preparing for this moment all her life. 'Look, I haven't come here to cause a scene. That isn't the intention at all. I've come for one simple reason. Christian Lemmerich followed you up here because he thinks you may have the money

– or, at the very least, you know where it is. I don't agree with him. I think you have some cash, a nest egg that Guy left you. But there's a lot more, and I can help you find it – in return for my share.' Linda had become so accustomed to bluffing that she almost believed herself as she made this ridiculous offer.

'Your share? What do you mean, your share? You're due nothing at all. What possible reason could Guy have for leaving anything for you?'

Linda sighed and lowered her voice. 'Because he loved me and I loved him.'

If this affected Caroline she concealed it well. 'What rubbish,' she said robustly. 'You've had a nasty bang on the head, haven't you? I think you're still suffering from it.'

'I'm sorry. I can see all this has come as a bit of a shock for you. But we do need to get it sorted out. I only want what's fair for both of us.' Linda put her hands up to stop Caroline from protesting. 'I know, you and I are going to disagree about fairness, but that's the way it is. Life isn't fair. I think I've been let down, too. I worked bloody hard to get where I am. I had to look after my mother when my dad walked out. I did all my banking exams, got the qualifications and then, one day, I landed the job at AMS. I'd arrived. I was so happy, and then what happens? Guy comes along and screws everything up for me. I've been to hell and back for him, and I deserve some of that money.'

'How long did it take you to concoct that fairy tale?'

'It's no fairy tale, that's for sure. I wish none of this had ever happened. But it has, and I've got to deal with the consequences. So have you.'

'I'm trying to, believe me. Nothing you say can shock me, if

251

that's your intention. I've gone beyond that stage. But I don't know where you got the idea that there's some money lying around.'

Linda was impressed with Caroline's determination, but tried not to let it show. 'Lemmerich thought you had the money, didn't he?'

'Which makes him just as stupid as you. Now look – I'm sorry I have to do this, but if you don't push off I'm going to have to call that nice policeman in here and get you removed.'

'Answer me one thing, Mrs Mercer. What will you do without the money?' Linda stared hard at her and waited.

It was not a new question, but Caroline still had no answer for it. She had already discovered how quickly cash could evaporate when you were on the run, and she knew a lot more would be needed if they were to continue to hide. 'Survive,' was the best she could come up with. 'Like I always have.'

'Doesn't that sound a bit sad? Is that what Guy would have wanted?'

What had Guy wanted? Caroline had no idea; whatever his intended bequest, he had brought down so much trouble on their heads that it was impossible to understand what he'd been thinking of, and now this sly little woman was reminding her all too painfully of the problem. 'You tell me. You seem to be the expert.'

Linda sensed a change in attitude. 'I'm not claiming to be an expert in anything. All I want is what's due to me. I promise you, there's enough to go round.'

Caroline's confusion finally caught up with her. All the tenets, the beliefs so faithfully accrued and burnished over the years, crumbled in the face of so much turmoil, so many differing fears, demands and desires, and she wilted before the wreckage. She was no longer capable of taking a stand on anything, defeated by uncertainty. 'OK. Convince me,' she said as forcefully as she could. Linda smiled, but Caroline hardly noticed.

TWENTY-FIVE

Jane kicked him so hard between the legs that even her eyes watered. He fell to his knees and bent himself forward, presenting the tempting target of his face for her foot, but she resisted it.

'I'm really pissed off,' she said, 'and I'm in a hurry. Shall we try again?'

Gerry Grass looked up at her and contorted his face into a sinister rictus. 'I could have you arrested.' The hoarseness in his voice made him sound as evil as he looked.

'I don't think you're getting the message, Gerry. Think really hard about it, will you?' This time she did kick his face, a glancing blow that sent him spinning on to his side. Her foot throbbed from the impact. 'Did that help?'

He was breathing hard but he was still defiant. 'What difference does it make? Don't you understand, you stupid little cow? They already know, for Christ's sake. Why do you think they agreed to pension me off – gratitude? You are so bloody ignorant, you can't even see what's right in front of you.'

Jane listened to his words but couldn't add it all up into a single thought. 'You're not making sense, Gerry.'

'You want me to write it down? Read my lips – they know. They've always known. Stuff like this happens all the time.

They make a judgement, you either go or you stay. I stayed. I had some value for them, even with all that shit. I earned my salary, that's for sure.'

More than anything, as she gathered the full weight of what he was telling her, Jane wanted to kick him again, smash her foot into him until the flesh split and the bone splintered. She wanted to vent all her hatred on a single point of contact, get it out of her system now so that she could move on. But a more noble instinct constrained her and she merely looked away from him in disgust.

Grass shifted so that he was sitting on the ground. She had caught him as he walked home from the pub, stalking him until he went through the narrow conduit he used as a short cut to his flat. It was unlit and deserted; she knew there was no danger of being interrupted as she set about him. 'Don't feel so smart now, do you?' he asked. 'So what are you going to do? You can't go to Watts because he knows so he's compromised. You're right up the creek.'

'And you're prepared to charge an innocent man for something he didn't do so that you can protect your own little racket,' she spat.

'Anthony Tilt is scum. He's expendable, and nobody's going to care one way or the other. Face it – you've got nothing to go on.' Jane was silent, not wishing to give him the satisfaction of an answer. 'I did warn you, Fox. But you wouldn't listen.'

She turned away and moved as if to walk off. Abruptly she spun back to face him as he struggled to get up. 'What about Alan Apostle? Is he involved?' she asked.

'If you mean did he have an arrangement with me, then the answer's no. He's just some arsehole bent out of shape because his wife doesn't love him any more – and who could blame her?' Grass finally got to his feet and rubbed his hands together, looking at them as if he were surprised they were still there. Then his gaze turned to her. 'I never did like you. You're a superior bitch, and I truly hope you get burnt on this one.'

'If I do, you have my guarantee that you'll be right there with me.' This time she did walk away, her pulse almost bursting through her skin. As she went she broke into a nervous laugh, adrenalin-fuelled, thinking about a joke and adapting it for the situation: 'What's transparent and lies in the gutter? Gerry Grass with the shit kicked out of him.'

They had gone to The Lifeboat, a pub just along the coast from Holme where they served huge portions of good food and you could sit in a conservatory at the back with your noisy children and no one complained about them. Linda smoked and drank without eating a thing, happy to watch as Caroline and the boys tucked in to scampi, steak and plaice followed by sticky toffee pudding with cream and custard.

'What happened to your face?' little George had asked, too young to know better. Linda, normally so quick with a sharp reply, was silenced by the question; Caroline reprimanded George and, when coffee arrived, sent him and Hugh outside to play on the climbing frame. Caroline was a little drunk: she'd had three gins and was now swirling a large brandy in front of her. Linda was untouched by the Bacardi. During the meal it had been impossible to say anything in front of the boys; Caroline was still smarting from Hugh's unkind words and she was wary of reopening the fight. With the boys gone they had some peace at last.

257

'What's the deal, Linda?' Caroline knew she was slurring her words, but ascribed it more to tiredness than alcohol.

'If I tell you, can you handle it?'

'As you already know, I'm a tough old bitch. Try me.'

Linda looked around; satisfied that no one was listening, she drained her glass, then lit a cigarette. 'Twenty-five million dollars.' She pulled hard on the cigarette. 'That's what we took.'

'What's that in real money?'

'Sixteen million pounds – and change.' Linda shrugged as if to show that this was an amount with which she was very familiar.

'And when you say "we", what exactly do you mean by that?'

'What I mean is this. Guy came to me with this plan. It would never have crossed my mind. Basically, he'd worked out a very simple way of taking twenty-five million off one of his clients, but he needed my help to do it.'

'Why? He ran the company, didn't he?'

'Yes, but there were controls, regulations, audit trails and everything. He didn't understand any of that, so he didn't know how to get around them. I did.'

Caroline sniffed her brandy, then sipped a little. 'He used you, then.'

'It looks like that to you because you don't know how it was. We had something good, you know. It wasn't some squalid little office affair. You have to understand that.'

'I don't have to do anything,' Caroline said, raising one eyebrow. 'For all I know, this something you speak about is all a figment of your imagination. I did know Guy pretty well, and I think I'd have noticed if he'd been involved in anything like you describe.' She didn't sound convincing even to herself, having long since realised that there was a side – or sides? – of Guy which she didn't know at all. But she needed to show this girl that she was unimpressed and still in control.

Linda took a long drag on her cigarette and then had some lukewarm coffee. She seemed unconcerned by Caroline's hostility, impervious to her show of strength. 'To tell you the truth,' she said, 'it's not too important if you believe me or not. What does it matter? But I am going to get that money, and I'd prefer to have your cooperation.'

Caroline suddenly stiffened, as if someone had stuck a sharp needle into her backside. 'He didn't tell you,' she exclaimed, stunned by the realisation. 'He didn't tell you where he'd hidden the money. I don't believe it.' She started laughing, a big laugh that shivered through her whole body before leaving her. Linda winced and concentrated on tapering her cigarette in the ashtray. 'You stupid girl,' Caroline said when she'd finished laughing. 'Surely you knew better than to trust him, didn't you?' Then she was off again, making no effort to hide her amusement.

'That's funny?' Linda said bitterly as she watched Caroline shudder.

'So all this is a bluff,' Caroline said, dabbing her eyes with her hankie. 'You can't help me at all, but you're hoping I'll help you. Don't you think you're being a bit optimistic?'

'No, I don't, and I'll give you two reasons why. First, you haven't got all the money. I knew he was going to leave you some – we'd agreed on that – but you haven't more than a couple of million at the most. That leaves fourteen still floating around. Now, who's more likely to find it – you or me? I'm a qualified settlements manger. If Guy hid that money in the banking system, I know where to look. Do you?'

'So far I haven't done too badly. And anyway, if you're so clever, why come to me? Why not just go after the cash yourself?'

Linda looked at her empty glass. 'Do you fancy another brandy?'

'I need to go and see if the boys are all right. If they are, I'll have one.'

'I'll get you one anyway,' Linda said. 'I'll drink it if you don't.'

When they were both seated again, with double brandies in front of them, Linda leant forward as if about to divulge an important secret. 'Everyone thinks I'm a bastard,' she said, quiet and matter-of-fact. 'It's come to suit me, having that label. Sorts a lot of problems out up front. You know the kind of thing: "Watch out for her, she's a real bitch". People treat you with a little more respect. But that isn't really me. You know, my star sign is Cancer, like the crab – tough on the outside, very soft inside. Things get to me, upset me more than they should, but I don't show it. That's how it was with Guy. I fell in love with him, base over apex. I knew it would end in tears, and I knew I shouldn't have done it, but knowing that wasn't enough. I couldn't help myself – didn't really want to. I just thought I was so bloody lucky, after everything I'd been through, and that was enough.

'I promised myself I wouldn't get too involved, but things don't work out like you plan, do they? And then, when he came along with this scheme, I was too far gone to say no. I still believe he meant to go through with it.' She wiped a tear away from the corner of one eye, the first time Caroline had seen any real emotion. Then she seemed to shake off the sadness. 'Anyway, Guy was an incredible man, as you know much better than me. All the time I knew him, he was so devoted to you and the children. I know he loved you, and I know that sounds stupid and I can't really explain it except to say that maybe he was in love with both of us but in different ways. But I never forgot that, the strength of feeling he had for you. He didn't try and hide it from me – it was right on his lapel like a badge. I never had that, you know, not from anyone. You're lucky you did.

'So now, I look at you and the boys and I wonder what Guy would have wanted. You know, you said you'd survive without the money. Do you think he would have been happy with that? It doesn't sound very much like Guy, does it? I'll admit, I wanted all the money and I didn't care how I got it, but now I've seen you and the boys I remember how much you all meant to him and I know it's only fair that we should split it.'

It would have been easier for Caroline to dismiss this out of hand, to treat it with contempt and regard it as yet another ploy. But something about the way Linda had spoken – almost naked in its simplicity and honesty – suggested to Caroline that she was telling the truth, that this had come straight from her heart and could not be denied. Was it so fanciful that Guy could have swept Linda off her feet, overwhelmed her as he had Caroline all those years ago? Could he not have lied, deceived and cheated and yet still have maintained the façade of devoted love? She had known he had his faults, but had she known all of them? Was she really so perceptive, so infallible, that he would not have been able to slide this past her? So often they tell you that you only see what you want to see – and how closely was she looking?

She should also have been sickened by the implicit patronisation in Linda's offer, but she didn't even notice. What came to her most immediately was the thought that someone was trying to help her; Linda had seen her despair and was offering assistance. Caroline could be proud, mean and spiteful: she could tell Linda to get lost and hang on to what she already had. But that was not entirely what she wanted to do, much as she hated what Linda had told her. She wasn't sure why, but she was gravitating towards some accommodation with her.

'Fair,' Caroline said, the word sticking in her throat like a large pebble. 'What's fair?'

'Nothing much, but this would start to even things up a bit, I reckon.' The pallor that had shot through Linda's face when she was talking about Guy had not yet gone; her cheeks were hollow and her eyes were red, the bruising more prominent against her pale skin.

'There was something else,' Caroline said.

'What?'

'You said there were two reasons why I should do a deal with you. You've only given me one.'

Linda puffed out her cheeks. 'So I did. Do you need a second one?'

'It depends what it is.'

Linda lit a cigarette and smoked for a long time before speaking. 'OK. What I was going to say is that I have information to trade with – information I think you'll want.'

'Such as?'

'Such as I know who killed Guy. I know the whole bloody story, for my sins.'

'Then why don't you go to the police?'

'Not such a great idea. No, I'm only telling once I've got my share of the cash. I'm not going to be shafted again.'

The boys ran back into the conservatory, their faces flushed from their exertions. There were demands for drinks and crisps and Caroline had no more time to concentrate on Linda and her story. It would have to wait.

Much as she had expected, the house in Norbiton was empty. Jane cursed herself for being so flat-footed: how could she have sent him such a strong message and not expected him to bolt? He had done what any reasonable, terrified, guilty person would have done in the same circumstances. What made it harder for Jane was that Linda had also gone to ground, so there was no trail to follow.

Jane had it all worked out – now it was just a small matter of getting the evidence in order and persuading Watts that she had a strong case. She had identified the motive and opportunity for Guy's murderer; she knew what Grass had been up to; she understood the involvement of AMS; and she could place Linda Betts squarely in the jigsaw. She was bursting to tell somebody, but there was no one around who was suitable. Everyone she knew seemed to have a vested interest.

She had got into the house through the back door. The kitchen smelt musty and damp. Somewhere a tap dripped slowly and she wanted to turn it off. The floor was covered with deformed cork tiles with large burn marks on them. On one work surface there was a dirty knife and plate and an ashtray full of cigarette butts. He hadn't even had time to tidy up before he'd gone – or perhaps it was always like this. She's seen his office, and that wasn't any cleaner.

Jane walked upstairs and looked into a bedroom. The duvet, pillow and sheets had all been bundled up and thrown on to the floor; the mattress on the double bed was stained and aged. There were no pictures on the walls, no decoration of any kind. In one corner was a small pine table with a mirror on it: Jane could see a photograph slipped under one edge of the mirror frame and she walked over to take a closer look. It was Linda – younger, but unmistakably Linda. Jane sighed: it depressed her to see the human side of criminals, the small attachments and manifestations of feeling that made it more difficult to understand their motivations.

She went downstairs again. The stairs led directly into the lounge, and she walked across the sticky brown carpet to the front door. There was a pile of mail on the mat. She bent down to pick it up and check the postmarks. As she crouched forward the back of her head was smashed with something very hard and she slumped on to the floor, immediately unconscious.

TWENTY-SIX

Anthony Tilt replayed the message four times.

'Hi. It's Caroline Mercer. Sorry I've been so elusive. I'm coming back to London tonight and I really need to see you. I'll call you again tomorrow to set something up. Hope all's well with you. Bye.'

His mind was clear and his body was recovering. When she had left the message he had been out – a bizarre coincidence – visiting her house in Castelnau to see if there were any signs of life. He had seen the shattered window in the front, but couldn't tell whether this was vandalism or something more sinister. He wanted to break in but lacked the courage to do it. He stood outside for a long time, cursing himself for his weakness.

Back at his flat he was restless. Caroline was all he could think of, other concerns now submerged beneath his desire to see this through to its conclusions. But, every way he looked at it, there was still nothing he could do to expedite the matter: she was running the show, and he'd have to follow at her pace. Frustrated, he paced back and forth until his feet were sore.

He heard the noise coming from downstairs but paid little attention to it. There were voices, and a lot of banging – that was nothing unusual where he lived – and he only reacted when the voices got closer and stopped outside his front door on the first floor. Then it went silent. He waited, his heart suddenly thumping against his ribs. There were three loud knocks on the door. 'Mr Tilt? Mr Anthony Tilt? Open up, please – it's the police.'

More than anything he felt surprise. He couldn't grasp what was happening as all his conscious processes melted to nothing. He opened the door without being aware of it, and he barely heard what they were telling him, as if he were listening to someone else's dream. 'I'm arresting you in connection with the murder of Guy Mercer . . .' was all he managed digest. The rest – the words of caution, the phalanx of officers standing in front of him, the hand firmly clutching his upper arm – was all lost in a fog of confusion.

It was surprisingly peaceful in the car. Caroline had decided to set out at midnight, and had kept the boys awake all evening, playing Monopoly and eating fish and chips. Linda sat apart from them, smoking and doing serious damage to a bottle of red wine she'd bought from the pub. Caroline drank strong coffee and tried not to think about what lay ahead.

The boys fell asleep within twenty minutes of setting off, and the two women enjoyed the quiet for a few minutes. Then Linda spoke. 'What will you do? I mean, once we have the money?'

'I truly have no idea. I can't even think that far ahead. This whole thing has wreaked havoc with my powers of reason. I don't even know what I've got now, let alone what might be out there in the future.'

'I'm going to leave the country. Travel a bit, look around,

see where I want to end up – somewhere where it's always hot, I think.'

'We have to find the money first,' Caroline reminded her gently.

'I've been thinking about that, too. Guy would have told me, even if he didn't mean to. He would have said something. He wasn't good at secrets.'

'He was when it came to you. I had no idea.'

There was silence again. After ten minutes, Linda spoke. 'What about the will? Did that leave any clues?'

'That will,' Caroline replied. 'That was the most bizarre thing of all. Guy set up two trusts, neither of them funded or anything, obviously hoping I'd work out the significance of them. I cracked half of it. He's left some cash for me at a place that was important to us. But the other is still a complete mystery.'

'What was it?'

'Something called Hartmann. I didn't get it, and I still don't.'

There was another long silence, then Linda shouted: 'Jesus Christ, that's it!' Then she put her hand over her mouth. 'Sorry.'

'What? What is it?'

'I think I know where the rest of the money is – or at least how to find it.'

'Are you going to tell me?'

'When Guy and I were planning to . . . you know, when we were going away, he bought me this fantastic set of luggage. He brought it round to the flat and showed it all to me. I remember now, he winked at me and said something about it being the most valuable luggage I'd ever have. I laughed and didn't really take it in because it must have cost a fortune, and I thought that's what he meant. But he didn't mean that. The bags – they're made by Hartmann! The answer's got to be in one of the cases, hasn't it?'

'It sounds reasonable. It's worth a try, anyway. Where is the luggage?'

'At the flat I rented. I used it to transfer all my gear when I moved.'

'And that's where you want to go now?'

'Don't you?'

'Lead me to it. I hope you're right, though.'

They reached London at three-thirty in the morning. Linda had not slept at all, and Caroline had to marvel at her stamina – for such a scrawny girl she seemed to be pretty robust. Linda gave vague directions that got better as they neared Camberwell, and the big Volvo finally pulled up outside a five-storey Victorian house.

'This is it,' she said. 'I'm on the top floor.'

'Do you think it's safe to leave the boys here?' Caroline asked.

'This is south London. What do you think?'

Caroline snorted. 'OK. You go up on your own. We'll wait for you down here.'

'Are you sure?'

'Positive. I may just close my eyes for five minutes. See you soon.'

Linda got out of the car and walked up to the steps of the house. Once she had put her key in the lock of the door she made an O with her finger and thumb to show Caroline that she was in. She punched the timer light in the hall and walked slowly upstairs to her flat. The light popped off just as she reached her door and she had to fumble for a switch behind her on the landing wall. She slotted her key into the lock and turned it, leaning wearily against the door as it opened.

She flicked on a light and took a quick look around the flat. It still looked as if a whirlwind had passed through; the clothes she had strewn across the floor lay where she'd dropped them, along with the two suitcases. She leant back against the wall and closed her eyes, inhaling through her nose. The smell jerked her awake: she knew it but couldn't place it, even though it was so familiar. It was out of place, out of context, but that was all. She tutted and dismissed it, picking her way across the floor towards the bathroom. Without bothering to close or lock the door, she hitched up her skirt, pulled down her knickers and sat on the lavatory.

As a wave of tiredness washed through her she closed her eyes again and thought about bed. When all this was over she would sleep for a week – perhaps go to a hotel and live on room service. She liked this idea and her lips twitched with the beginnings of a grin. That would be the start of it. There'd be much more luxury and pampering to come, and who was to say she didn't deserve it? She started to dream about the pleasures ahead, when the money was in her hands and at her disposal.

'Hallo, you little slut.' The harsh voice shattered her fantasy. Linda opened her eyes and was looking straight up at Alan Apostle. She jammed her legs together and tucked herself forward into a protective position. He looked down at her with a leer she recognised – and the smell now made sense. 'Pull your pants up and get in here,' he said, turning his back and going into the living area. He sat down in an armchair and watched her through the open door as she sorted herself out.

Linda was speechless. She could say nothing; there was

nothing to say. If he was here, it meant only one thing. Investing all her effort in slow, deliberate movements which she hoped would conceal her shaking, she came out and stood some way from him at the edge of the living room. She studied him to see if anything was different, but the face and figure, like his smell, were as they had always been. The years apart had not lessened her disdain for him.

'Where is it?' He lit a cigarette and exhaled with his eyes looking towards the ceiling.

'I haven't got it, Alan, I swear. He didn't tell me where he'd hidden it. That's the whole sad truth – I trusted him so much I never bothered to ask.'

He puffed again on the cigarette and then inspected his fingernails, dirty, broken and chewed. When he spoke again she could hear the desperation in his voice, quiet but insistent. 'I'm not going to piss about, Linda. I'm in a lot of trouble and I need that money. Give it to me or I'm going to kill you.'

'You don't frighten me, Alan. You should know that by now. You never did. I mean, let's face it, what have you got that could frighten me?' Alan pulled out a large pistol from inside his jacket and pointed it at her head. 'Except that, of course. Now that does frighten me. It scares the shit out of me, actually, so why don't you just put it away and we'll talk this through?'

He didn't speak; he simply fired a shot in her direction. It was meant to miss and it did, but not by much. 'For fuck's sake!' she shouted. 'Have you gone completely bloody mental? Alan! Listen to me. I have not got the money. Shooting me isn't going to change that, OK? I'll be a poor dead cow instead of a poor live one, that's all.'

He scratched the underside of his chin with the end of the

pistol. 'Do you know how many times I've wanted to kill you?' he asked, his voice now quite different. 'You have no idea. Some nights I lie there and it's all I can think about. I imagine putting a gun in your mouth, or slitting your throat and all your blood spurting out on to my hand. I like that. It helps to calm me down.'

She was keen to keep him talking, in preference to shooting again. 'Why, Alan? Why do you hate me so much? I wasn't that bad, was I?'

'You don't understand. You never did. When you left me – one thousand, nine hundred and eighty-seven days ago – you didn't give me a backward glance, did you? It had all been a bit of a laugh and nothing more. So you don't know how it felt – how I felt – when you decided you'd had enough and just buggered off. I loved you, Linda, I really did. I would have done anything for you. But you didn't ask. You thought to yourself: "I'm bored", and away you went. That's not fair. That's not right.'

'So what do you want me to do about it?'

'What do I want you to do about it?' He said this as if he were really giving it a lot of consideration. 'Well, you could give me a blow job and tell me you're sorry and that you're coming back to me for good, but I expect that's asking a little bit too much. So, to answer your question, I'd like half the money – twelve point five million dollars.'

Linda decided that she must humour him; the gun was still aimed in her direction. 'If I had it, I'd gladly share it with you. You know that. But I don't. Simple as that.'

Again without warning he fired the gun; this time it was much closer and a large piece of plaster fell off the wall next to her. Her ears rang with the explosion. She stared at him incredulously, her mouth flapping open and shut like a startled goldfish. He didn't even appear to be aware of what he had done. 'I'm tired of this, Linda. Try telling the truth for a change – if you can remember how.'

'I thought you said you loved me,' she croaked. 'Funny way you have of showing it.'

'You're right. I did love you – past tense. Now you mean absolutely nothing to me.' Then he looked at her in a way which betrayed his last remark. 'What happened to your face?' he asked.

'I accepted a lift from a stranger.'

Alan suddenly snapped up from his chair and jumped across the room to where she stood. 'I've had it up to here with your smart-arsed remarks,' he said, pressing himself hard against her. His breath smelt of alcohol and cigarettes, which didn't surprise her.

'Point taken. So what do you want to do?'

He moved away from her. 'We've got a problem. I want the money, and you say you don't have it. You're a lying bitch – always have been – and there's no reason for me to start believing you now. So – what's to be done? I think we'll just sit here and see, shall we?' He walked back to his chair and settled into it, apparently prepared for a long wait. Then he looked at his watch. 'I've got a good idea. Every hour I'll shoot you. Say we start soon – at four o'clock – and then hourly after that until you tell me where the money is or . . . you die, I suppose. How does that sound?' He was smiling, as if it were a new playground game he'd invented.

'Alan, you're losing it. You really mean you're going to shoot

272

me because I don't know where the money is? What good will that do? For God's sake, Al, give it up.'

For the first time since she had come out of the bathroom Linda made a move towards him; as she started he fired the pistol downwards and the shot glanced the outside of her right calf, just above the ankle. She screamed at the sting of it and fell over, not from the impact but just from the shock of having been hit. She put her hand down to cover the wound as it began to bleed.

'You've got an hour to think about that,' he said flatly.

Jane woke up with the thrashing inside her head. At first she was unable to focus and saw only faint outlines but, as she blinked away the pain and fog, she eventually worked out that she was still in the house in Norbiton. She was lying on the dirty mattress she'd looked at earlier, and she was completely naked. She was not tied down in any way, but the bastard had done this to her, the worst thing he could have dreamt up. She shivered and her hands searched for sheets, blankets, a duvet, anything to cover her, but he'd obviously hidden them somewhere.

It all went through her mind, the whole horror of what he might have done, what he probably did do and what she would now have to deal with. She had no alternative but to cry, so total was her shame. He'd reduced her to this; it would ache badly for weeks, maybe months, as she tried to conquer the disgrace. She curled up foetally and bunched her fists tight, rubbing her knuckles into her face and smearing the tears across her mouth. Apart from her head nothing hurt; she conducted a mental audit of her body, focusing on each part to check if there was any

273

unusual sensation, and was only mildly reassured to find nothing obviously wrong.

After five minutes she forced herself to get up and look for her clothes. She found them, ripped to shreds, on the floor at the end of the bed. He had even broken the heels off her shoes. Her bag lay next to them, the contents spilled out like a punctured stomach. The car keys were gone, as were all her identification, her mobile phone and her purse. He had left only some make-up and other items worthless to him. Jane moved to the wardrobe and looked inside for some clothing, but it was completely empty.

Starting to sob again, she ran down the stairs in her search, looking for something that could help her – a phone, a blanket, whatever came to hand. She found the phone in the kitchen; it was dead. She looked in a tall kitchen cupboard, expecting to find a housecoat: a broom and an ironing board fell out on to her when she opened the door, but there was nothing else inside of any use. She ran out of the kitchen and up the stairs, this time to the bathroom where she looked behind the door. There was an old dressing gown hanging there and she ripped it from the hook. She put it on and wrapped it around her, the action seeming to steady her.

She drew in several deep breaths and then went downstairs and straight out of the house, barefoot but walking purposefully until she came to an all-night fried chicken shop on the main road. The man behind the counter hardly looked up when she came in.

'I'm a police officer and I need to use your phone,' she said sternly. This made him look up; when he'd appraised the situation he smiled and nodded his head.

'Yeah, right.' He went back to arranging portions of chicken in the display cabinet.

'I'm serious. You are now obstructing a police officer. Please show me where your phone is.'

'Show me your ID first,' he said, still unimpressed.

'I don't have it with me. It's been stolen. Look, please let me call the station. Or you can, I don't care which. But I have to get this sorted out.'

He was still smiling, unsure as to what to do next. Eventually he made up his mind. 'It's in the back,' he said, jerking his head. 'You'd better not be messing around.'

'Thanks,' Jane replied as she pushed through the gap in the counter and went to the phone.

After she had called the duty officer and explained her problem – which was greeted with much laughter and little sympathy – she called her answering machine and punched in the code to retrieve her messages. There was only one.

'Jane, it's Caroline Mercer. I've decided to come back to London. Linda Betts has turned up and there's a hell of a lot going on. Don't bother to come up here. I'll call you again soon.'

Jane felt too ill to worry about the message, and she sat, rocking and hugging herself in the back of the shop, as she tried to win some remission from her own discomfort.

TWENTY-SEVEN

The noise which woke her up didn't register with Caroline. She thought at first that it might be one of the boys, but she looked behind her and they were still asleep. She knew she'd woken up unnaturally, and whatever it was had surprised her because her heart was pumping too hard and her temples throbbed. She checked her watch: it was just gone five o'clock. The first reluctant light of dawn was starting to show itself; Caroline yawned expansively and rubbed her hands together.

It took a little time to sink in: where the hell was Linda? She must have been gone for a good hour at least. Caroline immediately rehearsed all the options. She could have found what she was looking for and decided to run off with it on her own; she might have got into the flat and crashed out on the bed; she might still be searching; or she could be in serious trouble. Caroline didn't know Linda well enough to be able to figure out which of these was most likely, and she felt so tired that she wasn't fit to find out. Her shoulders sagged at the thought of trudging up all those flights of stairs, but she steeled herself to the task. Having made sure the boys were dead to the world, she clambered out of the car and walked heavily up the steps to the front door of the house. She looked at the intercom and its

277

buttons: Flat 5 seemed to be the most likely, so she pressed that one. She waited a moment before buzzing again, this time for much longer.

She was about to try the others when she heard the electronic whirr of the door being unlocked remotely, and she leant her shoulder against it and went inside. In her weariness she let the door slam behind her. It was an empty, hollow sound that seemed to reverberate up and down the house; she wondered if anyone lived here apart from Linda. She turned on the hall light and began the long climb up the stairs, promising herself that, when all this was over, she'd join a health club and work out.

Her hands and face were glowing with perspiration when she finally pulled herself on to the landing in front of the door of Flat 5. She could see a little spyhole above the number on the door, so she positioned herself in front of it when she rang the bell. The door opened almost immediately; strangely, Linda was not standing there. No one was.

Caroline stepped in rather timidly and was immediately grabbed by her arm and pushed roughly through a tiny hallway towards the central living space. With her arm twisted in a half nelson she couldn't turn to see who was holding her, but she could see Linda. She was lying still on the floor, curled up so that her knees were pulled in towards her chest. Blood covered the carpet around her, and both her legs were injured. She had her eyes open but did not seem to see Caroline.

'What the—' she gasped. A hand was clamped over her mouth before she could say any more.

'Listen, bitch. You make another sound and I'll kill you. Ask Linda if you think I'm kidding.' Caroline looked into Linda's eyes but there was no emotion there, not even pain.

From behind, Alan shoved Caroline hard so that she careered towards an armchair. 'Sit.' Seeing him for the first time – and noticing the gun he was pointing at her – she did as she was told.

'Allow me to introduce myself,' he continued. 'I'm Alan Apostle. You probably don't remember me, but I used to work for your husband at AMS. I don't work there any more, of course – I got fired by the new management.'

'I'm sorry to hear that,' Caroline said, struggling to adjust to yet another crisis.

'Are you? Somehow I doubt it. Maybe you'll feel sorrier if I tell you what all this is about.'

'What a wonderful idea,' she replied. She looked across at Linda, who seemed to be drifting out of consciousness. 'But shouldn't we get her to a hospital first? Then we can have our chat.'

'Oh, don't worry about her. She's as hard as nails. She's had worse than this, I can tell you. Haven't you, my angel?' He leered at Linda as he said this, but there was no response from her.

Caroline's stomach was beginning to churn uncomfortably. Not only was she sickened by fear for herself, but she realised that the boys were now unprotected – sitting targets. She swallowed furiously to push back the rising nausea. 'What is it that you want?' she asked feebly.

'You should ask Linda that. She knows.' He looked over at her again. 'Doesn't seem to be up to much right now, though, so I'll fill in.' Alan leant against the door jamb and let the arm which held the gun drop to his side. He was panting, and he waited for this to subside before he began. 'Young Linda and I

were man and wife.' He wanted a reaction but Caroline showed
nothing. 'Yeah, that's right. We had a little house in Basildon.
Life was good, you know, we were both working so we had a bit
of money and I couldn't have been happier. Then one day, out
of the blue, she tells me she's leaving. Says she's had enough
and that's all there is to it. No discussion, no chance to reason
with her.'

'All this is very interesting, but what does it have to do with
me?'

'I'm getting to that. My life went down the toilet after that. I
couldn't hold down a proper job and I felt permanently sick.
When I did sleep I dreamt about Linda, bad dreams that made
me feel even worse. It took me a long time to get better, you
know. And then, about six months ago, things took a turn for
the better. I got a new job – office manager at AMS. And who
do you think I found on the first day there? Yes, Linda Apostle.
Except she wasn't calling herself Apostle any more, and she
wasn't too keen to let people know that we'd been married. Bit
of a bad shock for her, naturally, but I didn't want trouble any
more than she did. I probably would have agreed to some form
of armed neutrality, if you know what I mean. But Linda doesn't
like to leave things like that. She's very methodical, very
calculating, nothing's left to chance with her. So she comes to
me one evening and says we need to talk. Says she's got a
proposition that will make me very happy.'

Alan pinched his nose between his thumb and index finger.
'Some deal,' he said dreamily, as if he might fall asleep at any
moment. Then he seemed to remember where he was and he
straightened himself up. 'She wanted my guarantee of silence.
She said that if I agreed to it she'd pay me twenty thousand

pounds. I laughed when she said that – where the bloody hell would she get that kind of money from? She said she'd been careful and had saved up a lot, but I never believed that load of crap. I thought there was something odd going on. And then, when I saw them together, I knew.' He grinned at Caroline, a malicious look that showed he was enjoying the whole situation.

'Are we getting near the end?'

'You must have known. You can't ignore something like that. Your husband and her, couldn't keep their hands off each other. They thought they were being discreet, but I saw everything. It was obvious – she wanted my silence because she thought he was going to marry her, and she didn't want me putting my oar in and screwing it up. Can you imagine that, Mrs Mercer? Our Linda can be pretty bloody stupid.'

Caroline was frightened, puzzled, tired and sick, but she knew she had to hang on. 'Look, I'm terribly sorry, but I know all this and it's rather tedious to have to hear it again. Whatever your problem is with Linda, I'm sure you'll be able to sort it out between you. But I really have to leave.' She made the slightest movement forward in her chair; Alan snapped the gun up from his side and pointed it at her face. She froze.

'You just don't understand. You see, I'm over the worst part. I'm in recovery, as they say. Now all I want is the money – not the pissing twenty thousand, but twelve and a half million dollars. My price for silence and a quiet life. Now that can't be bad, can it, considering the alternative? Isn't that a good deal?'

Caroline thought about this, thought about the boys in the car and their little lives hardly even begun, thought of Linda and what she'd been put through, thought of her own misery and hardships. The formula seemed difficult to crack, so she played for time. 'If we had any of the money, and if we were to agree to give you some, what guarantee would we have that you wouldn't continue to pester us?'

'I don't think you're seeing it from the right end,' Alan replied. 'You should be asking yourself what'll happen if you don't give me half.' He jerked the gun up a little to remind her of what he might do. But, behind all the bluster and the threats, she could discern his own insecurities, the shortcomings and failures that had led him to this point. And, even more importantly, she knew that he hadn't found Linda's money either. With a gun pointed at her head, this gave Caroline a very small degree of comfort, but it was something to work on. Every so often she shot a discreet look at the suitcases on the floor, the ones that Guy had hinted were so valuable. Then she would glance across to Linda, who was neither awake nor unconscious – she simply lay on the floor and gasped without showing any other signs of life. Caroline winced at the very thought of her pain.

Alan's face screwed up and his dark, broken teeth appeared as he twisted his mouth. Caroline thought that he might have been about to burst into tears; instead, he screamed, a hoarse roar that jolted Linda back into full consciousness and pinned Caroline against her chair. It went on for a long time, until his lungs had no more air to expel and he stopped, snorting heavily. He had enjoyed that, Caroline could see: he had rid himself of a lot of frustration and tension. She hoped he would be calmer now, more reasonable.

'Alan,' she said as softly as she could manage. 'Alan, please let's get Linda to a hospital. She doesn't look at all well.'

He looked towards Caroline but not directly at her. He was

beginning to seem detached from the whole scene. 'Linda,' he said, as if he were trying the word out for the first time. He nodded but didn't continue.

'Come on, help me get her up,' Caroline said, and she rose from her seat. She was moving towards Linda when Alan fired the gun; Caroline, knees buckling, fell instantly to the floor and landed on her front. She covered her head with her arms and clamped her eyes shut, but she couldn't feel any specific pain.

'Stay there now,' Alan barked. 'It'll be much better for both of you.'

Caroline hadn't been hit, but the lack of injury didn't make her any keener to get to her feet. She took his advice.

Hugh was uncomfortable and he needed to pee. George was fast asleep, and he looked at him with all the disdain of the senior sibling. He had to slide through the gap between the front seats because his door was child-locked; he got out of the driver's door and looked up and down the street in the dawn gloom. No one about: he leant in towards the car and unzipped his trousers, fumbling to free himself before the gushing torrent erupted. He sighed and shivered with huge relief, smiling at the wonderful release.

The explosion made him jump so much that he sprayed the car door, his shoes and his trousers before he regained control. 'Jesus!' he shouted. It was a loud report, not one he'd heard before although he reckoned it wasn't a bomb – too short for that, and so near that he would have seen or felt the blast. It had come from above and behind him and he looked up towards the top of the house, but he could see nothing.

Having zipped himself up again, he connected the two things

– a big bang and the absence of his mother and Linda – and thought the worst. He put his hands on the side of the car and rested his weight against them, starting to turn over the possibilities. 'Think, you little worm,' he said out loud. He wanted to do something but he wasn't sure what it should be. He smacked the side of his face, repeating the word 'Think!' over and over.

Inevitably, if slowly, Hugh came to the conclusion that he should call the police. He didn't want to do this: it seemed too dull, too unheroic, but he accepted his own limitations and vowed to give them as much detail as he could. He looked up and down the road once more to spot a phone box, and saw the light of one glowing about fifty yards away. He opened the driver's door and peered in; George hadn't stirred. Locking it again, he sprinted to the box.

Jane stood in the shower for fifteen minutes. She rubbed soap over her body and rinsed it off before starting again, hoping that the monotonous routine would eventually erase the memory of what had occurred. Her revulsion was irrational, she knew: he had not violated her, probably hadn't even touched her, but she had been at his mercy, had been as vulnerable as she would ever be, and that hurt. She couldn't handle the shaming process he had put her through. He knew that, of course. That's why he'd done it.

She wrapped herself tightly in a thick clean bathrobe and went to the kitchen to get her coffee from the percolator. The digital clock on the oven flashed the time at her: five-thirty in the morning. She needed to be at work in three hours – could she recover, or should she phone in sick? Face it now or face it later?

In the corner of her eye she spotted the dressing gown she had taken from Alan Apostle's house; it was tossed over the back of a chair. She went over and picked it up, planning to bundle it into a black bag and dump it somewhere. As she carried it to the kitchen a small slip of yellow paper dropped out of one pocket. She stopped and scooped it up, about to crumple it when something told her not to. She read it.

47 Camberwell Park Road

That was all there was, but it was enough for her. Jane got dressed and had left the flat within five minutes.

285

TWENTY-EIGHT

He knelt down so that his legs straddled Caroline's back. She could smell him, the sharp odour overpowering all her other senses: it was the stench of a man whose life was rotting in front of his very eyes. She felt the cold hard tip of the gun barrel being pressed against the back of her neck.

'It's five to six and Linda and I have a date,' Alan whispered. 'Unless you'd like to take over, that is.'

'I don't understand,' Caroline moaned.

'Didn't I explain? How thoughtless of me. You see, I know Linda wants to tell me where the money is, but she needs to be persuaded. She's always been like that, you know – a bit of a tease. So every hour I'm helping her to remember the information – with this.' He snapped the gun so that it jerked against her skin.

Caroline swallowed, although the saliva didn't want to go down. 'Can we do a deal?' she said quietly.

'A deal? Like the one that bitch offered me, you mean? No way.'

'No – a proper deal. I will give you everything I have, all the money Guy left, if you'll promise to leave us alone for good.' She seemed to have to wait a long time for an answer.

'In three minutes' time I'm going to shoot her in the thigh,' he replied, apparently oblivious to her proposal.

'For God's sake, listen to me – please. I'm offering you everything I've got. It isn't all the money, I admit, but it's all there is. Isn't that enough?'

'You're trying to waste my time, Mrs Mercer. I don't appreciate that, but I'll try not to hold it against you. Now, shall I shoot you or her? It's your choice.'

He lay forward so that his mouth was next to her ear. She heard the rattling of his lungs as he breathed, mucus-filled tubes struggling to regulate the airflow. She couldn't believe she hadn't yet vomited. 'Don't do this, Alan.'

He began to laugh, a small crackling laugh with no real voice, and she could feel him shaking on top of her. 'That's funny,' he said. 'That's what your husband said – his exact words. "Don't do this, Alan." I can hear him now.'

Caroline tried to raise her head. 'What do you mean?'

He stopped laughing. 'Hasn't Linda told you? Well, well, what a surprise. I'd have thought she'd want everyone to know – especially you.'

'Know what?'

'His hand. Yeah, when I cut it, that's just what he said. You see, I had to do it. He had the case attached to his wrist, and I reckoned the money was in there. It wasn't though. I went to all that trouble for nothing. There was nothing in there – well, nothing valuable, anyway. I needn't have bothered after all.'

Caroline whimpered and tried to say something.

'Shh,' he blew into her ear. 'It's time.' He got up off her and took three paces back. 'So, Mrs M., what's it to be? Decision time.'

Caroline ground her teeth together and dug her nails into her palms. That he was serious was not in dispute, and she couldn't think of a single way to divert him.

'Me,' she said firmly. 'Shoot me.'

'Have you released the handbrake?' Jane shouted.

'You can always walk,' the taxi driver replied.

'It'd be quicker – no, just joking. But can't you step on it? I'm a copper, so you won't get nicked.'

'They all say that. You just sit back and relax, young lady. We'll be there soon enough.'

She hoped and prayed that he was right.

Hugh was too excited not to wake his brother, and now they were both standing on the pavement waiting for the police to arrive. His phone conversation had been tough: they didn't seem to believe him at first, and asked him a lot of questions about himself before they showed any interest in the incident he was reporting. Eventually he had managed to convince them that he was serious and that he wasn't playing silly buggers.

The first car to arrive came silently to the kerb; it was disappointing because there were no lights or sirens and it didn't go very fast. Two police officers got out and came up to the boys. 'Which one of you is Hugh Mercer?' one asked.

Hugh stepped forward and put up his hand. 'Me, sir.'

'OK, son, tell me what's going on.'

'I heard a big explosion coming from up there,' he said, pointing towards the top of the house. 'I think my mum and a friend of hers may be in there. They've been gone an awfully long time and they didn't say where they would be.'

Two more police cars arrived, and George was taken off to sit in one of these. Hugh felt more important because he was kept outside. 'Do you know why they might be in trouble?' he was asked.

'Well, not exactly, but Mum's had some big problems recently and it's all to do with my dad dying. I think it's got something to do with money.'

'OK. You've been very helpful, son. Now we'll see what we can do to sort this out. Why don't you come and sit in our car and get yourself warmed up? Don't worry, your mum'll be fine, I promise.'

Somewhat reluctantly, Hugh did as he was told. He was asked some more questions, and he listened as the messages on the radio bounced back and forth – heard them mention 'possible hostage situation' and 'armed units' – and wondered if his mum was safe. He didn't want to cry, especially not here and now, but he felt pretty miserable. Everything had collapsed since Dad had died; he just wanted to have him back and feel himself engulfed in one of his huge hugs.

At precisely six o'clock, Alan Apostle raised his arm and pointed the gun at Caroline Mercer. She still lay prone on the floor next to Linda, who had long since faded into unconsciousness. Caroline tensed every muscle in her body and winced, waiting for the bullet to rip into her flesh. Holding her breath so tightly that she was becoming light-headed, she started when the first noise she heard was not the explosion of the gun, but the doorbell.

'Shit!' Alan shouted. 'Who the . . .?' He ducked down and scrambled over to the window, pushing his head up just enough so that he could see down. He immediately ducked again and turned so that he was crouching with his back to the wall. Caroline allowed herself to breathe out, but nothing more. 'Change of plan,' he said abruptly. 'Get up. And stay away from the window.' Taking more effort than she might have expected, Caroline got to her feet. Her legs were shaking and her bowels and bladder were close to violent eruption.

'What now?' she asked.

'Time to say bye-bye. I don't need you any more.'

'What do you mean?'

'I mean there's a load of police downstairs and I have some serious problems to deal with and you're getting in my way.' He was getting louder and more frantic; when the bell rang again, long and insistent, his face twitched and Caroline could see sweat beginning to run down his forehead. 'So get out of here – *now*!'

Caroline looked across once more at Linda, a fragile figure whose skin was now almost pellucid. 'What are you going to do with her?' she asked. 'You must let her go or she'll die. I'll stay and she can go.'

'You didn't hear me. I told you to leave.' He stepped towards her and pushed the gun into her ribs. Caroline put her hands up in front of her.

'OK, I'm going. What shall I tell them?'

He seemed defeated by this question, and his shoulders sagged. 'What the fuck do I care? It's nearly over, anyway.'

She sensed his deflation and tried to use it. 'Why don't you come with me? Then everything will be sorted out and we can get Linda looked after. Isn't that what you want?'

Instead of agreeing, Alan stiffened and his face contorted. 'I'm not coming out without the money,' he hissed. 'That's all there is to it, see?' Using the gun he pushed her to the door. 'Get out.'

She opened it and sighed. There was no point asking for a change of heart. He was determined to see it through to the end, whatever it was he had planned. She stepped on to the landing and the door slammed behind her.

'What's the story?' Jane had jumped out of the cab at the far end of the road and had sprinted the rest of the way. She was blowing hard and her shins ached. She stood outside the house with a uniformed policeman in a bulletproof vest.

'We think there are two hostages, both female. We've seen one man's face briefly at the window, after we rang the bell. No other contact's been made. There's no phone in the flat, and it's the only one that's occupied. There have been reports of gunfire, although we haven't heard anything since we arrived.'

'OK. Let me tell you what I think is going on. The man in there is Alan Apostle. The flat is being rented by Linda Betts, his ex-wife. They aren't on very good terms, to put it mildly. I want to question Apostle about a murder that happened earlier this year. I went round to his house last night and he attacked me before escaping. I think he's holed up in there with Linda.'

'We think there's another woman. A young lad – Hugh Mercer – called us to say he thought there was a problem. He and his brother were left in a car on their own. We think their mother is up there too.'

'Oh shit,' Jane said. 'What the hell is she doing there?'

'Don't know, but the boys are safe and well. We've taken them off to the station. Look, how well do you know this guy Apostle?'

'He gives me the creeps, to be honest. I know him, and I know what he's capable of. I don't think I'd be able to talk him down from there, if that's what you're getting at.'

'Just a thought. We're bringing in a negotiator anyway, but God knows how we're going to communicate – probably through the bloody entryphone.'

As he was finishing speaking there was a commotion ahead of them, closer to the building. Jane looked across and could see the front door opening; she was also aware, in her peripheral vision, of a number of lethal weapons being pointed directly at it. Then, before anyone could see who was opening the door, they heard a voice shouting.

'My name is Caroline Mercer and I've been released. I'm unarmed and I'm coming out with my hands up.'

Jane marvelled at her composure. Most hostages would have been so happy to be free that they would have run out without thinking – not Caroline. She'd worked the whole thing out and wasn't especially keen on being riddled with bullets in an unfortunate case of mistaken identity.

Caroline came out slowly, arms raised as promised, and walked down the steps where she was greeted by two officers. Jane wanted to go over to her but hung back. She watched as Caroline was wrapped in a thermal blanket and given a drink, and she heard her say: 'Where are my boys? Are they all right? Where are they?'

Once they had successfully convinced her that Hugh and George were safe and well, she was ushered back to a police car. Jane came and leant in the window. 'Sorry,' she said. 'I was too late.'

'No, it's my own silly fault,' Caroline replied. 'I should

never have let Linda talk me into it.'

'Is she still up there?' Caroline nodded grimly. 'Not in good shape, huh? What's the damage?'

'I don't know, Jane. It looks as if she's been shot in both legs, and she's unconscious. He's a madman, completely off his trolley. He was going to shoot me next, and I don't think he was joking. God knows what he'll do to her now. You have got to get in there.'

'Or get him out. We're working on it. You should go and get your boys.'

'Yes. Although I expect they think this is such a lark that they won't want me to come and spoil it all.'

Jane was wondering when it would happen, and it turned out to be right at that very moment. Caroline took one huge sob and then fat tears rolled down her cheeks. She shook her head to show how abnormal this was and that it should be ignored, but Jane put her hand on her shoulder and rubbed it.

'We've got him,' someone shouted. 'On the intercom.'

Jane looked up to see what was going on. 'Caroline, I have to go. I'll catch up with you as soon as I can.' Caroline nodded briefly and continued to weep.

'This is a private matter,' Alan said into the receiver. 'You don't have to be involved.'

'I know how you feel, Alan – it is Alan, isn't it? – but you see we are very concerned about Linda. We think she might be quite badly hurt and we'd like to get her to hospital as soon as possible. You don't want her to suffer any more, do you?'

Alan was leaning against the front door of the flat. He had lifted Linda from the floor and moved her to the sofa, partly because he thought she'd be more comfortable but also because he needed to keep an eye on her and the sofa was simpler to move around. He had dragged it all the way across the room so that it was no more than six feet from where he stood. He looked at her on it now and wondered if she was really as poorly as she was making out. She could fake anything, the little bitch, up to and including death.

His thoughts returned to the conversation. 'Look, you're not going to soft-soap me with any of that compassion bullshit. Maybe it works on some of the loonies you have to deal with, but I'm different. There's nothing wrong with me, you hear? And there's nothing wrong with Linda either. I can take care of her.'

'That's good to hear, Alan. May I talk to her?'

'No you may not. I know your game. You just leave her out of this.'

'OK, no problem. But listen, Alan, whatever it is you want, couldn't we sort that out separately? You don't have to involve Linda any more, do you? Send her down and then we can talk about what you need.'

'That's it. Conversation's over. You're just insulting my intelligence by saying such a bloody stupid thing.' Alan crashed the receiver back on to the wall cradle and slid down the door until he was sitting on the floor, his knees drawn up in front of his chest. 'Got any ciggies, babe?' he asked Linda. 'I've run out.'

There was no movement from Linda. She lay on her side, one arm hanging awkwardly over the edge of the sofa with her hand splayed and drooping like a broken wing. She breathed irregularly and the noise of it disturbed him.

'Linda, cut it out,' he snapped. 'Come on, stop fooling around, for Christ's sake. This has gone far enough.' He crawled over to the sofa and put his face right next to hers: she was cold and very clammy and he knew at once that this was not an act. 'Linda,' he said directly into her ear, 'Linda, babe, come on. Don't do this. Don't do it, please.' He put one arm over her and rocked her gently as if the motion might revive her.

He stayed like that for several minutes, trying to infuse her with his body warmth as he moaned under his breath. He thought of how they had been, how happy his life was when he was with her, and how much he wanted things to be the same again. He remembered them as a young couple, going out on the razzle together and having so much fun, and then the past disappeared and he was a sad, lonely man with no one and nothing and it was all her fault and she had to be punished. When he closed his eyes he could see throbbing red blotches and he wanted to sleep, but he knew he had to resolve this problem first.

The buzzer went off again. At first he ignored it, squeezing his eyes tighter and listening to Linda's breathing, but it kept on going and he had no choice but to get up and answer it.

'What?' he shouted into the receiver.

'Alan, is everything all right? Do you want to talk?'

'No, no, just leave us alone. I've got some things to do. Just bugger off, OK?' He dropped the receiver so that it was hanging by its cord and, gasping now as if every movement was an incredible effort, he went back to the sofa and kissed Linda on the forehead, lightly and tenderly, and then stroked her hair.

He leant down so that he was very close to her face as he spoke. 'I'm so sorry, babe. But this is the only way out. It has to be. I didn't mean to do this. I just got so bloody confused. Forgive me, won't you? I'll always love you, you know that.' He kissed her again on the cheek and moved away to get the gun, which he had left on the hall floor.

He picked it up and held it as if for the first time, testing its weight and feel. He could hear a distant voice calling from the entryphone – 'Alan! Alan!' – but it was too vague to disturb him. When he was satisfied with the gun, he raised his arm and cocked his wrist so that the barrel was pointing towards the ceiling. Then he brought it down to a level position and looked over it at Linda. 'Goodbye,' he said.

They heard the gunshot loud and clear. It was amplified through speakers connected to the intercom, but they didn't need them to know what had happened. There was a collective flinch as it rang out around them, and Jane shook her head and closed her eyes.

The negotiator kept on calling Alan's name into his microphone, but there was no reply; there was no noise at all from the flat. Outside it was equally still as the assembled officers and experts tried to imagine what was up there and how best to deal with it. They put their failure to one side as they each considered the merits of alternative actions, none of them certain they could avert more tragedy.

They were starting to re-form in new groups, with new plans, when the negotiator put his hand up to demand renewed silence. He pushed his earpiece hard into his ear and strained to listen for activity; all eyes were on him. They waited, too anxious even to breathe, whilst he tuned himself into the room noise of Flat 5.

On the speakers near to Jane there was nothing, no sound of

anything but death. Then there was a crackle, like a hard object being banged erratically against the receiver's mouthpiece. People leant forward to hear it more clearly, but it disappeared, to be replaced by a rasping rattle: Jane couldn't be sure, but it seemed to be someone breathing into the receiver. Every fibre in her body shrank into cramps as she listened.

A weak, distressed message finally broke through. 'It's over.' The voice, though shattered, was unmistakably a woman's.

TWENTY-NINE

Caroline put the drink to her lips, winked at Jane over the top of the glass and took a sip. 'Mother's ruin,' she said wickedly, 'but then, I've already been ruined, so who cares?'

Jane had declined the offer of a gin and tonic, and took tea instead. She wanted to keep her head clear, at least until she was off duty: there was still a lot to do and say and she didn't want to be diverted. She looked around the room – the shelves with their pictures of a happy family, the mementoes, the little ornaments they'd given to each other – and tried to comprehend the depth of pain that Guy's death must have caused. Caroline hid it well – too well, maybe – but it was in her face, her every movement and mannerism. She was hurt almost beyond cure, even if she'd never admit it.

There was still a large contingent of investigators at Flat 5. The final gunshot had deposited the major part of Alan Apostle's cranium and brain on to the ceiling and, after they photographed it for posterity, someone had to scrape it off. Having made a superhuman effort to reach the entryphone, Linda had collapsed across the bottom of the front door and the first officer had to squeeze in through a very narrow gap. She was unconscious again and they raced her to hospital.

Jane had helped to supervise all the activity, and had made some private notes for herself, things that she might later use to her advantage. She'd also overseen the lads as they started to bag things up for further examination back at the lab, stopping them now and then to inspect the goods before they were sealed. When she was happy that everything was under control, she left and went straight over to Castelnau to see Caroline.

'So how are the boys?' she began.

'Fit as fiddles. They'll be dreadful tonight, but I'm trying not to think about that.'

'And what about the house?'

'I'm guessing that it was Christian Lemmerich who broke in. Nothing's been taken, nothing at all, just a bit of mindless vandalism. I've been burgled before, so I can deal with this.' Caroline sipped again at the tall glass.

'What do you know about Lemmerich?'

Caroline shrugged. 'Nothing much. What do you know?'

'Not much more than you. He's part of the investor group connected to AMS. But I still can't work out why he came after you, and why he kidnapped Linda. I was hoping you could fill me in on that.'

So close to success this was no time to come clean, so Caroline deflected the question. 'What will happen to him?'

'Linda doesn't want to press charges, but we can have him for what he did to you – as long as you're prepared to cooperate.'

'I'd be very keen to see him locked up for a long time. Don't worry, I'll help.'

'Come on, Caroline, you have to tell me. I know there's something you're holding back. I've always had the feeling that you were frightened of something, and you were right. What did you know?'

'We've been here before. Guy was murdered and that was enough to scare the pants off me. It's as simple as that.' Caroline was getting good at lying, much as it went against her code, but there was a reward that was worth it.

Jane knew that further questions would be fruitless and, with her own dilemmas to address, she felt that this was a line which should be dropped. 'OK then, let's talk about what else has happened.'

'You've worked it out?' Caroline needed to hear it from a recognised authority.

'Pretty much. The question is, how much do you want to know?'

Caroline put her drink down on the coffee table. 'That day, when I came home from the Cotswolds and you and your boss were here waiting to tell me that Guy had been murdered, I wanted to die too. I wanted to give up. I didn't want to find out what had happened. I knew it was going to be ghastly, and all sorts of things would come out and upset me even more, and I didn't think I had the strength to deal with them. But I have. These past few months I've been to hell and back and I'm still smiling – just. I've learnt a lot about Guy but, more importantly, I've learnt a lot about myself. I know what I'm capable of. Very few people get that chance. Very few of us are ever put to the test like I've been. It's different for you, of course, because you're always facing life-or-death situations. I have been – and it's made me a lot stronger. So, to answer your question – I must know everything.'

'Fair enough,' Jane replied. 'You know that Guy was big in

what is technically known as defalcation – taking other people's money, to put it bluntly. He'd been running a little scheme which I think was designed to test his theories, siphoning off small sums from just one client – his own shareholder, Investment Logistics. Effectively, he made sure they always got some income from their trades, but kept the major part for himself – way above the going market commission for his firm's role in the deals. He must have known right from the start that the money they were putting through AMS was hot – very hot. I don't know whether it's drug money or Mafia cash or what it is but, believe me, it's so hot it's molten. That's why they liked AMS so much. What Guy was doing was putting their hot cash into the repo market, where it became anonymous. Deals of twenty-five million dollars aren't at all unusual, and no one asks who is behind them. There's no requirement to report them to the regulators, so they are the perfect channel for laundering frauds.

'Knowing that this was what they were up to, Guy could see that he might be able to slice off a little bit of their wealth without their being able to do anything about it. The little deals he did at first were just markers – and, if they went wrong, he could always blame one of the traders or say it was an administrative screw-up. But, when they went right, he decided to go for the big one.'

'And how did Linda fit into all this?'

'He needed her to help him process the deals. Peter Verity had set up some pretty tight controls and no one person was allowed to do everything – there had to be signs-offs by more than one manager for a deal to be processed. With Linda on his side, Guy could achieve whatever he wanted. And she also knew how to set up dummy accounts on the mainframe and where to

302

send the money so that it couldn't be found, as well as leaving a false audit trail which led everyone off the scent.'

'You sound as if you've done your homework on this. I'm impressed.'

'Well, to be honest, Peter Verity himself helped me a lot. After he was fired he came to see me and gave a stack of documents and a very detailed explanation of what had been going on. That's mainly what I've used to understand the financial side of it.'

'And what's happened to Peter, by the way?' Caroline asked innocently.

Jane sighed, no longer surprised but still disappointed by the way in which Grass had manipulated the facts. 'I thought you would have heard. He was attacked and killed on Wimbledon Common.'

Caroline looked horrified. 'Why would anyone want to kill him? He was such an inoffensive little man.'

'This is all off the record, Caroline. Originally, Peter's murder was not going to be linked to the investigation. It was just viewed as a bizarre coincidence – and probably would have remained so if nothing else had been uncovered. Now, of course, we'll be paying more attention to it. But, at the time, no one was particularly keen to look for ulterior motives.'

'Meaning?'

'Meaning his murder was all part of a much larger web of deceit – a huge cover-up.'

Caroline shook her head in astonishment. 'Go on.'

'This is where it starts getting complicated. Your husband is murdered and someone's cut his hand off. Apparently he's on his way to the airport to fly to Nice and meet up with Linda.

303

Someone knows about this and intercepts him. It was my theory
that Christian Lemmerich, or one of his henchmen, had killed
him. They'd discovered his fraud and were making him pay.
The hand, I thought, was either some obscure Mafia sign or,
more likely, because he'd had a briefcase chained to his wrist
and they wanted what was inside it.'

'You were right, in a way,' Caroline said. 'Alan told me
that's what happened.' Then she winced and inhaled deeply.
'I'm OK,' she said, putting one hand up. 'But I think I'll have
another drink.' She fetched one and rearranged herself on the
sofa.

'But I was wrong about who did it,' Jane continued.
'Lemmerich and his people didn't have anything to do with
Guy's murder. They only got involved once they found out about
his scam – and, by that time, he was already dead. This is where
it starts getting complicated.'

'It already is, if you ask me.'

'They killed Mira, I'm sure of that. We know there was a
device fitted to the car, and I can't believe Alan Apostle was
clever enough to do that. What I don't know is whether they
meant it for Mira or for you. But they were very rattled by Guy's
death. They got very nervous – not, I don't think, about the
money, but more about the fact that it would all come out and
they'd be implicated. Fortunately for them, they had an ally
right where they needed him.'

'What do you mean?'

'My former boss, Gerry Grass. He was on the take from them.
Had been for years. When this came up they simply told him to
find a suspect and charge him, and forget all about the financial
side of the investigation. Losing the money was painful for them,

304

but it was of secondary importance. You know the self-storage unit you went to? Gerry insisted on going there himself to search it. I think he was sent there by Lemmerich to clean it up and remove all traces of their involvement with AMS.

'Gerry wasn't stupid – he knew which side his bread was buttered on, so he agreed to all their demands – even to the extent of getting Anthony Tilt arrested.'

'Anthony's been arrested?' Caroline cried out. 'What the hell for?'

'Don't worry. He's going to be released, after everything else that's happened. But Grass aimed the whole investigation at getting Tilt. That's what he was being paid to do.'

'If you know all this, why haven't you done something with it?'

'The problem, Caroline, is that I'm not the only one who knows. Gerry's boss knew, but turned a blind eye. Gerry was a good detective and it didn't seem to matter that he was accepting bribes now and again, especially from a group of people who didn't cause much trouble in the first place.'

'You're saying they condoned it?'

'Pretty much. But Gerry knew that his police career had come to an end, so he opted for early retirement. He'd accumulated a big pile of cash over the years and he'd bought himself a villa in Spain. I know that because I took a call from his estate agents – that's what first set me thinking about him and the case.'

'Did you ever confront him about it?'

'Oh yes. In fact I really lost my temper and gave him a bit of a going-over. But he wasn't in the least bit contrite – he told me what had been going on and pretty much dared me to try and take it any further.'

305

'Will you?'

'As soon as I'm finished here. But I have one more thing to tell you, and that's the worst part. I don't know how, but Alan Apostle got wind of what was going on between Guy and Linda. He latched on to that and wouldn't leave her alone. I know he went round to her flat once, after she was back from Corsica, and beat her up. He admitted that to me when I first went round to his house. But he said he'd just been drunk and the whole thing was a big mistake, nothing for me to be interested in. In fact, he'd been round to see her because he thought she had all the money. And the reason he thought that was because—'

'Was because he'd already been to see Guy and found nothing.' Caroline spoke quietly, finishing the sentence without any evident emotion. 'He killed Guy, didn't he?'

'Yes. He went round there on the Saturday night and confronted him. Guy would have let him in because he knew him very well. Alan obviously told him that he knew everything and that he was determined not to let them get away with it unless he had his share. Unfortunately, Guy refused and . . . well, we know the rest.'

There was a pause while they both struggled with private anguish. The only noise in the room was the clinking of ice in Caroline's glass as she drained it. Her eyes had reddened but there were no tears. 'So what happens now?'

'I have to try and put all this information together into a coherent package. Linda's going to help me, I hope.' Jane left the implicit message – that she'd like Caroline's help too – hanging in the air, but to no avail.

'How is she? God, I haven't even asked after her yet.'

'That's hardly surprising, with everything you've been

through. The doctors say she'll be fine, but she's not likely to be running in the next Olympics. Either Alan knew exactly what he was doing with the gun, or he didn't have a clue, because both shots failed to hit anything too serious. She lost a lot of blood, but she'll recover.'

'I must go and see her.'

'I think she'd appreciate that.'

'She knew about Alan, didn't she?'

'I can't say for sure, but I think she must have suspected he was responsible. It must have torn her apart.'

'I'll have to try and find it in my heart to forgive her. She did try to tell me but never got a chance. Anyway, it wouldn't have made any difference if I had known.' Caroline shrugged and rolled her eyes.

'There's one big unanswered question in all this, Caroline.'

'What's that?'

Jane had to smile. 'You're good, I'll give you that. There's twenty-five million dollars unaccounted for.'

Caroline's face was blank and inert. 'You're asking me about that? Don't you think, after all this, that I'd have told you if I knew where it was?'

'I've thought about that a lot. It's a big number. Greed makes people behave in very strange ways – I've seen the consequences of that often enough to know. What I can't be sure about is you.'

Caroline took this in before replying. 'Tell me something,' she said. 'Has that money ever been reported as missing?'

It was precisely the question Jane didn't want her to ask. 'No,' she replied quietly.

'I see. So what's your interest in it?'

'Oh, come on, credit me with some intelligence. I'm a detective, and it's my job to worry about things like that. That isn't an insignificant amount of cash, after all.'

'So you're formally investigating it?'

This was all too sharp; Caroline had obviously thought it through very carefully. 'Not as such. But we may get round to it.'

'And I'm sure you'll let me know if and when you do. But I won't be much help to you, I'm afraid. Guy's business dealings were a complete mystery to me.' She gave a beaming smile to Jane, who could not help but admire her poise. 'So is that it?'

'Yes, that's it. Unless you have any more questions – or, better still, answers.'

'Just one. What will you do now?'

'I have to say that I'm pretty disenchanted at the moment. All my life I've wanted to be a detective, and now this has shattered most of my illusions. We all know there are bad apples in the force but we're always told they'll be mercilessly rooted out. That seems pretty hard to believe right now. But I'll probably get over it. It's not the end of the world, and there are – or there should be – more important things in life. I'll survive – but thanks for asking.'

When they got up Caroline hugged Jane very tightly. 'You're a saint, you know that?' she said. 'And I wish you all the luck in the world.'

'And me to you,' Jane replied. 'We both deserve a bit of good fortune, don't we?'

'Too right we do.'

Linda's bedding was arranged over a frame so that it did not touch her legs. Without make-up her face was so pale it seemed bloodless, highlighting the bruises from Lemmerich's battering. She blinked incessantly, as if trying to dispel fearsome images.

Caroline held her hand and squeezed it gently. 'Jane Fox has told me everything,' she said.

'Everything she knows,' Linda replied. Weak as she was, there was still a spark of defiance in her voice. 'Did you do the same?'

'Funny you should ask that. The problem is, I'm not sure what I know.'

Linda puffed through her nose. 'Between the two of us, we've got the whole story. Or as much of it as really matters.'

'I suppose so.'

Linda turned her head on the pillow to face Caroline. 'Why did you come?'

'To see how you were.'

'Nothing else?'

'Everything else can wait, Linda. We're going to have a lot of time to sort all this out.'

'I don't understand you. Your life's been shot to pieces, and one way or another most of the worst stuff has come from my direction. You have every right to be very angry.'

'I know,' Caroline said. 'And don't mistake my diffidence for unquestioning compassion. I'm just too tired for anything else at the moment.'

'Perhaps you need a holiday. It could be arranged, you know. As soon as I can walk I'm getting out of here, and I'm going to take a trip. You might want to come with me.'

'I'm not sure I follow you.'

Linda raised one hand weakly and motioned towards the

stand next to her bed. 'In the top drawer,' she said. Caroline looked puzzled; she pulled open the drawer and looked inside. There was a folded slip of paper. 'Read it,' Linda ordered. Caroline picked it up and unfolded it. On one corner there was a bloody thumbprint; the centre was taken up with two simple lines of typed information:

UNION BANK OF SWITZERLAND,
LUGANO MAIN BRANCH 332.067.17.19

'What is this?' Caroline asked.

Linda smiled. 'You don't know much, do you? It's the keys to the kingdom, Mrs Mercer. It's your inheritance – and mine.'

'The money?'

'Got it in one. It's what I found in the suitcase. Guy left it there. It's the classic numbered bank account.'

'But how . . .?'

'It was on my mind, all the time we were there with Alan. I didn't have a chance to look before he caught me, but once he'd shot himself, I didn't have any distractions.'

'You mean you . . . I thought you were half dead.'

'So did I, but it's amazing what you can do when you need to. I managed to crawl over to the suitcase. It was tucked into one of those zipper compartments on the side. I always wondered what they were for. I got it and stuffed it down my knickers.'

Caroline shook her head in awe; this girl had strength in depth. 'So what do you plan to do with this?' she asked, waving the piece of paper.

'We're going to Lugano. I have no idea what the procedure

is, or what Guy had set up. We'll both need to be there, just in case.'

'I need to think about it,' Caroline said. 'It isn't as simple as that.'

'It is for me. The thinking can wait. For now, I just want to get that money and deal with the implications later.'

'Perhaps. It seems to me, though, that this is a pretty good time to appraise what's happened – for you and me.'

'I've been through that already,' Linda said, her voice fading.

'And what conclusions did you draw?'

'Nothing very profound, I'm afraid. But then that'll be on my tombstone.' Linda's eyes started to close.

'You're tired. I'll come back and see you again when you're stronger.'

'Bring your passport,' Linda replied weakly.

Caroline patted her hand. 'It's an option I'll bear in mind,' she said.

She took the boys with her and drove straight to Anthony's flat. He was weak and pale, thinner than she'd ever seen him and obviously in the last phase of shock, but he smiled when he saw her and he was nice to the boys, and he sounded enthusiastic when she suggested they go to Hampstead. On the way, as the boys fought over their Game Boys in the back, she gave him a précis of events. Occasionally he would ask a question but for the most part he was quiet, trying to assimilate all the data.

When they were sitting in the pub garden he shook his head in astonishment as he sipped his mineral water. 'That's quite a story,' he said. 'How's it going to end?'

'That's a great question, and one I can't really answer. The money doesn't really solve the difficult problems, like what happens to the boys and where do we live and all that stuff, but it buys me a bit of time. For now, I'm just going to try and recover and get my mind in order. Then I'll think about the future.'

'If I can help . . .'

Caroline winced. 'That's so sweet,' she said, 'but I wouldn't dream of asking you. I've put you through quite enough as it is. I feel terrible about them arresting you.'

'I don't feel so good about that myself. I may be many things, but I'm not a murderer.'

'You know I never believed that, don't you? It's important to me that you understand that.'

'Of course I know that – although, when you disappeared and I got your letter, I was worried that you'd decided my intentions weren't honourable.'

'You had nothing to do with that decision, I promise. I always intended to get in touch with you again.'

'That's the nicest thing I've heard for a long time,' Anthony said, a little smile crossing his face. 'So – what's next?'

'There are still a lot of things to sort out. Someone told me that Guy had bought that house – you know, Shadowlawn? But I can't find any evidence of that.'

'Did you ever think of going back to the self-storage unit? He might have left some of his important papers there – like title deeds. It's worth checking out. Shadowlawn wouldn't be a bad place to live, if it was properly renovated.'

'Don't I know it. That's a good idea of yours, and it's something I will follow up on eventually. And one of the other things I have to do is pay your bill, by the way. How much do I owe you?'

'You really want to know?'

'That much, eh? Well, I'm good for it. You know that, at least.' They raised their glasses and drank together. The sun was warm and they both basked in it. 'Actually, there is something you could do for me, if you're still interested in working for me,' she said.

'Is it dangerous? Because I'm not really up for that.'

'I don't think so. At least, it shouldn't be. The thing is, when Linda gets out of hospital and is fit to travel, she and I have to make a little trip to Lugano. I'm going to deposit the boys with some understanding friends, and I imagine I'll have lots of free time. But I'm very conscious that I should have the best possible legal advice on tap, just in case anything unexpected turns up. I don't suppose you could recommend anybody, could you?' She raised one eyebrow.

'Hmm, that'll be particularly difficult. You're asking for a special kind of expertise that's very rare. I might even have to step up to this one personally.'

'Well, that would be awfully decent of you – if it wouldn't be too much of an inconvenience.'

'Think nothing of it.' He stretched his hand across the table and she put hers on top of it.

Caroline felt safe for the first time in many months. She could also sense a very small change within her, almost too slight to detect, but there nonetheless: she was finally learning to deal with Guy's legacy. The pain, though present, was lighter. She thought to herself that she might actually be able to make it all work: to cherish the past but live in the present. She was rediscovering hope.

313